KU-580-816

THE FALL OF THE HOUSE OF ROBSON

THE FALL OF THE HOUSE OF ROBSON

Keith Tomlins

Book Guild Publishing

Sussex, England

FIFE COUNCIL LIBRARIES	
HJ236876	
ASKEWS & HOLT	02-Mar-2011
AF	£16.99
GEN	DP .

First published in Great Britain in 2011by
The Book Guild Ltd
Pavilion View
19 New Road
Brighton, BN1 1UF

Copyright © Keith Tomlins 2011

The right of Keith Tomlins to be identified as the author of
this work has been asserted by him in accordance with the
Copyright, Designs and Patents Act 1988.

All rights reserved. No part of this publication may be reproduced, transmitted, or
stored in a retrieval system, in any form or by any means, without permission in writing
from the publisher, nor be otherwise circulated in any form of binding or cover other
than that in which it is published and without a similar condition being imposed on
the subsequent purchaser.

All characters in this publication are fictitious and any resemblance to real people,
alive or dead, is purely coincidental.

Typesetting in Baskerville by
YHT Ltd, London

Printed in Great Britain by
CPI Antony Rowe

A catalogue record for this book is available from
The British Library.

ISBN 978 1 84624 511 4

1 JANUARY 2008

No. They couldn't. Not today. Think of the distance. Impossible ... They could have tried ... No, the icy roads. Better safe than sorry ... No first foot? Who's to be first foot? ... Like my dress, the frost patterns on the panes. What did I do with it? ... Little Amy will be first foot ... Not fair, Pa, she always is. Let me instead. Why Amy? ... Don't want to anyway, Maddy. Staying up so late ... It's Amy's duty, whether she likes it or not ... Me next year then, Pa? ... Being woken up time after time by my father ... Derek'll ring of course ... Don't know about Daphne. Think she rang yesterday ... There's old Mrs Mullins's son. How did he get here? He risked the weather. Trust her to ... No paper. Boy's day off. Or he forgot me ... The television news ... That scoundrel being knighted. Wants locking up. Where is this country going? ... He looks like that actor. He's aged badly. MBE or some BE. He deserves it ... What? No more news? No good telling me what the weather was like today. Useless people ... Where's that silly little girl? Day off also, I suppose.

2 JANUARY

'Course I'm here? Where else would I be?'
    'Can you come down and open up, Mrs Robson?'
    Impatient hussy.
    'Can't shut this stupid window. Told Derek to fix it.'

'Don't even know your name.'
    'Tracy – I did tell you.'
    'Listen, I never forget a name.'
    'How are you today, Mrs Robson?'

1

'How would you be all on your own? Nobody to do things.'

'Did you enjoy that lovely dinner that your daughter-in-law brought you?'

'Have you looked at the clock? It's not time for dinner!'

'Yesterday.'

'Too salty. Threw most of it away.'

She's rummaging around again, the nosy little devil.

'Your bin's empty, Mrs Robson ... Where did your dinner go?'

'Down the toilet. Can't have smelly stuff like that around. No bin men.'

'Did your son, Derek, phone you? ... What are you eating today? ...'

How many more daft questions before I get rid of her?

'You're my first foot. Fancy that, you! Not even a member of my family!'

3 JANUARY

'Well, Mother, ready to go to lunch?'

'You're a fine one, Derek. I've had lunch.'

'Well ... I'll re-book it for dinner. I did tell you about it on New Year's Day.'

'You think I'm far gone, don't you? Nobody saw me on New Year's Day.'

'On the phone! ... Oh, it doesn't matter.'

'Doesn't it, Derek? Not worth a visit any more?'

'The weather, Mother, was ...'

The same old excuses I had when he was little. Couldn't cut the lawn, hang out his washing ... the weather.

'It was a sunny day, Derek.'

'That was yesterday, Wednesday.'

He thinks I can't remember the weather.

'Then why didn't you come yesterday, Derek?'

'Work ... Managed to take a half-day today.'

He has to earn his keep, I suppose, and keep that greedy wife of his. She begrudges me a crust, she does. There I am in wet rags with my begging bowl and she passes by on the other side ...

'Mother!'

'No need to raise your voice!'

'I've been asking you whether you want to go out to dinner tonight.'

'I understand if you can't afford it.'

'What do you mean. Mother?'

First it's lunch, then dinner, then he's hoping I'll change my mind.

'There are some meals in the freezer, Derek. We'll have one of those.'

See. He's gone straight there. I always fed him well, not like that dopey wife of his.

'Fiona's meals are all still here. What have you been eating?'

What's his wife got to do with it? *I* cooked most of that stuff.

'Cheese on toast and so on, Derek ... didn't feel like anything big.'

'Well, we'll have this chicken in the special sauce, Mother.'

I knew it, still eating my grub, the mingy devil.

'Seen Mrs Mullins recently, Mother?'

'She bores me to tears. Always talking about that son of hers.'

'How *is* Stephen, by the way?'

'How should I know? Haven't heard from old Mrs Mullins for days. In fact, I haven't seen a soul for ages ...'

3

'Hasn't Tracy called on you, Mother?'

'That silly little chit. What use is she?'

'Shopping ... washing ...'

'She doesn't do my washing. I wouldn't allow her. Look what rubbish she wears. She wouldn't know how to clean decent clothes.'

'Mother, she takes your washing away and brings it back ...'

'She only sends it to your sister, you fool.'

'Daphne doesn't do it!'

So it's Merlin with his magic wand. He'll be telling me next that his fat lazy wife is doing it.

'You'll be staying the night, won't you, Derek?'

I'll make the bed in his old room, all his old belongings around him ... he used to play happily for hours ... too much reading though ...

4 JANUARY

'What are you doing here? Thought you could burgle an old woman ... Take that!'

'Mother, it's me – Derek!'

'Derek, how silly of me .... Why did you ... change rooms ... not tell me you were here?'

'This has always been my room ...'

'Is your leg OK?'

'Hopefully. Just as well that it's a thick duvet. You oughtn't to have that crow bar.'

I'm a defenceless woman and I don't need protection?

'Go back to sleep, Derek. It was a mistake.'

'I need to drive to work, so I might as well get up bright and early.'

'You said you had time off. Besides, it's Saturday.'

'That's tomorrow. Tracy will call on you tomorrow, she even has to work on Saturdays.'

'So what, I had to, or you'd lose your job in those days.'

He rushed off quickly to his dear wifey. No time for me. A selfless person brings up selfish children.

5 JANUARY

Just look at them bringing all those goods in, all on credit. They can't afford all that. Just had a new TV and there's another. TV in every room, I bet. All on tick. Greed today and grieve tomorrow, that's today's motto. Oh, God ... Mrs Mullins ... what a relief, she's going the other way ... arthritis, can't get around well, can she, not as sprightly as me. Too cold for me to venture outside though ...

'Another young girl murdered, Daisy.'

'Tracy.'

'In every paper there's another ...'

'Where was that, Mrs Robson?'

'Luton, or was it Leicester?'

'They've arrested a young man for it.'

'That was quick, Daisy. Wish the police were as sharp here.'

'She was killed last year, well last week, same thing.'

'Don't be so silly, this happened yesterday, must be in another place then.'

'What date is the paper? Oh ... the 29th of December ... er ...'

'You didn't believe it was today's news, did you, until you saw the date?'

'You're right, Mrs Robson, different place.'

Salmon crossing the river ... sunset, better close the

curtains on an empty day. Walking with the pushchair along the shore, the waders, plovers and lapwings with their black neck scarves, wrapped up like us against the winter chill, Derek copying their calls, thinking they were talking to him ... I think he hears them still, doesn't seem to follow what I'm saying ...

6 JANUARY

'Who is it? Why are you saying it so softly? Who did you say?'

'Daphne, Mother. Are you wearing your hearing aid?'

'Ugly-looking thing, showed me up, would you like to advertise that *you* are hard of hearing? ... I got rid of it.'

'We'll have to buy you a better one ...'

'More like it ... huh, those NHS fob-offs. Why are you ringing so early? You woke me up.'

'It's gone nine o'clock, I'm phoning from the Guild office ... Make sure you have your dinner today ...'

'Are you talking to a little child?'

'In the freezer, Mother, there's a nice piece of pork, cooked in ...'

'You know I hate sloppy food, too much sauce ...'

'I did that one myself, it'll be just right for you ... or there's some haddock ...'

'Not Friday, is it, Daphne? Why should I have fish?'

'It's Sunday. Just look at the labels and see what you like best ... I must go ... Fiona will phone you tonight.'

Will she indeed? What's the point in ringing anyway, if you can only talk for a few seconds? ... What does she do in that office? Not like I had to slave in that factory, working my fingers to the bone ... or watching that belt go round waiting to grab things – at least it was lighter work than humping those boxes, the young lads were amazed at how many I could carry in my younger days ... now everything whirls round like that conveyor, you don't know where you are or why you are doing it ... you can't stop it and make something happen ... Why not? ...

7 JANUARY

'Oh, Mrs Mullins, do you know where Mrs Robson is? She isn't coming to the door.'

'Amy is in the garden. I've just heard her chatting to somebody, Tracy.'

'Did you recognise the voice?'

'Mainly heard her talking, didn't really think.'

'Helloooo ... Mrs Robson. It's me, Tracy ...'

'I've looked over the fence but I can't see her anywhere, Tracy. And, of course, nobody would have popped in to see her yesterday, I should have thought of that ... Ah ... she could be in that shed on the other side, sorting things out. I'll give you the stepladder so you can tap on the shed over the fence.'

'Ah, there you are, Mrs Robson!'

'Just checking that nothing was missing, Daisy. I thought you were those lads come back again. You scared the life out of me banging like that – you nearly broke the shed wall.'

'Lads, Mrs Robson?'

'Two of them. They sometimes jump over the fence at night and disappear into the shed. I'm too frightened to go out at night and see what they're up to.'

'Of course ... You shouldn't. Has anything been taken?'

'No ... or yes ... some tools that Derek uses here for DIY,

I'll get him to do an invention or whatever they call it to see what's missing. Better put the lock back on.'

'Wait, Mrs Robson! The key's on the shed floor. You need a padlock where the key stays in until you lock it again.'

'There, it's locked, Daisy ... no .... D ...'

'Tracy. Do you always lock it?'

'Do you think I encourage burglars?'

'Then how do they get in?'

'God knows, my dear, but they do. Seen them with my own eyes. You're not insin ... instigating that I'm seeing things?'

'Of course not, Amy.'

'Amy? You cheeky little snippet – I could be your great-grandmother. I'm Mrs Robson, when I'm at home.'

'Ever so sorry, only they encourage us to call people by their first name when we get to know them a bit.'

'Do they indeed? Goes to show what the world is like to day. Familiarity ...'

'Hello .... Tracy here ... bit worried about Mrs Robson, thinks she has burglars in her shed but she says she always has the padlock on .... yes, she must forget to lock it at times ... Oh! I forgot to ask who her imaginary visitor was ... the one supposed to be chatting to her in the garden ... will talk about her case after my other rounds ... Yes, bye.'

8 JANUARY

I'm used to the waiting though ... Alfred all that time at sea ... interminable stretches of life ... the sands at low tide ... high tide returns, still no ship in dock ... the seagulls mocking me over the harbour ... another ship berths ... but not his ... knew he wouldn't come back that time ... the foreboding froze us into statues, no words or gestures possible, he just went ... the kiss came blown from the gangplank ... the hand hiding his face ... tears perhaps ... knew before the telegram came ... they wait for weeks in case a survivor or a corpse washes up on a shore ... then only presumed dead ... there is no death without a body ... walk along the shore ... others can go to cemeteries ...

'You look sad, Mrs Robson, been meditating again?'

'It's his anniversary around this time, Daisy, did you know?'

'Your husband's ... Stanley's?'

'That feckless twerp! My first husband's, of course ... never had the proper date ...'

'Lost the marriage certificate?'

'His death, dear. Lost at sea in the war.'

'Oh, I'm dreadfully sorry, nobody told me ... Kind man, I'm sure.'

'The loveliest creature you could ever meet ...'

'Tracy here. Mrs Robson's still going on about her first husband ... We need to bring her records up to date, need to phone her son or daughter. If somebody else takes over from me, I don't want them to be embarrassed, will explain all when I get back. Bye ...'

She's gone again, didn't listen for long, no time, I'd imagine – chatting to her friend on the phone, I bet ... then on to the next poor old soul and fill in the papers ... nothing on television ... a lot of idiotic young people gossiping to one another ... or people selling pointless gadgets ... Mrs Mullins will probably call on me ... pass the time of day at least ...

9 JANUARY

'Not on that chair, Maddy.'

'It's Madge.'

'That's what I said, Madge. Not on that chair, it's not long ago that Derek bought me that ...'

'For Derek only is it? I thought you'd had it longer than that, Amy ... How's Derek?'

'He'll always have work, so many criminals, all need to be tried ...'

'We never heard of all these crimes in our day, did we, Amy? Everyone was too busy to get up to mischief ...'

'Such a clever man, I don't just say it because he's my son, how he can remember all the details, and he can argue the hind legs off a donkey ...'

'Stephen has just put a new bridge in place ... over a river ... all kinds of complications there were ...'

'Yes, Madge, very involved, and of course they don't admit it. You have to prove every detail, otherwise ...'

'Every little detail has to be just right, Amy, or the bridge would collapse, wouldn't it?'

'It couldn't collapse ... Derek can argue black is white, so they don't get away with it. He hates retrials ...'

'Oh, the number of trials they do, Amy – no, they call them stimulations ... to see if it works ... better safe than sorry.'

'I need stimulation as well or so they say, and I hope they don't want to try me out. They think I'm going gaga, you know, I can see it in their faces ... You're my first visitor in days, Maddy ... Madge ...'

'Stephen doesn't often come either, he's got a new project already, the main road at the bottom of ours needs resurfacing but the gas mains are a real headache ...'

'Can you smell gas? That girl just out of school is always reminding me to switch the taps off ... probably thinks I want to gas myself, the little numbskull ...'

'You're lucky, Amy, you've a daughter too – wish I had one, they're more use than sons ...'

'Huh, that's what you think, and with a son always working and he's got a family to look after, they've got pots of money, should have servants, not that I see much coming my way ... That greedy wife of his sees to that. Shall we have another cup of tea?'

'You haven't made me one yet ...'

'Course I have, Madge, you knocked it back in a jiffy, so you don't remember it.'

She was here for hours and all about that Stephen of hers again, never listens to my news of Derek. I expect that bridge'll collapse, serves her right if her bus is going over it at the time ... At least, though, it's a living soul to converse with ... The vicar used to put his sanctimonious face over the fence, so tall, he thought he was nearer heaven than the rest of us ... keeping your son away from church ... lovely voice Derek had when he was little, best lad in choir by far ... keep him away indeed, he's off playing football, and who has to wash those filthy muddy shirts, not you with your lily hands holding the chalice ... save his soul, and what about mine, is mine lost beyond rescue? ... See him next Sunday, Mrs Robson, and the apparition would vanish as quickly as it came, like I'd imagined him ... hara.... haranguing me over my own fence, the cheeky so-and-so ...

10 JANUARY

'So who were you talking to in the garden again last night, Mrs Robson?'

'What's that got to do with you, you impudent little waif? What's *your* name, by the way?'

'Kelly. I bumped into Mrs Mullins on the way in and she told me about it. It's not the first time that ...'

'So that's it, that gossip, and so what? Aren't I entitled to have conversations in my garden?'

Madge's hearing isn't so good – in fact she hears noises that were never made ... And I can't imagine how she gets around on the ice with her handicap ...

'Where are the tea towels, Mrs Robson?'

'In the kitchen drawer by the sink, of course.'

'They have vanished.'

'Leave those dishes to drain, Kerry, then you don't need to wipe them.'

'Oh, here they are in the dresser drawer.'

'Whoever put them in this room? What a silly place. Must have been that other girl who calls.'

'Tracy? She wouldn't move your things around without permission.'

'Are you instigating that I told her to shift them?'

'So long as I've found them ... Usually I only see you on Fridays, Mrs Robson. Tracy comes on the other days. This week I'm here today as well as tomorrow.'

'Isn't today Friday?'

'No, tomorrow is Friday, Mrs Robson.'

'You're trying to confuse me.'

Don't know why they bother to come. She's meant to have put the vacuum cleaner round, looks dusty in that corner still, won't move furniture, damage themselves, to think what I used to hump around at their age ... The seagulls are wasting their time as well, all that rainwater on the field is frozen solid ... Daphne could watch the gulls for hours, giving them all names, thought she could recognise them when they came back ... this control is playing up again, can't get the channel ... the rain running down the channels, Derek splashing through them on purpose to aggravate me ... all adverts, no use to me, what can I buy now? ...

11 JANUARY

Forgot to phone Mother yesterday, have to tell her I was out at friends', but she'd be jealous not getting out herself ... I had to do shopping or ... will have to listen to her litany, don't think I can face it ... and the accusations, not remembering she was all on her own ... tomorrow I'll tell her I had a headache, but then she might be unwell, or something may be wrong ... phone later ...

That nagging refrain grinding my head, you don't care about your old mother ... you care too much, life is rewound for her, can't fast forward to the moment when ... erase that, never think of it ... take a brandy and get it over with ...

'Mother – it's Daphne! *Daphne!'*
  'You're yelling again. It's not working.'
  'I'm glad you're wearing it.'
  'What?'
  'Aren't you talking about your hearing aid?'
  'You know I don't need those ridiculous constraptions. The television control is playing up, it won't change the channel.'
  'On the bottom right there is a button with plus and minus – if you are on channel two you press plus to go to channel three or minus for channel one – try it ... What? I can't hear ...'
  'Now who needs a hearing aid? I can hear you perfectly well and I never have trouble hearing the TV.'

'That's because you have it too loud – Mrs Mullins can't get to sleep next door with the racket ...'

'An outrageous thing to say, wait till I get hold of her ...'

'You pressed the wrong button, the one at the bottom left is for volume.'

'Left? I pressed that one, yes, and it's still Channel 4.'

'Not the left one, the right one.'

'The left one is the right one? Well I pressed the right one then, according to you, but that was wrong, my dear.'

'At least the sound has gone back down again.'

'It's not the sound I'm worried about ... Oh, I'll have to get Derek to show me, he's much better at those things. Don't expect you'll be down to see me just yet. You haven't even managed to phone me in weeks.'

'It was a few days ago. I was unwell, I ...'

'There's always something wrong with you. You are the one who needs to see a doctor, not me ...'

'I had to see some friends ...'

'Oh, that's great, see some friends, not your poor old mother, she ...'

'I do need a life of my own ...'

'I think that's the doorbell. Just as well somebody is bothered about me. Speak to you another time, Daphne.'

Should have phoned before ... it's my fault she's in a bad mood ... no, Dr Devonshire insists I mustn't keep blaming myself ...

12 JANUARY

'Ooh-ooh, Maddy.'

'Not Maddy, *Madge*! What are you doing out here in the street, Amy? You'll catch your death of cold.'

'I've a bone to pick with you, Madge. Somebody tells me

that you have been complaining about the noise coming from my house.'

'Don't know who that was, I'm sure. I ...'

'So you didn't say anything?'

'Well, Amy, you could turn the TV down after midnight, so that ...'

'That's rich. I hardly have it on, can't get the programme I want.'

'Well next time you do and it's late at night, turn down the sound a little, there's a good soul. Just off to get something for Stephen's dinner, he'll be round tonight.'

That's it, rub it in, little milksop Stephen sucking up to you again – course, only child, stands to get all that cash you've hidden away, not to mention the house – pity my kith and kin don't think about that ... Where's that Daisy or that other young hussy? Never know when they're coming ...

'You saw Kelly yesterday and the day before, so we haven't neglected you. Remember, I'm Tracy ... I have a day off in the week, as I always come on Saturdays.'

'Think I'm losing my marbles? I know perfectly well who you are. If you only have one day off, why did the other girls have to call two days in a row?'

'You're still very sharp, aren't you Mrs Robson. Friday is my day off, but on Thursday I had to go to meetings about my clients.'

'Sit down, dear, you look worn out – too much on your plate today, I bet.'

'Mind if I have a cuppa with you? Yes, we're short-staffed and I've taken on extra visits.'

'Have you got a boyfriend? I had one at your age, took me out to dances, danced properly in those days, not this razzmatazz you see on the television.'

'I expect you've got some photo albums ...'

15

'I've no pictures of my boyfriend, too long ago, there aren't any albums, unless my children ... they were going to get me some and stick in all the pictures, they're in some boxes somewhere or other ...'

'If you fetch them out, Mrs Robson, we'll have a look at them some time. Here's one of my boyfriend.'

'Handsome young fellow. Aren't you lucky! Been walking out with him long?'

'Four months, three weeks ... and two days ...'

'I used to count up the days like that when I first dated Alfred. Dressed up to the nines he was for our first date, bet your whatshisname just flings on a T-shirt and a pair of jeans ...'

'It's Tracy here about Mrs Robson. Seems to have eaten a proper meal today ... Yes ... must get her son or daughter to hunt out her photos, she likes to go on about the past, photographs could help me bring it back to her ... Yes, on to Mrs Jeffries, will phone again from there.'

13 JANUARY

Sunday? The church bells ... Who took my wedding dress? ... The height of fashion then ... The photograph was here ... Who put it away? ... No time for a honeymoon in those days ... and no money ... straight back to work on Monday, not even a day off, don't know they're born today, didn't even stay in a hotel, two nights at my auntie Ethel, couldn't even give us a decent breakfast, had fish and chips one night for dinner, she said it was a treat for us, know what they'd do with that now, throw it straight back at her, that's what we should've done, tiny little thing I was in those days, wouldn't even have said boo to a mouse, put upon I was by all, couldn't do enough for my mother, never grateful she was for it neither, always thought more of that rogue Bertie, God, the trouble he'd get into and never his fault, at home I got the blame, scallywag could do no wrong, hit out at the scapegoat instead, load all the sins onto it, that's what I call original sin, don't agree with that church version, we're all born innocent until they drag us through the mud ...

Those bells still ringing ... don't expect wedding bells, Stanley loathed the inside of a church, the stench of incense and all those starched collars and stiffer faces looking down on us sinners ... I didn't polish off Alfred you know, a Nazi torpedo got him for your information, and I'm entitled to marry again, Alfred's brother Stanley has nowhere to go to convalesce, they brought him back to England after his ship had been torpedoed, so he has to stay here with me now, anyway he wants to help me grieve for Alfred ... Oh, the tittle-tattle: her husband scarcely gone and she's taken his brother in, nursing him indeed, if we all nursed like that, we'd be in Gomorrah ...

Those boys are back, not content with raiding the shed, now they want to break in to the living room ... Oh, it's Mrs Mullins, what the devil does she want?

'I've been ringing the bell for ages, Amy.'
    'It probably doesn't work any more or you've worn down the battery – another job for Derek, I must draw up a list for him – what else was he to do now? ... What are you calling on me for, Madge?'
    'Oh, you remembered my name. Thought you don't have those girls popping in on Sunday, so I'd keep you company ... Stephen couldn't come this weekend after all ...'
    'All on your own like me – there should be a place to put us old ones, like that cycling centre where they could turn

us into something new ... The young prefer their own company ...'

'No, Stephen is very good, he usually manages a visit. It's that blessed bridge, developed complications, so they need him to come to the rescue, even on the Lord's Day ...'

'Derek might make it to the Lords, they have those Law Lords, you know, whatever other judges decide, they can find a way of making it appear wrong, ever so clever they are ...'

'But Derek isn't a judge is he?'

'Don't you worry, he already counsels the Queen, all his clothes have to be made of silk, he'll soon make his way further up ...'

'The only way to keep the bridge up is some kind of suspension – they can suspend such heavy things ...'

'That's the worst that can happen – when a trial is suspended, it gets held up for weeks sometimes.'

'Well, Amy, this has to last for many a year and with all those HGVs.'

'Mark my word, he'll make it to the top. Derek has a GV, or is it CV, second to none, he says, whatever that is.'

'In design and construction Stephen's second to none ...'

'Well, nice of you to call on me, Madge – quiet otherwise, today.'

'I hate Sundays, Amy, when Stephen doesn't come.'

'Never stop at one child, I always say, you must have two ...'

'Let's not go over that bridge again, Amy.'

'Ha! Ha! Bridge again.'

All she can talk about is building bridges and moaning about not being visited. I should be the one to moan, I'm like that old mare in the field that nobody has any more use for. Well at least they don't tell it to eat its dinner, as if there's any point in that – what do I need the energy for, sitting in my armchair? ...

'Well, it's a bit late to call me now, Daphne, I'm half asleep. What? My hearing is poor in the evening. Ring tomorrow ... You're busy tomorrow? ... Been somewhere nice this weekend, I suppose ... You think you could give me time of day ... What? Course I'm listening to you but you should be listening to your poor old mother ... Phone tomorrow then ... Bye.'

14 JANUARY

Just a quick call to Mother – I couldn't face it before going out, or how to get her off the line – I'd have been late. It's very bad of me to keep putting it off. I'll ring her from the Guild office when there's a spare moment. That hearing aid ... and that TV remote ... about time Derek sorted things out – why do I have the weight on me?

'It wasn't my fault, you know ... going away like that, I mean ... Who? Who do you think I mean? ... Derek's father, Stanley ... couldn't settle after the war ... no, your father wouldn't have been the same if he'd made it through, different character ... OK, Stanley was a father figure for you ... I don't know if you upset him, that day ... he was in a funny mood anyway ... oh, so he said he wasn't coming again? Well you might've told me ... That's always your get-out, isn't it? You don't remember, Mother ... I didn't remarry just for you to have a father figure around, course, you were too young and at that age you only think of yourself. What about me, the loneliness after the absence of

19

my husband in the war years, you didn't think about that ...
Oh yes, you'd better get back to your charity work ...'

Fancy calling from that office again, no time to discuss
anything properly. She probably did get on Stanley's nerves
that day, but blames me instead, call the kettle black, won't
bring the idle jerk back at any rate ... Couldn't find a job?
How did he expect me to manage with his child and
another to boot, didn't know where the next halfpenny was
coming from ... What's that racket?

'I've told you a thousand times, Daisy, you're not having a
key to my house ...'
    'It'd save me all the waiting, Mrs Robson, and I'd have
more time for you, I've been banging for ages out there and
it's freezing ...'
    'Roused the whole neighbourhood I should think, never
heard a row like it. Just ring the bell ... What do you want to
do here anyway?'

Where has that Daisy gone? ... She'll tear the carpet hoo-
vering like that and mind she doesn't break any of my
ornaments, clumsy little ha'p'orth, mementoes mean
nothing to her generation, of course ...

'You have your check-up at the doctor's tomorrow, Mrs
Robson – I'll take you if ...'
    'Will you indeed? And what do you know about my ail-
ments? Derek or Daphne'll be here ...'
    'They rang our office to say they couldn't make it, so ...'
    'The very idea! I'm the last to find out! I suppose they'll
say I didn't answer the phone or didn't catch what they said,
they believe I'm not all right up here ...'

15 JANUARY

Must call on old Gertie Stokes, all on her own as usual, I bet. Never married ... no children ... no strife ... just herself to worry about ... no wonder she has lived for so long ... but now nobody who cares about her ... poor old soul ... just pop round for a chat ...

'Morning, Mrs Robson. Surprised to see yer. What can we do for yer, ducks?'

'What are *you* doing in Gertie Stokes's house? I wasn't aware that she had children ...'

'Who? Gertie Stokes? Oh, that old dear! She popped off a few years back – gave us priority to buy 'er house, she did ...'

'So, you took the house off her, did you?'

'Took it? It was all legal of course, put it in her will. We paid for it, yer know. I've never mentioned it to yer before, but since yer ask and yer also looked after 'er, and with all the filthy rumours going about implying that we wangled it off of 'er and even that we helped to bump 'er off ...'

'She's dead, then.'

'Long gone ...'

'Must have been recent, because I never heard about it. Oh, you're Mrs P ... , C ...'

'Partridge, dear.'

'Well, let's get things straight – you didn't do anything for her. I was the one on call night and day ...'

'Now let's not squabble about this, dearie, we did our bit to help the lovely old lady.'

'Never in your life. And you'd better keep away from me, you'll find me a harder nut to crack than old Gertie Stokes, I'm telling you straight.'

'No need to take that tone with me, you old witch.'

'Oh, a witch am I now, well if you do me in, I'll haunt you until you go to hell.'

Banging the door on me like that. What dreadful neighbours you get today, and to think that that villain replaced
harmless Gertie Stokes. Wait till I tell Daphne all about it.

'Oh, there you are Mrs Robson, out in the street. I was about
to phone your daughter. Where have you been? You've
missed your doctor's appointment.'

'Are you my keeper, Daisy? Am I a little child who's not
allowed out?'

'You know the doctor forbids you to leave the house
without somebody to assist you. If you fall down in the
street, you ...'

'So the doctor controls me now, does he? Probably wanted to put me away today, anyway. I might as well be a robot.
For your information, I just called on Gertie Stokes, only to
find that she's no longer of this world and a ghastly woman
has taken over her house, Mrs Pheasant, I think.'

'Ah yes ... it was you who called us in to care for Miss
Stokes, because it was getting too much for you. You were
ever so kind to her. That couple Mr and Mrs Partridge were
also on the scene, for want of a better word, and managed
to get ownership of the house after Miss Stokes passed
away.'

'Polished her off, don't you think?'

'She died of natural causes, according to the doctor.'

'No post-mortem, for sure, that would have thrown up
something. If Gertie Stokes should have left anybody anything, it should have been me. Not a penny did I get, but
don't get me wrong, I wasn't after that kind of thing.'

'No, the neighbours here know that you looked after
people from the kindness of your heart. There were other
old folk apart from Miss Stokes, weren't there? So the social
services told me.'

'Not sure who they were now ... But what do you think of
that couple diddling Gertie out of the house? It's ...'

'I'm afraid that as a professional I'm not allowed to comment.'

'Well come and see me one day when you're not working and we can have a chinwag about it ...'

'No, I can't do that either. Look, let's go into your house, because I have to look at your pills.'

'A chemist as well, are you? ... Oh, God!'

'Whatever is the matter, Mrs Robson? Have you had a bad turn?'

'The key. I forgot the key ... Oh, no, here it is.'

'That's a key to a padlock, to the shed, I think.'

'Then I'm locked out! *Aaaah!*'

'No, don't scream like that – look there! We've just had a key box fitted, there's a key in there.'

'So that's how you get in. No wonder I see you suddenly standing next to me in the sitting room as if you were a ghost.'

'No, it wasn't there before. We installed it because you don't answer the doorbell.'

'The very cheek of it, you just take my key and come in anyway ...'

'I have to, in case anything has happened to you.'

'Well, you must show me how to get the keys out of that constraption, if I've forgotten my usual set.'

'Tomorrow – I'm running badly behind time today. I'll just take a quick look at a few things inside.'

16 JANUARY

'Hello, Daphne? This is Tracy, your mum's main carer ... It's about her tablets. They're in a real mess ... Oh yes, we give them to her regularly, but sometimes the tablet we are supposed to give her isn't there any more. We don't know if she has already taken it or if she has disposed of it ... Well, it'd be a good idea to have the chemist put the pills in a special holder which your mother wouldn't know how to operate, so they would remain there until we could give them to her at the appropriate time – they charge a few pounds a week for that service ... Then you need to write to her chemist to make the necessary arrangement, including payment, as she won't act on our recommendation. Oh, and your mother is interested in having the code to the key box, but of course we won't tell her ... Yes, she would hopefully forget it if we did, but we'll try to avoid giving it ... The hearing aid? She won't wear it, however much we persuade her, and I know you have done your best ... Otherwise, she's the same as ever ... Anyway, speak again sometime. Bye.'

'There you are again, popping up like Marley's ghost, giving me the fright of my life.'

'You didn't hear the bell, Mrs Robson, so I used our key.'

'My hearing is still perfect. I'll get Derek to check the bell.'

'I see you had a boiled egg for breakfast.'

'That was yesterday. Wasn't hungry today. What do I need to eat for? Stuck in here like a horse in a stable, no exercise.'

'I cleared up yesterday's breakfast, so you must have had an egg last night then.'

'It's bad enough telling me what to eat, now you are trying to tell me what I have already eaten. You might as well open me up when I'm dead and use the contents of my stomach for medical research.'

'Hello. Anything the matter? ... I told you not to phone me at work. It's not the time to be romantic ... Look, I've got to go. Ring me tonight.'

'Your boyfriend?'

'Er ... how did you know?'

'Tell by the look on your face. You young ones can't get enough of one another ...'

'He's not meant to phone me when I'm on duty.'

'Can't resist you, dearie – you should be flattered by his attentions.'

'Embarrassed more like it in this situation.'

'Oh, don't mind about me – after I left the factory because my father thought a girl shouldn't be doing all the heavy work, I used to work in a shop and my boyfriend would keep nipping in to ask me if we sold the most ridiculous items, never letting on who he was, until the owner caught us walking out together and I was threatened with the sack if he came in again.'

'Now, that's a giggle.'

'Wasn't at the time. At any rate, I shan't be splitting on you.'

17 JANUARY

'Where's all your dirty laundry, Mrs Robson?'

'All done, Daisy. Couldn't leave it stinking in that basket.'

'But you haven't got a washing machine any more.'

'Thank goodness you mentioned it. Who took it away? I was looking all over for it yesterday.'

'It broke down.'

'Then Derek should have had it repaired.'

'You were having real trouble using it ...'

'Fiddlesticks! I could use it as well as you. Now I have to bend down over the bath tub and all that emptying the bath and rinsing ... and the wringing isn't easy either with my arthritis ... and how am I going to dry it?'

'Well, where is it now?'

'On the line, where else?'

'But it's raining today. Has it been out since yesterday?'

'No, I only just put it out.'

'Then I'll bring it in.'

'No you jolly well won't. I'm not having all those wet things in here. All that damp would make me feel even worse. I forbid you to touch them. They can stay out till they're dry.'

I can't cope with all these calls about Mother. About time they phoned Derek, I have my own life to live. Keys, hearing aid, washing, tablets ... I'll take a few too many myself one day, not that she'd care, probably think me selfish. She's having trouble using the phone, so at least I get fewer calls from her, but now Tracy does the phoning for her instead.

18 JANUARY

'Hello Amy, haven't seen you for ages up this end of the road ...'

'Well, you must have left your glasses indoors then, Mrs Thompson, T ... T ...'

'Turner. Still the same perky Amy, I see. When I was down your end, Mrs Mullins said that you couldn't get out and about these days.'

'If you believe her, you'd believe the Prime Minister.'

'Always good for a laugh, aren't you?'

'Don't know what the world's coming to. People spending like nobody's business and they still want to have money on the cheap and what will they do with it? We used to have to make do ... How's that son of yours?'

'Nigel is still the same. Still at home. Still singing the same song up and down the street.'

'Thought I heard him yesterday or the day before. At least you've got him by your side. My Derek rarely comes to see me, he ...'

'Your Derek is a distinguished gentleman, you don't know how lucky you are. I love Nigel to bits, but ... well, it's hard to have them dependent on you all your life ... When I pass on ...'

'Don't speak too soon, you're a young woman yet ...'

'Ha ha! Anyway, Nigel always loves to see you. Pop in and chat to him for a bit.'

'Hello? Oh, it's you, Daphne. It's Kelly here ... Tracy's day off ... Oh, well, you couldn't get through to your mum because she's ... You've a complaint? ... Ever so sorry if we keep phoning you, Daphne ... I understand that it puts a lot of stress on you ... We only do it in emergencies, and we do have to have a relative as contact ... Look, I'm in your mum's house and ... No, she hasn't done anything silly here, the point is she isn't here at all ... Don't get into a panic ... Have you any idea where she is? ... OK, I'll phone Mrs Mullins in case she's there, and if not, I'll alert the police. Bye for now.'

'Oh, what a wonderful morning ...'

Oh God, I forgot to shut the front door and a drunkard is coming in singing at the top of his lungs, or ...

'Who are you?'

'No – who are *you*?'

'I'm Kelly, Mrs Robson's carer. Look, this is not your house, so get out this instant.'

'That's a fine way to speak to young Norman, Kerry.'

'My name's Kelly, Mrs Robson.'

'And mine's Nigel, not Norman ... Haven't been in your house much, Aunt Amy, forgotten what it looked like ...'

'Who is Nigel, Mrs Robson?'

'A son of a friend who lives up the street. I've just brought him in here to keep me company.'

'Where do you live, Nigel?'

'At 55. Nigel always do a good turn. Turner is my name.'

'Well, you can do your good turn for the day by just having a chat with Mrs Robson while I pop out to get her a bit of shopping.'

'What are you spending my money on, now, Kerry? I'll have none left at this rate.'

'The money isn't in its usual place, Mrs Robson ... have you moved it?'

'The audacity of it. Whose money is it? I'll put it where I like.'

'Not to worry. I'll pay with my petty cash and you can refund me later. You have no bread left, although Tracy said there was enough till the weekend ...'

'It must have gone stale and I gave it to the birds.'

'I always like to feed the birds, Aunty Amy, especially the robin.'

'Always looked after God's little creatures, that's Norman for you.'

'Oh, what a beautiful morning ...'

'What did you throw the bread away for, Mrs Robson? ... Well you can give it to the birds, Nigel, while I go out for a fresh loaf and a few other things.'

'... So you see, Mrs Turner, she has declined quite rapidly in the last year and she can't possibly look after Nigel even if she does invite him into her house, and Nigel is certainly not capable of seeing to her.'

'Well I never, Kelly! Fancy that! Dear old Amy Robson going rapidly downhill ... The life and soul of the street she was, always bustling back and forth, but if you stopped her, she always gave you a conversation to cheer you up ...'

'I'm going shopping for her, so could you fetch Nigel back?'

'When I get there, I'll stay a bit with her first, otherwise she might take offence. The trouble is how to persuade Nigel not to visit her in the future.'

19 JANUARY

Too many papers. Must sort them out before Derek comes, otherwise he'll ask me whether I'm reading them ... don't want him to stop paying for them ... Two days till Christmas ... Eeh, and I haven't sent my Christmas cards ... That Daisy will have to get some for me ... I must go and fetch the money ... Somebody's been sneaking a look inside this case ... The money's gone! I've been robbed! ... Wait till I get my hands on that Daisy ...

'Most of your money is still in your post office account, Mrs Robson, but we left you with enough cash for the week ... Anyway, it's just as well that you have the pension paid straight into the account now, as we didn't like taking you to the post office to draw it and sort it out each week, it's not really our responsibility ...'

'Daisy, how would you like people nosing into all your affairs? I'd rather go and draw the pension myself at the post office as usual.'

'That's not the way it is any more ...'

'That's it, another change, take it or leave it, nobody consults us old folk, we just do as we are told, why did we bother to grow up?'

'Anyway, Mrs Robson, not to worry, as there couldn't have been much money under your bed.'

'So you're the one who found out where it was, you little thief!'

'Mrs Robson, please, you told me this morning that you looked under your bed and the money was gone. I had no idea where you kept it. It's supposed to be in the cash box in this drawer, but it's empty.'

'And who has the key to that?'

'You have one and we have one – I mean, the carers do, me and Kelly.'

'Why should you break into my box?'

'We don't, we buy things for you, Kelly did so yesterday ... We keep a list of all that we spend, for your son Derek to verify.'

'There you go again. My son keeps tabs on my money and you spend it for him ... Anyway, there is something I need today and I don't feel like going out ... What was it? Ah, cards!'

'A card'll be hard to choose – whose birthday is it for?'

'Birthday? No, Christmas, of course, a pack of Christmas cards.'

'You want to buy them now while they're cheap and ...'

'They always reduce them just before Christmas.'

'And after as well. How big a pack do you want?'

'Fifty.'

'As many as that? I'd get Derek to address them for you next time, if I were you. You addressed them to yourself this Christmas gone and he had to apologise to everybody you normally send cards to. Anyway, it meant you had loads of cards. The postwoman said that you were the most popular person on her rounds!'

'You make me out to be the village idiot! As if I'm gaga – sending cards to myself ... If I did you might as well put me away ... And what do you mean, this Christmas gone? We haven't had it yet!'

'How do you work that out?'

'Unlike your young generation, I read the papers and keep myself up to date, that's how!'

Must call her son, can't bother her daughter right now, as

she's had it up to here. Oh, she'll probably forget about Christmas by tonight or tomorrow ... but Derek had better stop those papers. They help her pass the time of day, but she gets them into a muddle and they add to her confusion about the date. And the money, oh dear, this must be our most difficult patient.

20 JANUARY

It's about time one of my sisters called to see me. How old are their children now? Talk about children, Derek's haven't been here for ages. When did they last come? 1990 something? Lovely little girl he has, sweet little thing, always pleased to see me, why doesn't he bring her down? I could look after her for a week in the school holidays to give Fiona a rest – Fiona, that's her name, I don't know why I sometimes can't remember it – what was it about Fiona? She hasn't exactly encouraged her son to stay with me either ... What's his name? – He could be useful, as his father is always working. Is Derek a judge yet? Will be soon. I can picture him now with all his teddy bears and so on pretending it was a courtroom, passing sentence on some scoundrel or other ... He won't be wanting for work these days ... He used to watch that television series about trials, what was it called? And then I had to be in charge of the jury and help the toys decide... Why am I sitting in this chair all morning going over the old days? How long have I been here? It might be afternoon. Two o'clock, good job the old clock works better than me, Alfred's engagement present it was, had to save up for it for weeks in those times, get it on credit for a year or two now, no doubt. People think what a paltry present for a betrothal, but it was precious then, and still is of course, couldn't part with it – Derek wouldn't pay for the chimes to be restored, wasn't worth it for the cost in his estimation, or so he said – well, of course it wasn't his father's present, I should have asked Daphne ...

'Oh what a beautiful morning ...'

What's that? Somebody singing?

'Oh what a beautiful morning ...'

What on earth is he singing? Take a peep out from behind the curtains ... Oh, some suspicious figure is moving away ... Oh no, it's young Norman ... ooh-ooh, Norman! ... Too late, he's gone ... My chance of a visit today gone down the drain ...

Where's the piano? Always been here in the front sitting room ... Daphne must have taken it away ... I thought I heard her playing it only the other day, but she wasn't here ...

Soon be dark outside. Make sure all the curtains are drawn and the door locked ... *Aaah!*

'It's OK, Amy, it's only me.'

'Oh, you frightened the life out of me, Maddy.'

'Madge. Why do you insist on calling me Maddy?'

'That's my sister's name. You've brought it back to me ...'

'Thought you'd be all on your own like me. Stephen wasn't able to come again. That blessed bridge ...'

'Just in time for tea. I'll pop the kettle on.'

'Amy, I've just had a visit from that Partridge couple who took over Gertie's house...'

'Nasty kettle of fish, if you ask me, Madge, wouldn't touch them with a bargepole ...'

'You can say that again – they were asking me too many personal questions ...'

'Probably wanted to know how much cash you had and where you kept it.'

'In the bank, of course.'

'You must be daft! The banks are sure to waste every-body's money! I keep mine well hidden away, nobody'll get their hands on it.'

'Anyway, Amy, where's that cup of tea? ... Oh, the kettle isn't switched on. Look, let me see to it ... Ooh, that's a nice-looking cake ...'

'Somebody left it for me and I've just got it out.'

'Must be getting back. What's the time? Oh dear, Amy, the big hand has fallen off your clock, but I can see it's some-thing past five ...'

'I was just looking at the clock today, trying to see if it would chime again if I turned the hands round – perhaps it fell off then.'

'Oh, dearie me, here it is on the floor, but it's broken into bits. I'm ever so sorry, Amy, I hope I didn't tread on it.'

She should lose some weight, she's ruining my armchair and I bet she crushed that clock hand. Always having tea and cake here, don't know why she doesn't invite me in to her house ... nobody gets inside there, bet it's a right tip, that son of hers was always untidy, so I don't suppose he does much to sort it out, not that he's there except in a month of Sundays ... Madge Mullins said it's Sunday ... can't be, as nobody came to give me a lift to church, must get to church next week.

21 JANUARY

'So your clock's been in the wars, Mrs Robson.'

'Why, what's the matter with it, Daisy?'

'It has only the hour hand. You can't tell the time prop-erly with it. You'll have to get another one. You don't have a watch, do you?'

'It got lost. When I was last in hospital, I think. You don't know the history of that clock, do you?'

'Oh, yes, I'm sorry – you'll want to keep it for sentimental reasons.'

'I can tell the time perfectly with it. Right now it's ten o'clock, no, just past it.'

'Twenty past.'

'You see! That's good enough for me, sitting here all day – if it comes to that, what does it matter whether it's ten or two o'clock or whatever?'

'Well, at 11.05 you have to be at the doctor's, so please go up and get ready.'

'You might have told me earlier – that's not much notice, is it?'

'It's on your little noticeboard in the kitchen.'

'That's Daphne's idea – I don't need to look at that to know what's going on ... Now I have to change in a hurry.'

'Well, I've had a quick wash down ...'

'Oh, you haven't changed. Don't you want to take those old house clothes off?'

'Of course I did, I changed after washing. And what's wrong with these clothes anyway? They were a Christmas present from Derek's wife, F ... F ...'

'Let's just pop up and change the pullover and skirt.'

'Heavens above! You want to dress me like a little girl now!'

'Why did the doctor say I had to go to hospital?'

'For a check-up on your waterworks.'

'That doctor is far too old. Not like my proper doctor. How do you know he's got it right?'

'He's not sure, that's why you ...'

'Huh, not sure, and all the money he gets paid ...'

'Your usual doctor left to be in charge of another surgery.'

'Hospital. How I hate hospitals! They send us old folk there to get rid of us. At my age, I'd be lucky to get out again.'

'Come now, Mrs Robson, things are a lot better there than you think.'

'You haven't heard the news recently. Old folk lying around on trolleys. They hope they'll pop off and it's another patient they don't have to treat ...'

'We'll have to ask your daughter to take you, when the hospital appointment comes through.'

'That's another thing. By the time it does come, I'll be pushing up the daisies, Daisy!'

'Hello, Daphne, it's Tracy. Have you got a minute? It's about your mum's visit to the doctor ... She's OK generally, in spite of not taking her tablets regularly ... The chemist will put them in that special box next week, so thanks for arranging that ... but your mother has to have a check-up ... You know that she has had some pain when passing water? ... Yes, so could you take her to the hospital? ... Probably some time in February, but given her age they might speed it up more ... Oh, and could you sort out her clothes when you come? ... I know it's yet another job for you, but she has a lot of old things that are no longer fit to wear ... and the new things, presents, I suppose, as she doesn't get out to buy anything, the new things are all jumbled up with the old and scattered around in different places in the bedrooms. It might help her to decide what to wear each day, especially if she has to go out ... That's all – well, there are one or two other little matters, but nothing to worry yourself about ...'

22 JANUARY

Who's that snooping around the back of the house? Not those boys again. A funny-looking man nosing about. Take a look at the front. Only that P ... woman ... Mrs Pheasant? Evil inscribed on her face. Wouldn't be out of place in those American horror films they make today, can't get any of the old thrillers any more, all done to scare you to death now, Daphne says I must stop watching them as it's the films that are giving me nightmares. There's a face out of one if ever there was. She's waving up at me, look away ... What about the back of the house? ... That peculiar man has gone ... Better check downstairs ... Somebody's trying to break in ... What's Daphne's number? ... Can't find my little phone book, that Daisy has moved it again ...

'Go away! I'm calling the police! No point holding up that card, I don't know you.'

He won't go, I'll indicate to him to go round the front and I'll keep the chain on the door while I talk to him.

'Cowan's the name, madam. Do a lot of jobs around here. You see what it says on the card ... Couldn't help noticing that your fence is falling down, that's not good security.'

'Eeh, that'll be those boys who keep jumping over it at night.'

'What did I tell you, very unsafe for a lady of your age. Nobody could jump over a fence that I put up. Your one could be flattened by a burglar in seconds. I have recommendations from your neighbours, Mullins and Partridge, and ...'

'Oh, you must be the nice man who put Madge Mullins's new fence up. Well, how much would it cost?'

'Give you the estimate right now ... removing old fence ... panels ... posts ... coat of preservative ... labour ...

you're looking at just over eight hundred pounds, shave off the odd quid, call it eight hundred dead.'

'What? Where am I to get that sort of money? I'll have to talk to my children.'

'The thing is, love, I'm only around your neck of the woods for today, busy schedule you know, and I've given you my best price, which only holds for today. I've got the necessary materials in my big van and can start as soon as you give me the okey-dokey. You'd be forking out well over a grand – a thousand pounds – for any other fencer ...'

'Funnily enough, I've just come across my nest egg. I'll recount it and see if it's enough ...'

Two hundred and fifty, two hundred and seventy, three hundred ... no, start again ... Twenty, forty, sixty, eighty, a hundred ... two hundred ... three hundred ... four hundred ... no, oh, it's no use, I'll get him to count it for me.

'Just right, love, eight hundred pounds. So, I'll take that and be making a start. I've left you with forty pounds to spare for your other needs.'

Those panels don't look too sound and he's bringing in some flimsy wooden posts – I'd better ring Derek.... But I don't know his number ...

'Thanks for the tip off, Mrs Mullins.'
    'Just make sure she gets any money back, Tracy.'

'Amy, we just caught that villain in time.'
    'Madge?'
    'Mrs Robson, did you give that man any money?'
    'And you're here again out of the blue, Daisy. I gave him the money from my nest egg, for the fence. You'd better ask the man how much it was.'

'The police have just arrested him in your garden, Mrs Robson. They have been looking out for him for a while. Well-known con man.'

'Oh Amy! Just as well I saw him talking to that Partridge woman and then he knocked on my door with her recommendation. Those Partridges are in on it, for sure.'

'Good morning, I'm Detective Sergeant Johns ... I'm afraid it will be difficult to prove any connections the suspect has, but we found ... let's see the notes ... one thousand, three hundred and seventy pounds on him in an envelope marked with this handwriting ...'

'That's Mrs Robson's writing.'

'Naturally, he claims it was only eight hundred pounds you gave him and he put his other money in the same envelope, but he can't say where the other cash came from. We'll need the banknotes as evidence and we'll have to await his trial to see how much money you'll get back, Mrs Robson. At least he hadn't got round to demolishing the old fence, which he would have used for his next job. You were getting a fence that he pulled down elsewhere, that's his method ... But I do think your fence is genuinely in need of some repairs.'

'Such a pleasant, honest-looking man, and he did *your* fence, Madge ...'

'Not on your nelly! The little lying toad! You'd better get your Derek to see to repairing yours.'

Mustn't open the door to strangers again, can't trust anybody, surrounded by evil people. No call from the children. I might forget what to say to them by the time they ring. That Daisy knows she has to find my phone book. It's her fault, I would have rung somebody instead of letting that nasty ragamuffin in ...

23 JANUARY

'Why are you ringing me so late at night, Daphne? ... Don't be silly, it's not eight in the morning ... Eeh, I must have slept in this chair all night then ... but why didn't you ring me yesterday when I needed you? ... Something terrible happened yesterday ... A man ... man broke in here and stole my money ... You know what happened? You're telling me what took place and I was the one who was here? ... I'm supposed to have given him the money? I didn't even know where it was ... You're not searching this house for hidden money ... He's taken the lot, I tell you ... Yes, you'd better come at the weekend ... Well, I could probably add to your list of things to see to if I sit down and put my mind to it ... About time you stopped doing all that volunteer work and took care of me ... OK, on with your work, then ...'

I'd have no life if I devoted myself to looking after Mother ... They have asked me to chair the Guild, but as secretary of the Trust, would I have time for that *and* looking after her? Mother would make sure that I never left her side, far too possessive – she drove all those boyfriends away, all – well all three of them, and two were quite serious, but she used to drop little hints about me, silly things I'd done when younger ... I thought it was just to embarrass me then, but I realise now there was a more sinister motive, and they were only too aware that she would have been a millstone round their neck if they were to marry me. Well, Dr Devonshire says I mustn't have her living with me anyway, otherwise I'll be more doolally than her.

Daphne might as well have married for all the use she is, what was the name of that lovely young man? Ever so polite to me, he was, would have made a good son-in-law, ever so attentive, always bringing me little gifts, don't know why they broke off, she has an awkward character, blessed if I know where it comes from, not from me ... and Alfred was the kindest person you'd ever meet, don't see his like today, so her difficult nature must come from my mother – now she was a tartar if ever you saw one, fierce temper, nobody liked to cross her, my dear father didn't understand what upset her ... Daphne doesn't need the money any more, no children, must have put a fair bit by for a rainy day ... She could give up that volunteer work today, but it's a good excuse not to have to do things for her poor abandoned mother ... How long have I been sitting in this chair? Must wind the clock up, it must have stopped, can't still be ten at night ...

24 JANUARY

'Didn't see you yesterday, Daisy.'

'You were fast asleep in that chair, must have had a bad night, so I let you sleep. Your daughter said you were all right, as she had spoken to you in the morning.'

'She hasn't phoned me in donkey's years.'

'You didn't warm your dinner yesterday. What a shame! Your daughter-in-law prepared it specially for you.'

'Couldn't have been hungry. What do I need the energy for?'

'To keep you going.'

'Going for what. Going to the looney bin? That's where they'll want to put me.'

'I think you ought to have meals on wheels, as they come ready to eat ...'

'What did you say? That sloppy muck, I'd rather be in the poorhouse.'

'No, no, they really do tasty food now ...'

'Don't waste your breath. Do you want to poison me off?'

'It's my day off tomorrow. Kelly will call and do your main shopping as usual. It's best left to the same person to keep account ...'

'So that's where all my money has been going. I'll let you into a little secret ... I'm broke, my money has all vanished.'

'Not to worry ... there's some in the cash box, we put forty pounds in there that was left over after you paid that swindler to mend your fence.'

'What? I've hunted everywhere for some money, and you've hidden it from me again.'

'We've explained it all before, Mrs Robson. In any case, your son or daughter will have to bring some more cash soon.'

'Huh, a likely outcome!'

Must send a text message to her son's mobile. He needs power of attorney to draw money from her account. Takes time – he ought to start the procedure now – perhaps with his legal connections he can speed it up.

25 JANUARY

'Excuse me, am I going barmy? Wasn't there a post office here?'

'Ah, you're Mrs Robson, aren't you? ... Didn't they tell you? The post office was shut down a couple of weeks ago. The other one's almost a mile from here. You'd best take the bus.'

'Get off at this stop for the post office. Next time, remember your bus pass, dear.'

'Somebody told me it is Friday, so how do I get my pension from here?'

'We don't issue pensions any more.'

'What? That greedy grasping government has even stopped our pensions! No wonder I'm running out of cash.'

'It must be being paid into your bank account.'

'I don't have one.'

'Well, perhaps we still have a form you could fill in ... Yes, here you are ... and you can open an account here to have the pension paid in, then when you next come, you can withdraw the amount you want.'

Gosh, that old lady looks remarkably like Mrs Robson, but she's walking the wrong way from her house, and we're a mile or more away from it anyway ...

No, she's not at home ... oh God, that probably was her. Back down the main road quick, before she gets run over.

'What's happened?'

'An old dear put up her umbrella to stop the traffic and went charging across.'

'Is she all right?'

'She is, but a couple of vehicles collided ... fortunately, the drivers and passengers seem OK.'

'Kerry? Kelly?'

'Yes?'

'Would you believe it? Road rage I call it, they won't even stop for a defenceless old lady.'

'You must use the crossing, Mrs Robson. What am I saying, "use the crossing"? You shouldn't even be out of your house.'

'A prisoner in my own home, am I? Might as well lock me up for good.'

'Yes, Officer, I'm one of her carers. You won't get much sense from her about it. Let me get her back home. Here's my card. I'll tell you all I can find out about the collision, but you'd be better off asking the passers-by.'

'What's this form crumpled up in your hand, Mrs Robson? ... Request to have pension paid into a savings account ... But your pension is paid in to your account at that post office already!'

'Well, you might have told me, Kerry, to save me the journey there.'

'So that's where you'd been!'

'Couldn't find the one at the bottom of the road, they'd moved it.'

'I'm so sorry about all this, Mrs Robson. I was later than usual, as I did your shopping on my way to you.'

'And so now you mind-read to work out what I want!'

'No, Tracy drew up the list yesterday and showed it to you.'

'She did no such thing! Whatever next?'

26 JANUARY

'So, Mother, these clothes can go to the charity shop, and those are only any good for a jumble sale.'

'Daphne, you'll be giving *me* away to a jumble sale before long! What am I supposed to wear now?'

'You still have a few things left, and I'll take you out to the shops this afternoon to replenish your wardrobe. We'll have lunch out first at your favourite restaurant.'

'I didn't order this, Daphne.'

'You definitely did, Mother, but we'll swap over if you want.'

'Excuse me, waiter, but the food's not properly cooked.

You must have changed your chef. When I was last here, the food was of a much higher standard.'

'I'm sorry, but my mother is very particular.'

'I'll bring her another one.'

'I should think so too.'

'Mother, you said you didn't like that dish anyway ...'

'Fiddlesticks! *I'll* decide what I like and don't like.'

Big mistake. Derek would say, 'I told you so, Daphne.' Can't take her out anywhere decent any more, as she always creates a scene. Telling me not to pay the bill for such tripe was the last straw. Right to the manager's face ... She *would* demand to see him, of course. I'll never be able to go in there again ... Oh help, now to the shops ...

'You're right, madam, you have an excellent eye for quality, the very finest material and the best cut ...'

'My mother doesn't go out any more, except when I take her, so what she really needs is some everyday clothes.'

'I'm out today, aren't I? I must have at least one going-out outfit.'

'Oh, very well, Mother. Could you please show us the kind of daily wear I mean?'

'My daughter is paying, as I have no more money. That's why she's trying to keep the cost down.'

'Not so, Mother. I just want to get you what you really need.'

'My mother has come over very faint.'

'Good heavens, she does look bad. It must be all that trying on. I'll call an ambulance.'

'Please. And I'll settle up for the clothes in this pile once they've seen to her.'

Another scene. Just because she couldn't get the silly

clothes she wanted. The hospital said there was nothing wrong with her. The heat of the shop is all they could think of, though they did think it might also be the repercussions of yesterday's road incident. And I get told off for not having her checked up after that! ... It's the last time I go shopping with her. Fiona can take the next turn.

27 JANUARY

I thought she would ask to go to church. I feel guilty about not waking her up earlier, but I couldn't have faced another outing. Ought to let her sleep after yesterday's exertions ... This house gives me the creeps, I hate spending the night here ... too many bad memories ... my father's death ... Uncle Stanley's rows with her and then they'd both take it out on me... always selfish she was ... no thoughts for a teenage daughter who'd lost her father ... But I had everything I wanted, she wasn't mean in those days, Derek had more of that kind of deprivation, but you want more than feeding and clothing and so on – a little bit of affection wouldn't have gone amiss ... The gulls are lost on the frozen lake, just as they used to be ... They were my friends, what were their names again? ... Absurd, sixteen years old and believing the gulls could converse with me ... I thought they were like me, I suppose ...

'Why on earth didn't you wake me up, Daphne? I had to go somewhere today. To see my sister Maddy, that was it.'
    'Aunt Maddy has been dead for two years now.'
    'I know I'm getting old and frail, but fancy keeping that from me. To think I missed my sister's funeral!'

Just have to put up with the recriminations, no use insisting poor Maddy has passed away when she won't believe me.

45

She thinks Aunt Ellen is still alive as well … How do you explain that she's the only one left? Brothers gone long ago, not much fun outliving your siblings … I tell myself that I must make allowances, but it's really tough some days … Oh, and that hearing aid, she wasn't wearing it yesterday, everybody had to shout at her …

'Mother, what is this new hearing aid doing in the drawer among all this junk in the spare bedroom?'

'Hearing aid, Daphne? Didn't work. National Health rubbish.'

'It's a private one. Derek paid a lot of money for this and he'll be angry if he comes and notices that you're not wearing it.'

'All right, for goodness' sake. I'll give it another try.'

'Why are you shaking your head?'

'Can't hear a blessed word you're saying, that's why.'

'You've turned the volume down. Look, leave the control in this position.'

It's no use, she'll not know how to regulate that aid. Mention Derek and she wants to please him though, amazing the influence a son can have! Perhaps he'll sort it out and that wretched TV remote … and he still hasn't cancelled the papers … Oh, God … I clean forgot about her washing … mustn't let her do any more of it … and her photographs, now where are they? She could have thrown them away when having one of her stupid clear-outs … I'd better stay on for another day and then I can see Tracy as well … Must phone an apology for absence at the Guild meeting early in the morning.

28 JANUARY

'What on earth's up, Mother? ... What time is it? ... Half past four! ...'

'Oh, it's you, Daphne. I thought my sister Maddy was here. Don't look at me like that. She does come from time to time you know.'

'You didn't wake me up for a chat thinking I was Maddy?'

'No ... oh, goodness me, I nearly forgot ... didn't you hear them?'

'Hear who?'

'I think it must be those two boys again. I heard them in the garden.'

'I didn't hear a sound, but then I'm at the front of the house. I'll put the security light on and look out of your bedroom window.'

'Since when do I have a light like that?'

'A year or two.'

'Then you must show me how it works and I'll keep it on all night.'

'Think of the electricity bill!'

Nobody there. Last time Derek was here, she woke him up believing he was a burglar. We must get to the bottom of this ... boys getting over the fence ... If she lived with me, maybe she would sleep better, but then I might develop worse insomnia than I have now ...

'Morning, Mrs Robson. Oh, you're here too, Daphne.'

'This is the young lady who helps me, Daphne. Daisy, no ... D ...'

'Hello Tracy.'

'So, you two know each other, well, well. I never know what's going on behind my back.'

'We'll probably have five or ten minutes in here, Tracy, before she wanders around the house and finds us. There are so many things to discuss, though. Derek has agreed to enquire about power of attorney ...'

'But your mother would have to agree with it and sign the forms.'

'There's the rub. What can we do about this urge to do washing? She always had a thing about cleanliness, would wash clothes thoroughly even when they were worn briefly only once. A psychological thing, but we won't go into that ...'

'I get it in the neck, Daphne, for not making the house look spick-and-span, as she says. We can only do light work ... Perhaps she doesn't like the idea of paying to have her washing done?'

'That also ... and her independent spirit. If Derek and I controlled her money, we would have to write cheques for that type of thing, but when we come, we could always bring cash for her shopping and so on. All the money she withdraws with you now at the post office goes into that cash box, so we shouldn't find money lying about the house.'

'It's difficult sometimes to get her to understand why she is taking the money out of her account ... and signing the form is a bother too ... oh, and it would be helpful if you could locate her photos, as they would help me pass the time of day with her and perhaps cheer her up.'

'Might depress her more, Tracy ... why do any of us want to revive the past? Better to leave part of it at least in that old musty charnel house in our minds ...'

'Hmm ... you were born just before the war, weren't you?'

'Yes, I stopped doing paid work and collected my state pension long ago, so I could look after Mother ...'

'No, that's not why I asked. What I meant is, you couldn't have much memory of your father.'

'Went down on his ship not long before the end of the war, just when we thought he would come through it all unscathed ... I had only seen him for brief periods when he was on leave ... But the way life has turned out for me, what was the point in me being born? ... I often wonder.'

'Don't look at it that way, Daphne. You've led a very good, useful life ... Er ... your mother's second husband, Derek's father, didn't stay around long, according to your mother.'

'A long story. We haven't got time for that. I can hear Mother padding around. Finding the photos is nigh on impossible. No idea where they are, and she won't let you snoop around the house for long without following you and putting you to the inquisition. Before I go, I need to talk to the neighbours to see if they've seen anybody trying to break in around here. It's amazing that she can perceive people outside without her hearing aid ...'

'You did well to get her to wear it today, Daphne ...'

'*There* you are, Daphne – and you here too, Daisy! What are you two plotting?'

29 JANUARY

So, Daphne claims she was here yesterday ... She's trying to spoof me again. Only my sister Maddy was here, at least she cares about me, but I bet your life she has taken some of my things again ... About time Derek called ... What's this food on the top shelf of the fridge? Who put it there? Needs eating, if you ask me ... I feel like cooking one of those delicious dinners like I used to do, but they don't bring me any meat and vegetables ... This had better warm up on the hob, doesn't have the right taste when you put it in that micro con ... constraption ... Watch the news ... depressing rubbish ... murders, bankruptcies, people losing their jobs ... and their heads ... where's the paper? Have they delivered it? But it's the same kind of thing there ... This hearing aid is making everything too loud ... how do you turn it down again?

'I'm so pleased you opened the door just after I rang the bell, Amy.'

'I always do, Madge.'

'No, I usually have to bang the door for ages. Oh, I see you're wearing your hearing aid.'

'It's deafening me. Turn it down, will you?'

'Is that better ... I said, *is that OK, Amy?* ... It's no good, I'll turn it back up a bit, otherwise you won't hear a word I say. There. *There!*'

'No need to shout, Madge.'

'You can turn the TV down a good bit now ... Can't you smell burning, Amy? The smell is getting stronger.'

'I don't cook any more, so you can't.'

'Oh, it's the saucepan! Your dinner is ruined and the pan has had it too.'

'That's because you called and I forgot all about it.'

'Ever so sorry, Amy. I'll bring you a bit of dinner when I cook mine.'

Her saucepan is wrecked and she claims she hasn't eaten today, but the remains of a meal are in the bin – she must have warmed something up. At least she can hear me today. She's had her tablets for the evening ... How long can this go on?

'That's it, Daisy.'

'That's what, Mrs Robson?'

'Your little trick worked. I can now change channels. This one's no good, it's that government minister rabbiting on about his dud plans. Try this other one ...'

'I hope you can always get it back to the channels you like

best. I must go now. See you tomorrow morning, Mrs Robson.'

30 JANUARY

My sister Maddy has messed around with this television again. Can't get BBC. No point if I can't hear it anyway. Maddy has borrowed that hearing aid, most likely. I'll have to have it out with her. Where is she? Hiding upstairs. It's a real struggle to haul myself up step by step, other people have got stair-lifts, but I'm grateful I'm still able-bodied. She's not here. In the front garden? These drab winter days with a blackout up in the sky. If you open a window, that damp shroud seeps into your mind, soaks into your brain cells ... Come spring, I'll be back to normal, and I'll go out for walks without getting frostbite in my bone marrow. That was Maddy going downstairs. I'd recognise her shape any-where. Wait a minute, you ... a word with you ... She must have gone out of the front door ... Must have gone the other way down the street.

'... Morning, Aunty Amy, like to look at my new book?'
    'Oh, come in Norman, N ... N ...'
    'Nigel.'
    'It's full of beautiful pictures, Nigel. But it doesn't look new. Is it a library book?'
    'No. It was a birthday present ... That's my favourite picture ... a garden full of birds ... like yours used to be, Aunty Amy.'
    'You're grown up now, Nigel, how old are you?'
    'Forty-three.'
    'Then you should just call me Amy.'
    'Ooh, that would be too daring.'
    'We'll go and feed the birds.'

'You in Amy Robson's garden there, Nigel?'

'Oh, Aunty, it's Mum, calling over the fence there. I'll have to go.'

'I've told you hundreds of times, you mustn't pester Mrs Robson.'

'He's no bother, Mrs T ... just keeping each other company.'

'Oh, that book, he won't go anywhere without it recently, Amy. His fifth birthday present.'

'Can't remember the other four presents, Mum.'

'He's being serious there, you know. I meant he's had it since he was five, Mrs Robson.'

'He's looked after it well then.'

31 JANUARY

Maddy was always the clever one, outwitting us all. Went to work in the factory at fourteen like me, but she soon worked herself up to a better position on the production line, unlike skivvy me. If it's tough, give it to Amy, she'll stick it out, that's always been the story. Nothing she can't handle when it comes to physical effort, pile it on her, she loves it. Maddy would have time to file her nails, while I was wringing with sweat. Well she's not going to get the better of me this time, having free board and lodging here and making off with my things like she always used to, I'll put a stop to that ...

'Oh, I knew there was something I had to tell you, my cooker's packed up, Daisy ... Daphne'll have to order me a new one.'

'It has been disconnected, Mrs Robson.'

'Whatever for? How am I going to eat warm food?'

'You're not supposed to cook any more.'

'There you go again! I'm in the kindergarten. Anything else I'm not allowed to do in my own home?'

'Please, Mrs Robson! You burnt a saucepan and its contents badly. There could have been a fire.'

'That must have been my sister Maddy. She's always interfering with my things.'

'You'll have to take these meals from the freezer and warm them up in the microwave.'

'Sorry, Daisy, I can't make sense of that constraption.'

'Then, as I've told you before, you can have meals on wheels ...'

'I'd rather be put in a wooden box than shovel that slime down my throat.'

'You *will* be in a wooden box if you stop eating.'

1 FEBRUARY

Mother used to think that as her son I'd inherited her sympathetic spirit, detecting the good, shutting out the evil in others – 'Derek looks for that redeeming feature, refuses to accept the negative,' she'd say, and I'm sure I was better than I am now when I was defending even the indefensible, rescuing the lost cause ... But then the gnawing of the conscience, the rescue of villains, enabling a further spate of crimes, the inexcusable profit-making from what was more plausible as felony than falsely accused innocence, and so then the sudden switch to prosecution, the hunting out of flaws in the defence, detecting the kind of errors I myself would make at the beginning of my career, the breaking down of alibis, the hounding of the cornered victim, squeezing the verdict out of the jury, crushing what might have been a seed of innocence ... Have I become more callous, more vindictive, like my mother became, as I age? She wishes to live to see the day that I become a High

Court judge, but, huh, there is only one real judge above ...
I would have to balance the tolerance of my early career
with my later more shrewd, not to say cynical, self in order
to make it that high up ... Anyway, better ring to say I'll see
her tomorrow – like a murder trial, it won't take further
postponement ...

'Yes, tomorrow, see you tomorrow ... many jobs to do for
you, I know ... about eleven ... o'clock, I mean ... see you
then ...'

She could hardly hear what I was saying – so much for the
hearing aid Daphne fitted on her ... Need an early night,
the driving down, the litanies to listen to, the impossible
problems to try to sort out, the driving back ... Why won't
she accept the idea of living in a nursing home?

2 FEBRUARY

'What time do you call this, Derek?'
  'Eleven, like I said.'
  'The day's nearly over. I expected you at eight o'clock.
You could have stayed the night even ...'
  The usual exaggeration, but what time does she think it
really is? Ah, that clock ... it has stopped completely now, so
she has no idea ...
  'You need another clock, Mother.'
  'Don't you start on that subject as well! Course, it wasn't
your father who bought it, so it means nothing to you –
typical attitude – as a matter of fact it was my sister Maddy or
that Madge Mullins who broke it, neither will own up to it
though.'
  'Be that as it may, it won't tell the time for you any more.'
  'Nobody has time for me any more, come to that, Derek.

At any rate, time is meaningless to me sitting here cooped up like an old hen day in day out, day and night – what difference does it make, let alone what hour it might or might not be?'

'Well, keep the old clock on the sideboard and I'll get you a little one for the mantelpiece.'

'What in heaven's name is the use of a little clock? How could I see the time?'

'What happened to your reading glasses?'

'That fat Mullins woman walked all over them, I think. Course, she knocked them down in the first place, as I always keep them on the side table.'

'We ought to have you tested for long-distance vision.'

'Are you casting aspersions on my family? None of us from my great-grandfather downwards ever needed glasses to see down the street. Reading the paper, well, that's different, but blindness was never one of our failings.'

'Maybe you need another operation for cataracts. Your left eye was never done ...'

'So you'd put your poor old mother through that again, would you? That clumsy foreigner nearly poked my eye out last time and I haven't really seen clearly since.'

'It was a lot better than it had been before the operation.'

'God, I've lived too long – my children know how my eyes work better than me. Whose head are they in?'

She hasn't eaten yet – let's look in the bin ... No dinner in there this time, but ... fancy putting the TV remote in there! Better say nothing, just clean it up and show her again how it works ...

'It's all very well you going on about this and that television button while you're here, but when you go I won't be able to make out which is which again, and another thing, can't you afford to pay for my papers any more? At least I can keep up to date with the help of them, even if the television is useless.'

Could go along with the idea of starting up the paper again but do nothing about it, we'll see ... The days and dates are just as big a mystery to her as are the hours ...

'I can tell by the look on your face, you're thinking, she can't even read the paper without her glasses, and she probably can't make head nor tail of what's inside it, her brain cell count is going down rapidly ... oh, and I don't have that little box with the television like other people, you know, the one that sends in more channels – about time you sorted that out for me ...'

She can't manage to find the channels she's got, but better at least promise to buy her a digital receiver. While I'm upstairs, I'll take a look at her room ... At least – her wardrobe is in order ... strange rearrangement of the drawers ... so that's where the hearing aid got to ...

'Now it's my ears which are meant to be defective! Put that stupid constraption back in the bin where I left it. If there *is* anything wrong with my hearing, it was brought on by that appliance! It damaged my eardrums, it was so loud.'

'So, Mother, I'll have to be heading back home. One last thing though, the chap is coming to fix your fence next week, weather permitting.'

'Nothing wrong with that fence. Alfred put that up with a good deal of sweat and toil, I'll have you know ... If your father had done it, you'd wouldn't be so prejudiced against it.'

3 FEBRUARY

Eeh, the church bells, it must be Sunday – why hasn't Hilda come to take me to the service? Perhaps she's not well ... Won't take me long to walk there ... Daphne must have given me that for Christmas, I'll wear that ...

'Like a lift, Amy? Only you seem to be going the other way ...'

'Ah, Reverend Spoon ...'

'... er, Spooner.'

'Quite, Reverend. But you should be going to church like me, not the other way into town.'

'Join the two others in the back, Amy, if you were intending to go to worship today.'

'Never missed a service in my life on the Lord's Day. People have taken me to church, like Elsie and dear old Hilda ...'

'May she for ever rest in peace.'

'Why, whatever happened to her?'

'Went to our dear Lord a few months ago ... I'm Mrs Fox, by the way, and that is my husband, who is unstable on his feet now ...'

'Well, you might have told me, Reverend! The least I could have done was to have gone to her funeral.'

'I thought you were there, Amy ... oh, but of course I must have been mistaken, with all the mourners present ... By the way, I'll arrange for another parishioner to take you all home, as I have a christening after the Communion.'

4 FEBRUARY

'Whatever's the matter with you, Daisy?'

'Tracy, not Daisy. I've had a row with Sam ... you know,

my boyfriend ... over the weekend, Mrs Robson. He's been seeing another girl.'

'Typical fecklessness of these young lads today. Such an attractive girl as you, what more does he want? Mind you, my second husband ... second? ... Yes, he was the second ... anyway, Stanley was always after other women. My mother did warn me. She said he had slitty eyes, like those people who live in far-off lands, whatever you call them, and have hundreds of women.'

'You do say outrageous things to make me laugh, Mrs Robson!'

'Just the truth, dear. You just sit there and I'll look after you for a change. Like a cup of tea? Course, just what you need to buck up your spirits ...'

'Come and have a look at the water in the kettle, Daisy. Our water supply must be contaminated. There was something about it on television ...'

'That was a film about secret agents poisoning reservoirs ... Oh, did you remember to put the tea leaves in the kettle before you boiled the water?'

'That's the way one always makes tea, dear.'

'And the milk's already in the teapot, I see ...'

'Horrible taste, Daisy. I told you somebody had been at our water.'

'Let me make us a cup of coffee instead, Mrs Robson.'

'Let me know where that boyfriend of yours lives and I'll go and give him a piece of my mind! If I'd known about this, I would have said a prayer for you at church.'

Must phone the vicarage and see if she really has been to church and how she got there. Need to make arrangements for Sundays if she insists on going, as somebody has to take her. Good mind to send her round to Sam's, let her loose

on him, that would teach him a right lesson! What a giggle
... Control yourself now. On to the next client.

5 FEBRUARY

Can't be snow. Haven't had that for ages. Sky like milk of
magnesia. Need some of that to keep me regular. Derek
tobogganing on the field, special days when the school
didn't snatch them from me and there was time to dote on
them a little ... What on earth is Madge Mullins up to?
Going out in ... well, it could be a blitz, what's the word? ...
Thought it was the German invasion, all those airmen
dropping down in their parasols, para ... Falling like flies
they were. We've had it, they'll round us all up, my father
said, we'll be herded into concentrating camps ... It was
only that big air battle, German planes being shot down,
what a relief when we heard the news ... knew we'd sock it
to them ... They'll never get hold of this country, my father
said ... he had that fighting spirit, that's who I got it from,
what I've got left in me ... Mind you, he did panic at
times ...

That's how I used to ice cakes, why don't I bake another
one? ... All crinkly icing just like that, nice when you don't
have to stray out in it ... No visitors today in this ... Loneliness is second nature to me anyway ... entertain myself
with my reflexes, remem ... mustn't brood on the past too
much ... There's Stan explaining how he couldn't get back
that night because of the snow, spent it with that other
woman, if my name isn't Amy – what was the hussy's name?
Always have excuses, men like that, my mother never liked
the shifty look in his eyes ...

'Ever so sorry I couldn't get to you earlier in the day, they hadn't gritted the roads, Mrs Robson.'

'Nobody has any grit today, Daisy.'

'I can see you haven't warmed up your main meal of the day ...'

'How do you work that out? Can you see the contents of my stomach now?'

'I can see the meal I left yesterday out of the freezer for you, Mrs Robson. Besides, I know from the number of meals left in the freezer. I'll pop this in the microwave now ...'

'Always checking up on me. Don't know why you don't put in one of those spy cameras to follow my every move ...'

'Now you've eaten you look a little better ...'

'Why? What is the matter with me, for goodness' sake, you'll have me out of here in an ambulance before long ...'

'Ah, I have some bad news for you ...'

'Derek's dead! One of those gangsters got his revenge for being put behind bars, I often warned him to be on the lookout ...'

'No, it's Mrs Mullins, she fell down in the snow and twisted her ankle badly. Fortunately, she was well padded up so didn't break any bones, but an ambulance took her in for a look-over ... I'm afraid she won't be able to come and see you for a couple of weeks maybe, and she may well have lost her confidence to go out ...'

6 FEBRUARY

I could have sworn that somebody told me something about Mrs Mullins – perhaps she's gone away to stay with that son of hers for a while ... Why can't I go and spend a few days with Derek or Daphne? Too much of a burden, when you can't be of much use. How I used to sort out the mess in their homes, a tidy parent always seems to bring up untidy children . . .

No, no answer . . . try again . . .

'Hello Madge. It's Amy.'

'I'm not Madge. It's Daphne here.'

'What are you doing at Mrs Mullins's? Your own mother needs help!'

'I'm at home. You dialled the wrong number – two is for me, five for Mrs Mullins.'

'What are all these other numbers for?'

'Mother, they only go from nought to nine on your phone; one is for Derek, three the carers, four the doctor – those are the important ones now.'

'Well I'm blowed, what a funny phone. It didn't used to be like that, why did you change it?'

'To make it simple for you to phone people.'

'You call that simple! You can see that it doesn't work, because I want Mrs Mullins.'

'Put the phone down and dial five.'

No use, I'll have to go round and see her. Where's my coat? They've hidden my coat . . . and my shoes . . . Trying to stop me going out, are they? The sun's out today and the snow is melting, so I don't need a coat, just pop there in my slippers . . .

'Morning, Mrs Robson.'

'What do you want with me, you . . . you . . .'

'It's only me – Mrs Partridge. From my window I saw yer slip up in the snow and get all wet – my! And in yer slippers too! Yer'll have to come in to my warm 'ouse and dry out, ducky.'

'Not on your nelly! I'm going to knock on Mrs Mullins's door.'

'No point, ducky, she's tucked up in a bed that I made up for 'er in 'er living room. You know how I like to take care of poor old dears like ...'

'Like me, that's what you are instigating, aren't you? Well, you can keep your filthy hands off me, you scoundrel!'

'No need to take on like that ... No point knocking on 'er door, I told yer, Madge's ankle won't allow 'er to get to it.'

'Think I've got a screw or two loose, don't you? So how does she open it to you?'

'No need, ducks, I've got her key, see ...'

'I'm going back home to phone Madge.'

Madge's blood as well, like poor Gertie's. Well, she'll never suck up to me ...

7 FEBRUARY

I wonder whether Mother managed to dial Mrs Mullins ... At least Madge has a son, it's the ones who have no family who ... Who will help me when I get to my mother's state of mind? Who knows whether even Derek will be around ... Perhaps his daughter? In fact, Lucy should really be asked to pay a visit to Mother to assess her – after all, she is a psychiatrist, and she did do a placement with old people. Why hasn't Derek seen to it? We ought to have a professional opinion about her ability to live alone ... Careful now, they'll be asking me to take her in ... Derek might assume that it would be the natural thing for me to do for company for myself as well ... Huh! He's very selfish, career-minded ...

'Derek Robson has requested our next item for his sister Daphne. If you are listening as usual, Daphne, your brother has fond memories of your playing this piece on your piano when he was a young teenager. For those who know it less well than Daphne, it's Schumann's Fantasy in C.'

I'm dreaming ... Derek thinking of me? Yes, the radio *is* playing the Fantasy, yes, fantasy and passion – that's what Derek heard in the piece as a teenager himself, he said I was a young woman of passionate fantasy. Wretched ingredients for success in life, collision guaranteed with Super Nova reality. But fantasy has been squeezed out ... look at that dried-up lemon in the mirror ... anti-ageing cream makes no impression. As for passion, Mother poured too much water on that – the boys and then the men were not worth expending it on, in her estimation ... Must get back to playing the piano, all the music is still there.

8 FEBRUARY

'Kelly here. Your mother has caught a chill. Tracy said that she didn't look her real self yesterday ... Apparently, she fell down in the snow on Wednesday ... perhaps she didn't dry out or change her clothes ... No, Mrs Mullins can't do anything for her, because she tumbled too and twisted her ankle badly ...'

What *is* Mother's real self? I never made that out. About time Derek went to see her. There are still things to be sorted out ... the cash situation – does he check the bills? Has he requested power of attorney? Perhaps he'll be in tonight – still need to thank him for the radio request ... Why do I always think ill of people, often just when they are thinking kindly of me? Don't start on that slithery slope ... Ring Mother now ... no, later, when I have gathered strength ...

'It hasn't snowed this year, Daphne, so how could I have caught a chill in the snow? Besides, you never allow me to go across the doors, keep me cooped up in this budgie cage, I could go raving bonkers ... There's no need to hide it, you think I'm far gone already ... I was reading one of my old books, what was it called now? Anyway, the man is trying to prove that his wife is loopy ... Course I still read ... I've taken to books because my sister keeps coming and nicking the newspapers ... She's a sly devil, always was, doing things behind my back ... What do you mean, Derek stopped the papers? What business has he to cut off my one outlet to the outside world? ... The television? It keeps getting stuck on the same channel, it ought to be seen to ... Perhaps I *ought* to have a cold, then I'd get you paying more attention to me ...'

It might be better not to phone her at all and avoid all the abuse – she won't even remember tomorrow that I did phone today ...

9 FEBRUARY

'Don't take on like that, Mrs Robson – everybody's worried about you; your children must have phoned, and even Mrs Mullins – you probably didn't hear the phone ringing ...'

'Daisy, don't you start up about those hearing constraptions again, none of them work.'

'Kelly was pleased with you yesterday, you ate all your meal up ...'

'Good little girl, aren't I, teacher's pet with Kelly, are you going to write a good report for me today?'

'Report?'

'Don't think I haven't noticed you writing in that little

notebook before you go each day. I must read it, where is it?'

'Oh, I take it with me.'

'Don't pull the wool over my eyes, they may have had cata ... contracts in them, but ...'

'Didn't know you had contact lenses – thought you wore, or rather *should* wear, reading glasses ...'

'Not lenses, those things they had to operate on ... anyway, they've gone and I can see all your little tricks. Kerry was writing in it yesterday – if you took it, as you say you did, she couldn't have done, could she? I was always top of the class at school, so you can't make a fool out of me ...'

'Pity you had to leave school at fourteen, otherwise you would have ...'

'Gone far like my children – well, like Derek, as Daphne has wasted her life.'

'I wouldn't say that ...'

'So you know the children better than the mother? When I want your opinion, dear, I'll ask for it. I can see you didn't leave school when you were fourteen. Besides, I was thirteen – as the eldest of six ... or was it seven? ... I had to stay home to help my mother look after my little brothers. The welfare officer caught me one day as I opened the door, thinking it was my sister Maddy back from school. He said I had to go back to school or my parents would go to jail, but my mother invented some illness for me, so I never got back to learn anything more, but that doesn't mean I can't read and write – I learned before all the other children did when I was very young and would read novels at the back of the class while they were struggling with their acrobatics, their alpha ...'

'... bet.'

'Don't take words out of my mouth! What were we talking about?'

'Mrs Mullins. Perhaps you should give her a call.'

'Kelly? Yes, it's Tracy. We'll have to hide the notebook about Mrs Robson, as she knows about it. I'll ask Daphne if she can think of somewhere and I'll let you know.'

10 FEBRUARY

'Well, I've come in like you asked, Maddy.'

'Madge!'

'Yes, Madge, I'm not supposed to go out either, but they can't keep me prisoner for ever. What's all this about the Pheasants?'

'Partridges. Can't keep them away from the house, Amy, they're into my things upstairs, say they're only going to the toilet, but they must have solid constipation, the time they take up there, and I can't get upstairs because of the ankle ...'

'Eeh, I wouldn't put it past them to be robbing you.'

'More likely they're nosing into my affairs to see if I'm worth all the trouble they're taking over me. Do stay, I know you'll see to them ...'

'Give them short shrift, that's what I'll do ...'

'That's them now, I bet. Go and open the door to them, Amy.'

'Do I know you?'

'It's me – Mrs Partridge, ducky.'

'Mrs Robson to you. That's beside the point, I wasn't aware that you lived here.'

'Just popping in to see Madge ...'

'That won't be necessary. You can see that I'm already here.'

'You need 'elp yerself, poor old soul – how can yer look after somebody else?'

'How can crooks look after anybody? Mrs Mullins's son

will be calling on you soon, and my son, Derek, did you know that he was a barrister?'

'No need to take that attitude! Only doing a good turn!'

'Take a turn somewhere else then. If Mrs Mullins tells me you've been in here again, I'll let the law loose on you. Good day.'

'Brilliant, Amy!'

'Knew I'd soon fettle them.'

11 FEBRUARY

There's no point in the Reverend Spooner asking me why Mother didn't answer her bell yesterday. Nice of him, though, to have gone round to offer her a lift to church. She wouldn't have been out somewhere, would she? Why didn't he ring Daphne instead of me? If I can't make it down to her next weekend, I'll ask Lucy if she'll pay her a visit. Daphne has some bee in her bonnet about getting a mental health assessment done on Mother. Back to the notes on the brief – some bastard preying on old people ... Hope she doesn't fall for any of those con men again ... Oh, what was the name of that chap who tricked her about her fence? Hmm ... hope it's not the same chap as the one here, otherwise I'll have to drop the brief. Must ask Tracy, as she was there at the time ... Hmmm ... 'Uses contacts around the neighbourhood, no proof as to their involvement though' ... sounds like those Partridges ...

'Thank you, Tracy. Cowans was his name, you say. Thanks – this is another fellow then, so that's all right ... Oh, of course I'm concerned that the crook who tried to swindle my mother is brought to justice too, but ... oh, you mean that I should come down and see to her problems? ... No, no, that's all right, I don't mind you saying that – you're only trying to help ... As a matter of fact, I had next weekend in mind to come down anyway ... Yes, I understand that you have to hide the notebook. I'll take a look at it when I get there, but go ahead and I'll jot down your concerns now ...'

Those lads were in my garden again, but my sister Maddy says that she invited them in, whatever for I'll never know, trust her to encourage such hoodlums, they've damaged another panel of my fence with their ball games, why don't my children see to these repairs? Another day is going by and still nobody pays attention to me after all I did for them, working my fingers to the bone day after day and they don't think twice about it – fit for the junkyard, that's what we are. My advice to the young would be don't grow old and be forgotten, but they'll be taking pills to keep them young by that time, selfish lot ... Where is that girl who pops in and what time is it? ... Soon time for bed ... How long have I been in this chair? No television and no papers, can't remember what book I was reading ... it was the red one, but then there are a lot of red ones ...

12 FEBRUARY

'Why haven't you been in to see me these past few days, Daisy?'

'You used to complain that I popped up here too often, Mrs Robson! I was here yesterday in fact.'

'Well, you must have crept around like my sister, because I didn't see or hear you. What about the day before that – Friday?'

'You mean Sunday. We don't come in on Sundays, but perhaps you ought to have a visit from someone.'

'I should jolly well think so! Leaving me on my own at my age, it's an utter disgrace!'

'If you were in a ... in sheltered accommodation, Mrs Robson, you would have somebody to attend to your needs all the time.'

'Don't twist what I say! I'm talking about help here. Nobody is moving me out of my own house, it took a lot of scrimping and scraping to pay for this place, you know, and money wasn't so easy to come by in those days. You spend it like water now ...'

'Oh, I see that you've brought out some photos.'

'Those are the only ones I could find, Daisy. My sister must have borrowed the others and she took a loan of some of my cash while she was here too, without letting me know, because I can't find any money ...'

'Don't you look lovely in this one! Is that Derek? Or is it Daphne's christening?'

'Hideous outfit. That was all you could afford in those days. We put her christening off for a while and then there was a war on, as we used to say. Should have made the dress myself as I usually did, but Alfred persuaded me to buy one.'

'So it's Daphne ... What a beautiful smile!'

'She always was a happy child, skipping and singing. I don't know what's got into her these days.'

'The cares of the world, eh?'

'Don't be silly, she hasn't a care in the world, always had plenty of money and no children, not like her hard-worked, hard-up mother.'

'Hmm ... who's this then?'

'That's the one I wanted you to see, that's my interfering sister Maddy. If you spot her in this house, let me know and I'll throw her out without more ado. You can keep her photo, then you will recognise her when she next gets in. I should never have given her a key.'

'Well, I'll put the photos away in this drawer for now, and

perhaps we'll have a little look at the others when I get time.'

13 FEBRUARY

What's Amy up to at this time of night, banging around? No point phoning her, as she won't hear and my ankle's still not up to going out. Besides, it's three a.m. Must ring that Tracy in the morning. Dearie me, Amy's shouting at somebody, perhaps there are burglars. If it goes on, I'll dial 999.

Must have dozed off ... It's that racket next door at Amy's again that woke me back up – is somebody moving the furniture around? Burglars! I'm going to get the police!

'Yes, Mrs Mullins, I understand your concerns, but we need the code to her key box to get in. Her family didn't register it with the police and it's not the social services' job to inform us ... I can hear the noise down your phone though, definitely an argument with someone ... just a relative, perhaps?'

'She has no brothers or sisters left alive, and she wouldn't quarrel like that with her children or grandchildren – or would she?'

'Well, of course, whoever it is would open the door to us, as we'd let them know it was the police. We can wait a bit, and if it goes on, we'll have to break the door down to see if she needs protection. In these cases of dementia, we often find that the person in question is rowing with themselves.'

'It's OK now, Mrs Mullins, you should be able to get some kip. Mrs Robson has opened up to us. She claims that two lads came in through her back door. In fact the lock is completely loose. Things have been shifted around in the house and drawers emptied, so we'll have to investigate, even though it could still be her own doing.'

'She's not safe to be left alone, if you ask me, Officer. Will you tell her son or daughter about tonight, or do you want me to?'

'As it could have been a break-in, we'll inform them, but to save us time please let us have their phone numbers if you have them, Mrs Mullins.'

'They're in my phone book. I have had need to contact them in the past ...'

14 FEBRUARY

I'll have to see Mother myself this weekend and weigh up what went on that night. We can't have the neighbours woken up by her shenanigans and have the police called out again ... Steady on – it could have been a burglary – I should have checked that lock. She is always trying to tighten it with that silly screwdriver to make it more secure and has probably worked it loose. Apparently there's no real damage to the furniture, but a mess with all the drawers. Of course, she could have been having one of her clean and tidy-ups, which are an absolute disaster ... Daphne has taken it badly and is on some even stronger pills to steady her nerves, so I can't ask her to pop down again ... I wonder whether Daphne won't go bonkers as well at this rate. We must press for a mental check-up for Mother, with a view to forcing her into a home before we all end up in the asylum ...

'Derek? Why on earth are you waking me up at this time of night? What? Just to tell me you are coming on Saturday?'

'Can't you see that it is light outside? It's lunchtime, Mother.'

'I've got thick curtains to keep the cold out and it looks pitch black out there to me ... Lunch? You must have your lunch very early – not good for you, you'll be putting on weight again ... The back-door lock? Nothing wrong with that, I've fixed it ... My television? Huh, no point in sorting out that control thing as the programmes are utter rubbish – in fact, I'm going to write a letter to say I'm not paying for my licence next year ... What do you mean? I don't pay for my licence at my age anyway? I distinctly remember that it cost me about fifty pounds and that's far too much for an old lady like me ... Over a hundred pounds? ... They've put it up that much? ... Well, even if I don't have to pay it, I'm going to give them a piece of my mind, the bald-dash you have to put up with on that stupid box and they're milking us for it ... Didn't I say balderdash then? ... I eat up all my dinners, but I'm worried about where they're coming from. Are they hygienic? I mean, if they come on those wheels ... They don't? Fiona and Daphne take turns to bring them, do they? Well you could have fooled me. Can't they give them to me to put away, instead of hiding them? That Daisy girl has to locate them for me ... Derek, they do *not* show me where they are in the freezer! ... Clocks? What else are you coming for? I think you ought just to come down and see your poor old mother before she passes on – whoever heard the like of it, fix this and that – you'll be fixing me next with some drugs to keep me quiet, don't you think I don't know what they do to us poor old folk ...'

Daphne's right, you need a stiff brandy or whisky after phoning her, the ungrateful old bat!

15 FEBRUARY

'No, it's Kelly. It's Tracy's day off.'

'I don't have a Tracy calling on me, only Daisy. She's more friendly than you, why can't she come every day?'

'We all need a rest, Mrs Robson. Aren't you pleased, though?'

'What have I got to be pleased about? Go on, let's hear it.'

'Your son's coming to spend the weekend with you!'

'Oh, put the flags out! Whatever did I do to deserve such recognition? I'd better put my best frock on and curtsy, I suppose.'

'Don't be too bitter ...'

'There you go again with your nasty remarks. Daisy never talks to me like that ...'

'Really sorry, Mrs Robson, didn't want to upset you, I'll just get on with a few things ...'

Whatever does that hussy get up to? No re ... refinement in her, too blunt for my liking, and too clumsy, she'll wreck the beautiful furniture that I have preserved since Alfred made such sacrifices to buy it, going on longer tours of duty, not seeing me for months on end, they're mollycoddled today, couples can't be parted for long like we were ...

'Kelly here, reporting on Mrs Robson ... Yes, I've filled in the notebook, but I just wanted to get it off my chest ... Her mind's on form today, worst luck for me ... I mean, I copped one of her bad-tempered outbursts ... Tracy's right, Mrs Robson took a few chips out of her furniture the other night, goodness knows what she was doing with it... No, the trouble is that she blames me for every bit of damage she finds ... I'm just thankful I only do one day a week here ... Yes, I know Tracy finds her a sweet old dear and so on – perhaps she grows on you with time ...'

16 FEBRUARY

'Well, I won't be stopping today, Derek, now you're here. We've run through everything, I hope?'

'Thanks, Tracy, you're ever so good with her, it's very much appreciated by Daphne and me. I don't know where you find the patience to deal with my mother.'

'Oh, go on, she's a lovely lady really.'

'I must tell Daphne that, but she'll think it's a case of mistaken identity!'

The electric clock in the kitchen is working all right ...

'My watch must have stopped. Could you give me the time from the electric clock in the kitchen, Mother?'

'You rarely give *me* any time ... It's nearly twenty to ... past ... it's one, then another one and then two more ones, oh, why don't they have clocks like they used to? Just to confuse us old people, I think ...'

'Eleven eleven then.'

'No need to say it twice, eleven o'clock, I'm not deaf, and in any case, you've made me wear one of those hearing helpers ...'

'No, eleven minutes past eleven ...'

'For heaven's sake, what do eleven more minutes matter to me?'

'Just check your clock with the hands in the sitting room, the one you always go by, to see if it's right.'

'Of course it's right, never go wrong those old clocks ...'

She spends most of the day in the sitting room and doesn't realise the clock has stopped working, which means she has lost the ability to read even the hour hand. The cooker is switched off, so you can't read its digital clock, and the same goes for the one on the microwave, as it is switched on and off by the carers as and when they need it ... Anyway, Mother has lost her understanding of numbers, so no type of clock is of any use to her ... No wonder her body clock is out of sync ... More urgently, I must find the back-door lock. According to Tracy, it must have been off all night – but did Mother take it right off? Try the shed ... Good, it's open ... Where's the lawnmower gone? Perhaps those boys do come and raid the shed at night and try to break into the house after all ... Ah, here's the back-door lock on the shed floor ... Now let's take a look at the garden ... What on earth has happened to the lawn? Bad case of moles? Oh, so, *there's* the lawnmower ... She can't have been trying to cut the lawn in mid-winter, surely?

'Do you really think I want to catch my death of cold out there in the garden, Derek? I've told you until I'm blue in the face, it's my two nephews who mess around in the garden ...'

'What nephews?'

'Why, Maddy's boys, she lets them get up to all kind of tricks.'

'Your nephews live in the States ... the USA.'

'So, you don't think I know what the States means! Well, for your information, they're back here on holiday.'

'Worse than Bertie Wooster's nephews, if you ask me.'

'Don't bring your friend Wooster into it. At any rate, you're the one who has to put a stop to them – why, aren't you a bar ... a law person? Take them to court and deal with them, a good thrashing is what they need ...'

'You can't punish people like that any more, Mother ...'

'More's the pity, no wonder there are so many young thugs about. Kid-glove tactics today, if you ask me. If only I was in charge of ...'

17 FEBRUARY

'Get up this instant, Derek.'

Oh, at least she remembered I was here. What? Five o'clock? What's happened now?

'Are you going to get your lazy bones out of that bed? You've got to take me to church. Old Elsie Lipton has forgotten to call on me again with her taxi.'

Lipton? She got too old to drive her taxi and shouldn't have been driving at all. Last time she took Mother to church there was a terrible accident … a bus and a sports car collided trying to miss Elsie Lipton's car as she pulled onto the main road … I had to rush down here, only to find Mother as right as rain and old Mrs Lipton only suffering from mild concussion, complaining about the standards of modern driving … and half the passengers on the bus were in hospital with cuts and bruises and the poor car driver was in intensive care … I hoped that nightmare would not come back to haunt me … Anyway, how does Mother know it's Sunday? Even if I did remind her last night, she surely would have forgotten since?

'How do I look, Derek? … What's wrong? The dress is good enough for church, isn't it?'
    'You've put it on over your nightie.'
    'No … er, yes … well I just wanted to check if it would be all right before I got dressed.'
    'It's far too early, Mother. Lie down for another couple of hours.'
    'You know jolly well that I like to be on time for things, especially church. I'll go and have some breakfast.'

'Had your breakfast then, Mother?'

'I did have some porridge, but I was waiting to see if you wanted anything cooked.'

'The porridge is still in the microwave.'

'That must be yours.'

'I can't see your dirty bowl, Mother.'

'Then I must have washed it.'

'Tricky things, these microwaves, not sure if I can work yours. Can you help me out?'

'That's a fine thing – you come supposedly to show me a thing or two and I end up giving you instructions! ... Stupid constraption ... the thing won't start, even though I pressed all the buttons ... I'll make you some scrambled egg on the cooker ... Just sit down and rest, I expect those villains you deal with have worn you quite out ...'

Fifteen minutes already, but at least there's no smell of burning ... Oh, of course, the cooker is disconnected ... I'll pop it back on to see if she can still cook some meals ...

Another quarter of an hour at least – what on earth is she up to?

'It can't cook like that, Mother, it's virtually on zero, you need to turn up the heat ...'

'I've had strict instructions not to burn the house down and I'm following them to the letter, and now you're encouraging me to send the place up in flames. Sometimes I think you want to get rid of me, or is it that you want to force me to leave this lovely house of mine?'

18 FEBRUARY

'I had a wonderful weekend, Mrs Robson. I'm sure you did too ...'

'What? All on my own in this dreary house? What was so good about your weekend, Daisy?'

'My boyfriend took me away for a romantic weekend ...'

'Did he indeed? And you're not married!'

'In your day couples had to be married before they did that sort of thing, but today ...'

'I won't ask what sort of thing, Daisy dear. Anyway, I'm glad for you, he seems a nice young man ...'

'It was a Valentine's treat ... champagne was waiting in the room, which had a four-poster bed, and then there was a jacuzzi in the bathroom, it was just like in that film, and Sam ...'

'Proposed to you.'

'No, unfortunately not. It was only the other week that he was flirting with that other girl, so I suppose he was making up to me ...'

'Can't get my head round young people's goings-on today. Make sure he sticks with you. In any case, if he doesn't, he'll be the loser.'

I see there are some more of her old photos here in the drawer. Derek must have rooted them out.

'Who are these two fine-looking boys then, Mrs Robson?'

'You must be on the lookout for them. They're the devils who are causing havoc in my garden.'

'The photo was taken many years ago, and they look like little angels.'

'Always up to mischief if you ask me.'

'Oh, and this must be your second husband, because he's not the one in that wedding photograph on the sideboard.'

'You can tear that up! I rue the day I married that no-gooder.'

'But then you wouldn't have had Derek.'

'The things you have to go through to have a child! Childbirth was no joke in those days either. Born here in this room he was before the midwife could arrive, none of your plush hospital beds and drugs to ease the pain. Ask Mrs Mullins, she could hear me screaming next door, just like I heard her when her son was born, and when Daphne came into the world, it was even worse – for a start it was my first child and there was no help at all ...'

At least the photographs get her talking, but I can't get her on to cheerful memories somehow. Give the pictures a rest until another day.

19 FEBRUARY

'Here's a photo of you in a nurse's uniform, Mrs Robson! You never told me that you had been a nurse – I thought you had worked most of your life in a shop.'

'Do I look like the person who would stay all her days in a dead-end job? I left the shop when I married Alfred. Besides, during the war I had other jobs. When that cheater Stan finally left me and he didn't send any money home for weeks on end afterwards even with a young son at home, what was I to do? I became an auxiliary nurse while I was doing my training to become qualified. They made me lift all the heavy patients, no lifting aids in those days, just physical effort, but I was used to it from humping the factory packages around when a slip of a girl – I had more strength than any man, I can tell you – imposed upon I was – don't you be too willing, Daisy, or you'll have to do more than your fair share in life while idle loafers sit around ...'

'You passed your exams to qualify, then?'

'What's so amazing about that? Mind you, people around here, even my own children, didn't think I was up to it. Didn't they realise where Derek gets his brains from? Not easy to study at night after a hard day's slog and a young child to see to and nobody to explain things to me when they were hard to grasp, but I have staying power, you see, something lacking in most of the younger generation, not you, of course, my dear, and I got through. Medicines were the hardest to sort out, but even though I was a bit slow in ad ... in ministering them, the examiner said I wouldn't poison anybody and that was the main thing, the terrible things you hear today about overdoses or the wrong drugs given, wouldn't have happened in my day ... and without much money from Stanley – they didn't have ways of making deserters like him pay up properly in those days, I had to work on till sixty in the hospital and after that I was a matron in an old people's home ...'

'I bet it was a marvellous place with you in charge. Perhaps you ought to visit it, it might be just the sort of place you would like to go to yourself ...'

'You're talking to somebody who knows what it's like to live in one of those parking bays, they just park their old relatives there and visit them for a few minutes when they feel like it, and the old people gradually lose their person ... personality, identity, call it what you like, would you know who you were if you were herded together with others already gaga and nobody to speak to you for days on end? Of course I tried to chat with them, but we were always short-staffed and the nurses had their work cut out to put them on and off the toilet and in and out of bed, dress them and feed them and so on – just like the production line in the factory it was, you're not smart enough to persuade me to go and live in one of those old people parks ...'

'Hmm ... so when you retired for good, you looked after those old people like Miss Stokes ... Gertie.'

'How is she, by the way? I must pop and see her.'

20 FEBRUARY

The house hasn't had a good turn-out in a long while ... miserable curtains ... carpets getting worn out ... haven't been across the door in ages ... birds not fed ... television no sound ... must have dozed off ... Was that somebody in the other room? ... What's for lunch or did I already have it? ... Cold-looking day outside ... to think I used to put washing out on icy days ... must do some underclothes ... must be in the washing basket ... none in the drawer, I think ... Did I sleep a bit there? ... Too stiff to get out of this chair ... Recognise his face but don't know his name ... some government man ... sound won't get louder ... can't find the button to switch it off ... no paper today again ... I've dropped the book while having a nap ... not the proper book anyway, I must ask that girl if she took the green one ... the big green one, I've read the little green one ... Depressing house ... still, it's all you've got ... they're not shoving me out of it ... Daphne could bring me some new curtains, she did promise me some ... the door banged, better see who it was ... Did I check the door? ... I must have nodded off ... Ought to ring Madge ... can't find the phone book ... that's right, press this number, Derek said ... That was the police! What are they doing at Madge's house? Asking me if I wanted to report anything ... Should have told them about those two rascals ... always trying to break in here ... Something wrong with Madge ... those Peacocks have been in there, poisoned her perhaps ... Should do that washing ... or did I just hang it out a moment ago? ... Stomach pain ... couldn't have been lunch, I only had a bread roll ... need to eat something ... Where does Derek's wife put those meals? ... Dirty plate, that's odd ... Maddy's been here again and eaten my dinner ... this can't go on ... must have it out with her ...

'Maddy! ... Maddy! ... No use pretending you're not here ... you're out in the garden again helping your two boys over my fence, don't think I don't see through your schemes ...'

Check from my bedroom window ... poor birds, no food left, couldn't have put any out today ... What was I looking at the garden for? ... Oh, yes, the weather ... no good for washing, the clouds have come over ... Eeh! Somebody's walking across the ceiling, a burglar has got into the lobby, the lo ... the roof space ... those two boys, of course ...

'I know you're up there! Just you come down this instant! I can't understand why your mother doesn't deal with you ...'

21 FEBRUARY

'Good to see you lying on your bed, Mrs Robson, but you didn't change into your nightdress!'

'Got dressed, Daisy ... and then I ... I lay down again ... I was dog tired ... too much work yesterday ...'

'That must have been between my visits. Each time I came in yesterday, you were fast asleep in your chair and I couldn't wake you, except once to get you to eat a bit of dinner ...'

'Well, after you left I did some washing and ... then what did I do?'

From the case notes:

Patient may have gone to bed eventually last night but didn't undress. Found her still in day clothes on bed at 10 a.m. No sign of her doing any washing yesterday, although she claims it is the reason for her fatigue today. She had already eaten her meal today before I came in again at 2 p.m., but the remains of it were still very cold, so it was probably not properly defrosted nor even re-heated. Relatives: please insist on meals on wheels.

22 FEBRUARY

'Why, it's Madge! Thought you'd forgotten me.'

'I couldn't get out for just over a fortnight with that ankle, Amy.'

'What ankle?'

'You know, the one I sprained in the snow.'

'Snow? I didn't know that we'd had snow. Snow in April, well I never!'

'It's still February dear ... anyway, you didn't ring me up to have a chat, ever so lonely I was ... What have you been up to these past two weeks?'

'I went to London to see my father. He hasn't been well since my mother died, poor old soul, all on his own ...'

'Er ... yes, well ... hmm ...'

'Not on that chair, Madge!'

'Oh, yes, Derek's chair – sorry ... Anyway, where was I? Oh, Stephen managed to tear himself away from that bridge ...'

'God! He wasn't thinking of doing himself in, was he?'

'No, that new bridge he built. As I told you before, it developed complications.'

'Whatever did he build it for? I didn't think his garden was as big as Derek's.'

'I bet his garden is twice the size of Derek's, but the bridge I'm telling you about is ... .'

'Come on now, you would go across the world to see gardens, like that man on television does, and not find a garden as big or as beautiful as Derek's ...'

'The bridge is causing him some headaches, but Stephen's really bright, he'll solve the teething problems, just you see ...'

'Nothing wrong with my Derek's head or teeth, he comes from strong stock, but your Stephen is getting on a bit now and might need false teeth ...'

'So it was good of Stephen to pop round to see me last weekend. Oh, and Derek popped in to have a chat with him as well ...'

'The very idea! Coming to see you and your son and not putting a foot in here to see his long-suffering mother ...'

'Go on, now, Amy, he said he was just leaving after spending the weekend with you.'

'Well, I've never known my Derek to be a liar, but this is just too rich!'

23 FEBRUARY

Not being able to read Mother's case notes, it's good that I receive calls from Mrs Mullins now she is out and about again and can fill us in ... So, I'm a liar now, am I? Well, I've spent a lot of time making a case out for lies, but I must now make a case against them ... However, I failed to have this latest defendant put away ... Can't miss out next time, they'll think I'm losing my knack – and perhaps I am, with my mind too much on Mother and her woes ... Lucy's going down next Saturday, not a minute too soon ... If only she can persuade Mother to come to her senses ... What a silly thing to say! She's losing all sense rapidly ... She doesn't want to allow her children to tell her what to do but she'll listen to the advice of a grandchild – Lucy's always been her favourite ... As a psychiatrist, Lucy can also tell me whether we'd be able to get an independent assessment that would testify to Mother's dementia ... There you go again, Daphne would say, independent, but you want it to say that she's off her rocker ... Can't understand Daphne – she's driven crazier than me with it all, but she's terrified that she is being too harsh on Mother ... Then again, Lucy has put off going, knowing how hard Mother is to deal with, it's not like your own patient, where you can be objective and not feel personally insulted by any remarks ... Must phone Lucy now and make sure she does go, and doesn't attempt to put it off ...

'No, Mother, it's Derek here, not Daphne .... Nice to hear you using the phone again anyway ... You don't need a washing machine, your washing is done for you ... I can assure you that it is ... I know Mrs Mullins doesn't invite you in for a cup of tea, but she can't now, because you can't get out ... Well, the doctor doesn't advise you to go out, put it that way ... OK, Madge has never invited you to tea, but she comes over and makes the tea for you just like the carers do, doesn't she? ... Of course you can still make a cup of tea yourself, but it's nice to sit back and be waited on, isn't it? You always complained that all your life you waited on others, so you should sit back and enjoy it now ... Yes, yes, of course ... I know ... By the way, Lucy's popping down to see you next Saturday – won't that be nice? ... Not my wife, that's Fiona, I mean my daughter, Lucy ...'

24 FEBRUARY

'I think I know you from somewhere ...'

'I'm the Reverend Spooner, Mrs Robson, but call me Andy ...'

'If you are selling something, I don't have callers like that at my door, can't you see the notice?'

'No, I'm not even collecting for the new roof ...'

'Don't say my roof has gone – it has started to get very windy ...'

'I came to see if you wanted to go to church today.'

'So you have services on weekdays now do you? Why have you changed from Sunday?'

'But it *is* Sunday ...'

'Well, you can see that I can't go to church with these old rags on ...'

'You have time to change. I'm just calling on my way round to visit some sick people who can't make it to church today. Mrs Partridge has offered to bring a few elderly people to Communion, she's the lady who lives next to Mrs Mullins – she'll collect you in half an hour ...'

'The ruddy hell she will – excuse my language – you should be ashamed of yourself getting people like that to recruit members for your church – why, she has seen off more old folk than you've had years as a vicar ...'

'Even if that be the case – and one should not listen to malicious gossip, indeed it's the subject of my sermon today – we must remember that the good Lord welcomes sinners into the fold ...'

'The ones who re ... reap ...'

'Repent?'

'That's the word – did Mrs Pheasant make a full confession?'

'Well, really, Mrs Robson, that's a private matter ...'

'Too bad – she's not getting me into her car. Good day, Vicar.'

25 FEBRUARY

Another few days gone by and no visitors since that man with the funny name came round – Handy Spoon – fancy calling yourself that! He is in league with that Pheasant woman, whatever they call her ... and he's the vicar ... They'll be having black Masses at that church before long, mark my words ... The old priest was such a lovely fellow, whatever happened to him? ... These young people with their new-fangled ideas, come in all sinners, they say – well, I can send him a few more round from these parts and there won't be enough room in that little church for any good folk ...

'Talking to yourself, Mrs Robson?'
    'Who else is there to talk to, Daisy? I didn't hear you come in.'

'Now, you're talking to yourself, aren't you, Daisy?'
    'I was asking you a few things a while ago, but your hearing aid isn't in, Mrs Robson ... Not now, Sam, there's a time for that kind of talk, but not when I'm on duty ...'
    'Since when have I been called Sam, my little dear?'

She can hear when she tries to.

'By your red face, it's that boyfriend of yours who has been chatting you up on the phone again. I know, you can't get enough of one another – we were just the same, Alfred and I, but I must have told you before about the dangers of letting it interfere with your work ...'

'What I need to find out from you, Mrs Robson, is where the cash box is.'
    'That Pheasant woman's not getting her filthy hands on

87

my hard-earned money. I've put it somewhere safe until I can pay it into the bank.'

'But we need it to buy you some food.'

'Didn't you tell me that Derek's wife – or my daughter – brings all my meals?'

'Only the dinners – I have to see to breakfast and lunch. And all the food has run out.'

'Well, you'd better run after it then, because I haven't eaten it. I'm famished. I'll be nothing but skin and bone before long, you'll see ...'

From the case notes:

Cash box must be found. Meanwhile, I'm paying for things out of my own pocket.

26 FEBRUARY

Mother wanted Derek, I bet ... It's always me she rings, but she may have just dialled any number ... How can she be starving? Why wouldn't the carer buy her any food? What a ridiculous story! ... Thank God Lucy's going down on Saturday ... that's if she doesn't chicken out of it ... rather her than me though ... may God forgive me ... Put on another soothing record and keep off the brandy bottle, too early in the day to have a stiff drink ... Why not play the piano for once? ... Why have I started playing the *Appassionata*? Do I want to be reminded of Peter? He wasn't a bad sort really ... Couldn't face her as a mother-in-law, otherwise I'm sure he would have proposed ... That night I was sure he was going to, I'd put on the Beethoven quite low and turned down the lights, and all those silly tricks ... all that fondling during the Andante ... and then he sat up with a start at the onset of the Allegro ... as if with some purpose, as if he had decided not to put it off any longer ... He even went down on one knee ... or is that memory playing tricks with me? ... Then Mother rang ... at eleven o'clock at night, she rang ... She heard Peter's voice and was shouting some nonsense about me allowing men to be in my flat at that time of night ... and I justified myself by saying that we were only listening to music, music appreciation, nothing more serious ... Why didn't I bang the phone down on her? ... Peter took note of my abjectly apologetic tone, of course, and he'd had a basinful of Mother before, so he was furious, stormed out ... He could have laughed it off ... but he didn't have the courage himself to deal with that type of a mother-in-law, Derek said ... If he really wanted me, he would have made a joke of it, according to Derek ... Thank you, brother, for your kind thoughts! I listened to Derek and to Mother ... Why have I listened to others instead of hearing my own heart? ... We mean the best for you, they claimed. Huh, it suits Derek that I'm a spinster ... Nobody else in my life, so I should always be on hand to see to Mother ... I shouldn't have let the relationship slide – Peter might have made a good husband ... She's starving? Well, let Derek's daughter see to it ... Since Mother wanted Derek, let her have him ...

27 FEBRUARY

'I've found your false teeth in the rubbish bin, Mrs Robson. No wonder you're not eating your dinner.'

'Keep them there for all the good they are, Daisy. They're hurting me more than the real ones ever did. They're past it, had them for years.'

'No, these are the ones the dentist fitted when your daughter took you in December.'

'Could have fooled me – they're useless. I knew that silly

man wasn't up to the job. Took one look at him, I did, I could see straight away that he was incom ... incontinent.'

'Oh ... that reminds me, I've noticed that your underpants are a little ... well, wet ...'

'What do you expect?'

'Well, I ... er ...'

'When you wash things, they do tend to get a little wet in my experience. You're not instigating that I can't get to the toilet in time, are you?'

'Er ... about the problem with your teeth, Mrs Robson – would you like to go to the dentist again to ...'

'Never in my life! Have that clumsy idiot fiddling around in my mouth? ...'

'I'm sure he would ...'

'So you love going to the dentist, do you, Daisy?'

'Ha! Ha! OK, nobody really likes it, but ...'

'But nothing.'

'Perhaps I'll liquidise your food for you.'

'Gone back to being a baby now, have I?'

'Oh ... your blender broke, didn't it, when you put your frozen dinner in it?'

'You have me breaking up my possessions now – better lock me up quick before I ruin everything. Do you know, my children are afraid I'll do that and there'll be nothing left for them to inherit. So now you're taking sides with them ...'

From the case notes:

False teeth no longer suitable? Patient doesn't want to re-visit dentist, but patient's daughter asked to book appointment. Signs of incontinence – passing water – also.

28 FEBRUARY

Have to go and see Nan on Saturday. Strange to go in that
capacity. I last saw her – when? – on her 95th birthday ...
Wonder if she remembers that ... or her 90th birthday
party, that was a big one ... Who has the photos? ... And
before that I saw her at my graduation for my doctorate ... I
have been putting off going to see her too often ... but
Lionel is no better ... she used to dote on my brother, and
he doesn't repay her, so she says ... What Dad and Aunty
Daphne have to listen to! So now it's my turn ... Pretend it's
a family visit ... have to cheer her up ... but I need to go
through certain questions that they would ask if they were
assessing her ... Very difficult – she may be suffering from
dementia, but she's still alert and shrewd enough to detect
any funny talk ...

'Who? Lucy? I don't know anyone called Lucy ... My
granddaughter? Daphne doesn't have any children, unless
she's been keeping a dark secret from me all these years ...
Derek's daughter? Well, I never! ... You're coming to see
me? That'll be the day! ... Saturday? That's tomorrow! ...
Day after, I see ... So, young lady, how are your studies
going? ... Finished already? That must have been a short
course ... Doctor of what? ... A doctor in the family – you'll
be able to give me a good check-up then! Just a minute ... I
hope that's not why you are coming ... Of course, I would
love to see you again, dearie ... Didn't you have a brother?
... Lionel, yes, that was his name – and what is he up to,
dare I ask? ... Well, I'm not *that* far away, just you tell him
it's about time he called on his old nan, the things I used to
do for him – when your mother and father went out for the
night I used to look after the two of you, for that matter ...'

29 FEBRUARY

That granddaughter of mine, I wish I could recall her name, where on earth is she? Only last night, I'm sure she rang to say she was coming ... Of course, they'll say I was mistaken, but I never get things like that wrong ... They think I don't remember what happened yesterday ... Who's this now entering my house? ... That could be her, she must have changed a bit since I last saw her ... Lesley ... no, Lucy ...

'Lucy, is that you?'

'It's just me, Kelly.'

'What are you doing here? You're not my granddaughter!'

'I come every Friday to replace Tracy on her day off. By the way, did you know that this is an extra day in the year?'

'Whatever gimmick will that government think of next? Changing our calender, no, that's a thing you strain things in, you know what I mean.'

'Calendar, you're right, but the government hasn't altered anything, it's always been the case that every four years you get an extra day in February.'

'What do I need an extra day for? Time lies on my body like a dead weight, this year is never-ending as it is – can't I vote to miss today out?'

'Very funny, Mrs Robson! At any rate, March tomorrow.'

'Where to? Besides I'm not allowed out of doors. Why are you laughing your head off?'

'You do say such funny things ... no offence ... er ... I mean, you've got a good sense of humour.'

From the case notes:

No signs of incontinence today, but impossible to get patient to eat anything except soft food. Relatives: Blender or some such needed urgently.

1 MARCH

'So you're Lucy! My, you've grown a few inches since I last saw you.'

'You're shrinking, Nan!'

'My brain's shrinking, dear ... Oh, don't worry, they say it shrinks as you get older ... I ought to measure it, I suppose, just like I used to measure you on that wall.'

'You remember it, Nan! You used an indelible pencil and Dad was furious because he had just given you some money to have the room redecorated! Then he gave you an HB pencil ... and then he told me to tell you what height I was when I arrived each time, so you wouldn't need to measure me, but it made no difference, you still had to check it!'

'Why can't children stay little? Like that Peter boy ... We shouldn't encourage you to grow – you love being with old nans at that age ... we had so much in common, dear ...'

'The world wouldn't change if we didn't.'

'But why on earth do you young people want to change the world?'

'Is it such a lovely world then, Nan?'

'Well, to tell you the truth, dear, I haven't heard the news recently, but I've seen it – the television is stuck on that day-long news channel – but my hearing help has vanished, and anyway, I see horrible things ... earthquakes, fires, clones ...'

'Cloning could cure many diseases ... but I know, Nan, you don't like the idea of making a copy of somebody ...'

'That's another disgrace, man playing at being God – but I don't mean that, I mean those winds that rush through towns and blow them down or flood them ...'

'Oh, *cy*clones!'

'Anyway, who wants to have his double going around, dear? There was a sinister film about that once. Sometimes I think it's not my sister I see, because they say she's dead, but her double – they could have made a clone of her.'

'Where on earth have you been, Lucy? I was worried sick about you.'

'I told you, I just popped out to draw some cash for you and to pay back Tracy ... and also to get you a food blender.'

'I know you'd love a cake to take away, but I don't make them any more, dear.'

Well, we've broken the ice all right – perhaps tomorrow we'll get down to business.

2 MARCH

'What time do you make it, Nan?'

'Well, we've just got up and you said it was nine o'clock not long ago.'

'Isn't it a nuisance to you, Nan, not being able to tell the right time, even with this kitchen clock still working?'

'I only need the rough time, and that's easy to work out, Lucy.'

'How, Nan?'

'Well, the big hand goes round all the time and doesn't help you keep track of anything. So I go by the little hand.'

'You know when it's lunchtime, then?'

'Those girls come in to give me lunch.'

'But if they didn't come in ...'

'They don't come in every day. When the hand is on the left side of the clock, this side, you see, then it's morning, everybody knows that. And when it's on the other side, it's afternoon, simple, isn't it? At the top it must be in between the two, so it's lunchtime.'

'But it could be evening as well.'

'And I thought you were intelligent, Lucy! It's evening when it gets dark!'

'When do you go to bed, Nan?'

'Well, at night of course.'

'Evening and night look much the same, both dark.'

'Let me ask you the same question, Lucy – when do *you* go to bed?'

'Why, when I'm tired, of course, Nan.'

'Then you've answered your own question.'

'You'll have to ask me which number's which on this phone when I'm fresh. Could *you* study when you were tired?'

'But you might be tired and want to contact the doctor or Dad and not be able to ...'

'Let's face it, whatever number I dial, I'm going to get help, knowing the few people on that list your father made up. Fancy cutting my phone off from all those other people! ...'

'Which people, Nan?'

'Don't you have friends, Lucy? Aren't I supposed to have any any more? ... People from church, I might want to talk to them, but there is only silly old Madge Mullins available on that phone!'

'I've told you, Dad, she's quite plausible ... Not eating? Her lack of teeth would still be a problem if she were in a home, it's not a reason for putting her in one ... Disturbing neighbours at night? We don't know for sure that she didn't have a break-in, and besides, she hasn't caused any trouble since then ... Look, I'll write everything up as I would do for a patient of mine and you can read the notes to see for yourself that it's too early to convince anybody that she needs to be consigned ...'

3 MARCH

This trial is complicated, but less so than my mother's tribulations ... For goodness' sake, stop thinking about her or your work will go to pot! ... Suspect needs to be put away, according to the police ... She does too, really, creating disturbances and being a danger to herself ... Come on, stick to this trial ... Reasons for custodial sentence request ... ah, that'll be the crucial witness ...

'Hello, Robson here ... Lucy? Well, be very quick as I'm expecting an important call – one that's vital to my brief ... Of course your report on Nan can wait a day or two, so yes, email it to me at home, not here ... Bye dear.'

So, we've got testimonies so far from Hurd, Jenkins and Mullins ... no, not Mullins, Mullen ... though Mrs Mullins could put in a word or two for us ... For heaven's sake, concentrate ... This Mullen chap is none too reliable – there's a contradiction in his two pieces of evidence, surely ... Why hasn't that Mrs Hurd rung me to corroborate her evidence? I hope she hasn't been scared off ... Wonder the carers aren't scared off too, the way Mother goes at them at times ...

4 MARCH

'Now, that wasn't too bad, was it, Mrs Robson?'

'Not bad for you, you'll get paid a tidy sum, but it's my mouth you've been fiddling with.'

'Oh, no charge this time – after all, it's not long since we fitted these new dentures, and ...'

'Let's just hope you've got it right this time – I don't want to make a habit of being a guinea pig for your false-teeth experiments.'

'Thank you for arranging to see her so quickly, Mr Thompson, and for putting up with her cantankerous mood.'

'No problem, Tracy, just keep bringing them in to see me. Mrs Robson used to refer her patients to me, you know, in her nursing days. Very pleasant woman, if a bit matter-of-fact at times, but we all have a business side. Old age wears most people's patience down, I'm afraid. My wife says I'm getting a bit tetchy at home myself ...'

'Let's stop off at the department store on the way back, Daisy.'

'You don't need anything, do you, Mrs Robson?'

'I don't have the money even if I did, dear – that dentist has probably taken all I had.'

'No, he didn't charge you, even though your previous dentures looked a little damaged.'

'Damaged? I looked after them with great care. Put it down to bad workmanship, like everything else today.'

'Anyway, which store did you mean, Mrs Robson?'

'The one on the corner there. Oh, where is it?'

'Oh, that one. It closed down a few years ago – replaced by a supermarket.'

'And to think I used to buy some very refined items in

there – just goes to show that you only make money with shoddy, cheaper goods today.'

'We'll go straight back home then, shall we, Mrs Robson?'

5 MARCH

Ah, Lucy's notes on Mother ... 'Knows date from calendar, as carers have crossed out preceding days' ... Hmm, not always, I bet ... 'Has her own strange method of telling the time, but it works for her purposes' ... Daphne won't believe this ... 'Carers make sure she has her tablets and meals, they take care of money with help of relatives, no recent night-time disturbances' ... and so on and so on ... Best call Daphne ...

'I didn't think much would come of Lucy's visit, to tell you the truth, Derek. In fact, Mother rang me while Lucy was there – Lucy probably dialled my number for her. Didn't she tell you what Mother said to me on the phone?'

'I didn't know anything about the call, Daphne.'

'She was angry that the most junior member of the family was sent to visit her instead of one of us and that this junior upstart was interrogating her as if she were not right in the head.'

'Lucy must have been too embarrassed to tell me. What it all shows is that Mother can put on a passing performance when she feels threatened ...'

'Nobody's threatening her ... She gets paranoid though ... Oh, what are we to do, Derek?'

'Nothing. We'll just have to muddle along as we are. Look. Daphne, I'm going to have to get back to my notes for the trial now, as Mother's problems are distracting me seriously ...'

Of course, *I* have nothing to be distracted from like Derek does, and no children to send in lieu of me. God, I forgot to mention Mother's fence – that man never came to fix it in February.

6 MARCH

'Any odd jobs need doin', Mrs ... ?'

'Robson. Well, my fence is not what it was – perhaps you can take a look at it?'

'No problem.'

'Cash in hand seven fifty. Just say the day.'

'Where do you expect me to get all that money? You'll have to come back tomorrow afternoon.'

'Right you are, Mrs Robson. Tomorrow at two then. And I'll take a look at anything else that needs fixing.'

'What did you say your name was?'

'Fixin' Phil, that's me. I'm your man.'

Nice fellow, but I'll have to ask Derek or Daphne for the money.

'Any news from the family, Mrs Robson?'

'Get away with you, Daisy, nobody ever calls here. I haven't seen a living, or come to that a dead, soul – and there are plenty of those – in a month of Sundays. You'd think that one of the neighbours would call on me.'

'Your granddaughter came at the weekend. As for neighbours, you only really know Mrs Mullins, as all the others of your generation are dead, so Daphne tells me. Mrs Mullins's ankle started to play up again and she's a bit unsteady on her feet, so ...'

'Then she could phone me to say so!'

7 MARCH

'Oh, it's you again, Mrs Robson. I must apologise. I gather you came here in January about your pension and the temporary clerk didn't know you.'

'Nothing and nobody lasts today, everybody is temporal. I need some cash.'

'Are you sure? Your relatives usually draw cash for you.'

'So that's where my money's been going. To think that my own flesh and blood have been stealing it from me. Surely you can give me seven pounds and fifty pence?'

'That's rather a little amount, but ...'

'Little? I think it's a lot of money. You could buy a wedding dress for that in my day. Look, the man wrote it down on a piece of paper, no flies on me, you know, I always demand a written estimate, and it says seven pounds fifty for tomorrow for the fence.'

'It's seven hundred and fifty pounds written on here, I'm afraid.'

'What? That's daylight robbery! I'm not parting with that sum of money. My children can pay for it or jolly well fix the fence themselves! ... Anyway, I'll take ten or maybe twenty pounds instead. That should last me till the end of the month ... What are you whispering about?'

'Hmm ... I'll fill in the form for you ... There, just sign where I put the cross.'

'As if I don't know where to sign a form. I'm not illegitimate, you know.'

'That's not your usual signature, I'm afraid.'

'Well whose signature is it then, the Queen's?'

'All right, well, I saw you sign it ... Four fives or two tens?'

'Yes please.'

'Very funny ... er, a joke, I take it? ... Oh! ... Here are four fives ... five, ten, fifteen, twenty pounds.'

'You weren't here this morning, Mrs Robson, I was worried to death about you.'

'Might as well put me in the Tower of London then, D ... no, not Daisy.'

'Kelly. Did you pop out for something? ... Oh, what's this twenty pounds doing here ... and this scruffy note?'

'I went to get some money one day or other. I can't live on the pocket money my children give me.'

'There was no need for you to draw cash, as Lucy had left enough for you here at the weekend.'

'Then where did she hide it?'

'I'll have to ring Daphne about this note. Your children were going to have the fence fixed by a reliable person. This looks like the estimate of another cowboy to me. I suppose I'll just have to wait here, as it looks as if he's calling back this afternoon, so I need to be here to send him packing.'

From the case notes:

Another dubious person tried to persuade the patient to have her fence mended. As it was marginally a cheaper quote than the last one, the Partridges could be behind it again. Patient's son notified of problem.

8 MARCH

I sit here for hours on and off – or have I been here all day without moving? About time I stirred my stumps then. Ought to go and see Ma Mullins – Ma Mullins, that's what I used to call her ... there's something the matter with her ... what was it now? Didn't like the queasy look on her face last time I saw her, she'll not be long for this world, like poor old Gertrude, and then who will I have to talk to? Can't call this bunch of young creatures neighbours, they're always back and forth and won't give you the time of day, too busy making money hand over fist, and then there's those students in that house, scruffy-looking types, Derek and Daphne used to dress smartly when they were at university. That Daisy says they don't have any money – well, my two had to get by as well but they made the most of it, and of course those Peacocks or whatever they call themselves, full of their own pride they are at any rate, what have they got to be proud of ? They're probably scheming now to rob me of my sweat-earned cash ... That could be them now ... or just my stupid sister come to borrow more money – don't see how she can't manage if I can on my pittance of a pension ... or a burglar!

'Who's that? I've got my walking stick handy!'

'It's only me, Mother. I phoned you this morning to say I would be here by eleven o'clock.'

'Derek!'

'Put that stick down, you could do somebody an injury with it.'

'Oh, you don't care if a burglar injures your frail old mother ...'

'What time did you say it was, Derek? It can't be eleven at night, it's not dark.'

'It's still morning, Mother. A man I found in the yellow pages is coming to give me an estimate for the fence.'

'I can never find anything in those yellow pages, why do they colour them yellow? It damages my eyes.'

'Where are your glasses, by the way? You need them for reading – in fact, I think you need a check-up to make sure you don't need them for general vision. I meant to organise that when I came down in early February.'

'You just forget about me when you leave here, don't you? You meant to do this and that but ...'

'That'll be the man for the fence. Just stay sitting there and I'll deal with it.'

'Well, Mother, he has made a start and will finish it by tonight, or if not, by tomorrow morning. I'll stay the night with you, of course.'

'To what do I owe this favour? You're almost a stranger to your own mother. What's wrong with the fence, anyway? If you fix it, those two boys will be pulling it down again. Oh, and I've just put on my glasses, for what they're worth.'

'One lens is missing, the right one.'

'No wonder I couldn't see properly out of my right eye.'

I'll make an appointment with Mother's doctor to look at her eyes for cataracts. – In any case, she needs a new pair of glasses.

9 MARCH

'Nice to see you in church again, Mrs Robson. I trust your son is coming back to collect you after the service?'

'I walked here, didn't I? Oh, no ... well, I don't know what's got into Derek about religion, he won't hear any good of it these days. Mind you, there are some fanatics about who are enough to put anybody off.'

What on earth is Amy Robson singing? Still, mustn't discourage her ...

'I can't follow this hymn. I thought I knew the words ...'

'Yer've got your hymn book upside down, ducky. There, that's better. But not so loud, don't deafen everybody.'

'Mrs Pheasant!'

'Partridge!'

'Well! I'm moving to another bench.'

Why is she pushing past the others like that? Where is she going?

'There, back on yer feet again, ducky. Yer 'ad a nasty fall there.'
  'Get your hands off me, you filthy swine!'

Whatever is she saying to Mrs Partridge? Hardly a Christian sentiment, I think!

'A word in your ear, Derek.'
  'Yes, Vicar?'
  'We had one or two scenes in church with your mother today. It might be better if ... well, if she didn't come to church ... I'll visit her at home instead ... or one of the congregation could go along ... It seems that she doesn't take kindly to Mrs Partridge.'
  'She has her reasons, Reverend, but I take your point. I think a church service is too much physical and mental strain for her. But I would appreciate home visits to her from the church.'
  'I'm glad we see eye to eye on the matter, Derek.'

10 MARCH

'That was my son on the phone just now, Daisy. You'll not credit this – that priest Knife has told him that I'm not to come to his church again ...'
  'Knife? ... Oh, you mean Spooner ...'
  'Spoon? At any rate, he has his knife in me ... I don't see anything to laugh at, Daisy ... It's all down to that ghastly Pheasant woman.'

'Why, have you been quarrelling with her?'

'For your information, I never have a row with anyone, you ought to know me by now, you see enough of me, I'm the most easy-going person in the world, but I'm not going to let that ... that Pheasant become lovey-dovey with me, I know what she's after ... and fancy a vicar taking sides with her against a poor old innocent like me ...'

'Did Derek mention that you have an appointment with your doctor today about your eyes?'

'Do I normally go to see my doctor about my eyes?'

'He has to refer you to a specialist.'

'Specialist in what? They're not going to start tampering with my eyes again – I read the paper every day with the best vision for anybody of my age in the country, I'd could even win a competition ... Where is that wretched paper today, anyway?'

Well, that visit to the doctor was a waste of time – he can talk until he's blue in the face, he's not going to persuade me to have another operation on my eyes, and as for needing to wear glasses all the time, how ridiculous! Granted my eyes get tired with reading, but it's only natural at my age, nothing to be ashamed of – as Derek says – I'll just get somebody to find that missing lens and pop it back in so I can read the paper, watch television, for what it's worth, and so on ...

11 MARCH

'Oh, what a beautiful morning ...'

'Ooh-ooh, Norman! Norman! Why don't you answer me when I call you?'

'My name's Nigel-do-a-good-turn, Aunty Amy.'

'You must have changed it by that poll they use.'

'Don't climb poles any more, but I did go up the tree in our back garden, and guess what I saw! Little birdies are starting to make their nests. Have you seen any nests, Aunty Amy?'

'Come round the back garden, there aren't any places for birds to build their nests in this front one.'

'There's one in this tree, Aunty.'

'Mind you don't fall, Mr Do-a-good-turn.'

'Don't want to demolish that new fence of yours on my way down. I helped my dad to put up a fence once. Bit wonky, my dad said, and d'you know, he wouldn't let me help him do much DIY after that.'

'I could do with a son living at home. You must be of help to your mother now your dad has passed away.'

'Oh, there he is, Mrs Robson – he just disappeared! From my window I couldn't see him in the street any more. Come down this minute, Nigel!'

'Just counting the birds' eggs, Mum.'

'I'm at my wits' end with Nigel, Mrs Robson. Had to have the fire brigade out yesterday to get him down from the top of that big oak tree in our garden. They couldn't understand why a man of forty-odd would want to get stuck up there. They don't know that he has the mind of a child.'

'They say I have the mind of a child now, so perhaps that's why I get on with your son so well, Mrs Taylor.'

'Turner. Well, I'd let you keep him, only life is difficult enough for you as it is. I have strict orders from that young Tracy not to leave Nigel with you.'

'Oh, do you indeed? Since when does that little girl have the last say about who visits me?'

'Sorry, I tumbled onto your daffodil patch there, Aunty Amy. I could plant some more for you.'

'You're coming back home right now, Nigel!'

106

12 MARCH

'You'll break my door down if you go on hammering like that! Oh, it's Madge. Have you been away at your son's?'

'You've kept me waiting an age in this biting wind, Amy. It's my ankle, remember?'

'You didn't fall down the stairs again?'

'No, it hadn't recovered properly from that tumble in the street, but I can get about again now.'

'While you're here, Madge, just put this lens back into my glasses. Somebody left this handy little screwdriver in the case.'

'There you are, Amy. It's back in ... I didn't want to be a burden at Stephen's, he's got enough on his plate with that bridge.'

'He never had enough on his plate, if you ask me – my Derek used to eat twice as much.'

'My hearing aid is playing up. Yes, it's twice as much bother as he thought it would be, something to do with the suspension now ... Where *is* your hearing aid, Amy?'

'Suspension, that's the word I was looking for. That's what the defence asked for in Derek's latest trial ... *trial*, I said ...'

'Trial did you say? It's a trial all right, just think of the deadline coming up and the repairs to the bridge not completed. If his company get a fine ...'

'That's all they get now, Madge, a fine, they hardly ever go to jail ...'

'Why should Stephen go to jail? His bridges are always safe.'

'Safe? None of us are with those villains getting off scot-free ...'

'Hello, ladies. You two talking at cross-purposes again?'

'I'm not cross with her, Daisy.'

'We need our hearing aids seen to. We didn't hear you ring or knock, dear.'

'I just let myself in with the key nowadays, Mrs Mullins.'

They're bad enough at conversing when their hearing aids are in and working OK. Perhaps best not to mention the doctor's appointment until Mrs Mullins has gone.

From the case notes:

Doctor's appointment 17th March, but patient refuses to go, won't accept that her ears need attention. Refuses also to see specialist about her eyes.

13 MARCH

'Maybe you put it in the shed, Mrs Robson, let's have a look ... Oh dear, what a muddle the shed is in, somebody will have to sort it out for you ...'

'What do you mean, sort it out, Daisy? That's what I've been doing.'

'Well, well, here is a shoebox with some of your old photos in it. Let's forget what we're looking for and sit down and chat about some of the photos over a cup of tea ...'

'Well, look at that, Mrs Robson! Here you are on a tandem, you and your first husband, is it?'

'What's so surprising about that? We used to cycle for miles, once even to London ...'

'Surely not that far?'

'Do you think I've always been slow in getting around? When I was your age, I never stopped for a moment ... Only a few years ago I could walk up this street in a flash. When they saw a blur and couldn't make out who was whizzing by, they'd say, that's Amy Robson – just ask people along the street ...'

'You're always good for a giggle ... Oh, I meant it in the nicest way ...'

'I'm being serious now ...'

'No car in those days, I suppose, but why didn't you catch the train up to London?'

'No lolly for it ... besides, we liked to keep fit in those days, didn't need television programmes about getting our weight down, food wasn't as plentiful either ...'

Up the hill ... how much further? Splendid view at the top ... makes it worth it ... not much time to admire it ... your sister's expecting us at eleven o'clock ... pity she didn't live nearer ... careful downhill ... steep slope ... brakes are sound ... watch out for that object on the road, we don't want punctuation ... punc ... remember to put the bike round the back ... those lads nearly stole it when we propped it up against her front wall ...

'Still looking at those bike pictures, Mrs Robson? It's me, Tracy. I've come back to give you your supper. Wake up, Mrs Robson!'

'Why did you wake me up? I was having a lovely dream about ... now you've even made me forget what I was dreaming about.'

'Don't worry – most people forget their dreams.'

'If I forget them, I might as well pack it all in and croak. They're about all I've got left.'

14 MARCH

She couldn't afford much of a wedding, no more than the rest of us ... Ellen shouldn't have married him, what was his name again? My mother said he was a rotter, never liked the look of him. Father was flattered by his money of course ...

You're doing the right thing, Ellen, he said, he'll see you all right, my girl – all right indeed, he had more women than I take pills ... where *are* those stupid tablets, anyway? ... How many have I had, today? ... Where's that Daisy? ... Always on the prowl, he was ... and Ellen such an attractive girl, the beauty of the family, wasted on such a vampire ... They say men with money are only out for good-looking girls, they're the ruin of them ... Maddy told me she would never marry money to suit Father and what did she do? ... Where's that picture? ... Look at the sickly invalid, what did Maddy see in such a broken-down creature? You can't marry for pity either ... had to nurse him most of their married life, she did, what there was of it ... it made her turn bitter when he died, so young, she complained ... would have been better if Stan had popped off earlier too, for what use he was to me ... Maddy relied on the rest of us too much after that, lost her independent spirit, drifted too, wouldn't marry again, often no job – here comes Madge on the cadge, we used to say about Ma Mullins – well, Maddy was no different ... and she's still at it now, some of my best china has vanished ...

'What a good job Tracy found your photographs, Mrs Robson.'

'What's so good about it? What's your name again, dear?'

'Kelly. You told Tracy the photos brought back happy dreams ...'

'And a lot of sadness too ...'

15 MARCH

'What's the old dear doing in the middle of the road? I don't know how I didn't run her over.'

'Eeh, most of the tiles must be off my roof. The house is flooded ... Can you see where the damage is?'

'What's she on about? Her roof? ... I'd get back onto the pavement if I were you, dear.'

'Let me see to 'er. Come on, ducky, we'd best be going back in. Oh, the door has banged to in the wind. Where's yer key, Mrs Robson? ...'

'I'll get wet in there ...'

'What's the number to this key box, ducks?'

'You might as well go back to your house, Mrs Partridge ...'

'Thank goodness, Madge. I knew that God would send somebody to help me.'

'I'll ring Tracy to say we'll be waiting for her in my house, Amy ... She knows how to get the key out of that box of yours so that she can let you back in.'

'I can't see any flooding downstairs, Derek, but upstairs the rain must have come in overnight in the back bedroom where your mother sleeps – the bed is wet as well ... Oh, and the bathroom ... Can you sort it out and tell your mother she mustn't dash off into the road again?'

'Easier said than done, Tracy – we can't lock her in.'

'So, you like the bed I've made up for you in the lounge, Mrs Robson? You can still spend the day in your other room, your sitting room, that's where you entertain your visitors, anyway ...'

'Visitors, Daisy? Who do you call my visitors? There's only you ...'

'As for washing, I'll bring one of those bowls out of the shed. I'm afraid you'll have to make do with the kitchen sink until upstairs has dried out.'

'Wash in the kitchen sink, eh? I'm as dirty as the dishes now, am I? You know how I love my own house, but how can I live in it in this state?'

From the case notes:

Patient very disturbed and confused. Relatives contacted to see to repairs to roof and damaged rooms upstairs. Doctor's appointment cancelled for now.

16 MARCH

'It's Lionel. You remember me, Nan – Derek's my dad.'

'Then why didn't he come? Don't tell me, he's too busy with those scoundrels in court ... But where's your ... Daphne, your ...'

'Aunt? Er ... they thought it better if I came down, being young and fit, so that I can move your furniture ...'

'Where are you taking it to? I'm not ready for one of those people parks yet!'

'I'm going to move it away from the wet room to the dry one upstairs ... Your roof was leaking ...'

'Good heavens! Then get straight up there and fix it, Lionel, if you are so able. How long has it been leaking?'

'Mrs Mullins recommended a repairer to Dad yesterday. He came and put a plastic sheet on it ...'

'What's the good of that? I need those slanting things, sl ...'

'Slates. I'm afraid there are a lot of people like you waiting to have tiles put back on with this windy March weather.'

'This is driving me mad with worry. Half the roof bare and I just have to sit here and lump it ...'

'It's not leaking any more, Nan. I'll just pop upstairs and rearrange things.'

That's Maddy again, rummaging around up there. What's

she trying to get hold of now? I'll creep up on her in a minute and give her the fright of her life.

'Calm down, Nan. It's only me, Lionel.'

'I thought you were at university. Haven't I just been to visit you in that residence place of yours?'

'Oh, in my hall? ... That was some years ago. I'm lecturing now. You could come up to see me again, but I've changed universities ...'

17 MARCH

Just as well Lionel didn't let on that Daphne was away on holiday, as I don't want to disturb her – her doctor ordered a complete rest ... It's not as if she was looking after Mother, but she does get het up about everything ... Lionel thinks Mother has settled down ... washes herself in the kitchen sink ... does she ever wash anyway these days? Did they ever get to the bottom of that? Perhaps the carers need to wash her? At least she can't wash clothes in the bath now that the bathroom is out of action ... A pity she wouldn't have that downstairs toilet and wash basin put in, it would've come in handy now ... No answer from the roofer – he won't do the job till the end of the week at best ... He should give priority to her case, but then there are houses with families and young children on his list ... He's probably making a mint out of it ... an ill wind and all that ... At any rate, that cat burglar who came out of prison the other week won't find the weather to his liking ... But once spring and then summer are back, with people leaving windows open at night, the thieves'll be doing a better trade again ... 'Keeps you in a living,' Mother says ...

'It's Derek, Mother ... It's half past eight in the evening ...

Not seen a soul all day? I'm sure Tracy's been in to look after you ... No, she's not called Daisy ... What? You're in the extension in your bedroom and somebody has stolen the furniture from it? I can explain ... You sleep on the bed downstairs now, remember? Go back down and look, but mind you don't fall on those stairs. You are on the waiting list for a stair-lift, you know ... Yes, I know your legs are still as strong as an ox's, but you can't be too careful ... Are you on the phone downstairs now? ... What was that crash just now? ... Your stick falling downstairs? You should have both hands on the banister. We gave you another stick for upstairs, you shouldn't be taking the other one up with you ... No, it's not your sister's bed in the best room, it's yours ... They had to move it because of the leaking roof ...'

God, I shouldn't have mentioned the roof, she'll be worrying about it all night now. If only there was a respite home she could go into until these repairs are done and everything is back to normal ...

18 MARCH

Such clear blue – which is a deeper hue, sky or lake? Blue ... why is it associated with depression? Who made it the colour of immense sadness, Picasso? That painting still haunts me with its hopeless melancholy – *Mother and Child on a Beach* ... but surely I was happy then watching the seagulls? Yes, I must tell myself that those days with Mother were joyful ... not filled with joy, but still bright ... if not completely serene ... Is it me now or was it me then ... or her? What put a damper on it? ... No, I must believe that those were better days. It's beautifully peaceful here ... I might walk up the mountain a bit further today ... a relief to be cut off from all cares ... I shouldn't have left my mobile at home, Derek is

114

probably trying to contact me this very minute, Mother has probably fallen down the stairs ... Stop it, the doctor said I was not to return before the fortnight was up, that Derek would make arrangements for the body to be kept ... I shall have nightmares, with her frozen body haunting me ... How do I take my mind off it? ... Why did Father have to die? Couldn't he have survived that senseless war – all wars are barbaric futility – like those other men in our street who came back? ... But then a few didn't ... and the bombed houses ... terrifying ... Mother wanted to keep me with her in the cupboard under the stairs during the air raids ... I used to scream when the planes came over ... Perhaps that was what unhinged me ... Stop it, you're not going insane, you're just full of nerves ... no, guilt ... Repeat after me, there's nothing to be guilty about – the therapy only works for a certain time, sometimes not even for the rest of the day – and that doodlebug when the engine switched off just above us and Mother, full of her usual sense of doom, told me that it had our names written on it ... I was delighted when it took one of our neighbour's houses instead, then full of shame and remorse, because Mother told me off ... Well, I was so small, just a little child's reaction ... No, Mother was cheerful before the war ... and the house was full of my laughter, she said ... Did I used to be so happy? Mother had a deep sense of foreboding during the war, said she knew it when the letter came to report Daddy as missing presumed dead ... Why do you still call him Daddy? Derek asks. Well, I never grew up with him and he remained just that ... Derek says he didn't grow up with his father either ... It's not the same, Uncle Stan may have deserted Mother, but he was still around somewhere for Derek ... But it can be worse than a bereavement, they say, if your father is alive but doesn't come to see you ... Oh, get out of these blues into that blue yonder ... up the mountain ...

19 MARCH

'What's all that banging and crashing, Daisy?'

'Didn't think you'd hear it much without your hearing aid, Mrs Robson ... You're in luck, the man has come to fix your roof.'

'You call it luck to have my roof off ... I can't get to sleep with the racket.'

'It's not time for your afternoon nap ... It's only ten o'clock.'

'Ten? Then it's time for bed, Daisy.'

'In the morning. Didn't you sleep well last night?'

'How can I sleep? I'm sick with worry about my house. It's old and falling apart like me. I need to get away. I'll ring Daphne and ask her if she'll take me to her house for a few days' rest.'

'I could take you to that day centre we mentioned. You could have lunch there and sit and chat with everybody.'

'How many times have I told you, Daisy? I hate sitting around gossiping with a bunch of old people.'

'But you'd be the oldest one there!'

'You don't understand. When you get to my age, you don't want to be with people who have one foot in their tomb. Life is dismal enough as it is. You want to be with young folk, children, a source of life, people with a future, with dreams, impossible dreams perhaps, but nonetheless dreams ...'

'Do you daydream a lot in your chair, Mrs Robson? Last week with those photos, you ...'

'You don't want to know what I dream about.'

'Why on earth not? The dreams can't be that bad.'

'I see Alfred standing by my bed all dressed in black, calling me ... He wants to take me with him ... For some reason I tell him I can't go yet, I'm not ready, not dressed for it ...'

'Ooh, how morbid, Mrs Robson!'

'What did I tell you? They're not the sort of dreams for a young lady like you ...'

20 MARCH

'That banging has stopped, Daisy, but somebody's moving around above me ...'

'It's the decorator, Mrs Robson. He's making out an estimate of the damage for the insurance company.'

'What damage? Don't say there's something wrong with the rooms upstairs! Who caused it? My sister's sons have been larking about up there again ...'

'A bit of water came in through the roof. Don't worry, you won't have to pay for anything.'

'Eeh, I won't let them in through the front door, so they break in through the roof! How could I pay for it anyway? They've stopped my pension. I can't find any money anywhere in the house. How am I expected to live?'

'You're standing there too, Daisy.'

'Yes, it's me. The decorator has gone. I'm back down again.'

'No, in my dream ... you're standing on the other side of the bed. I think you're telling me not to go yet with Alfred, because Alfred is making signs towards you as well ...'

'Ooh, not that dream again ... I'll see you this evening for your supper and a bedtime wash ...'

'The very idea, Daisy! Needing somebody to wash me!'

'It's difficult for you to manage with just a bowl in the kitchen sink.'

'I never thought it would come to this – they don't think I'm capable of having a wash now. Why, I'm the most spotless person in the street – in fact, you could go for miles without finding a cleaner person than me ... Besides, I'm too tired, I haven't slept a wink in days, let me go up to bed ...'

'Your bed's just here in your best room as you call it.'

'It won't be best for long if I have to sleep in it. Whoever put my bed in here?'

From the case notes:

Patient extremely confused and having morbid dreams. Seems worn out. Doesn't seem to wash and won't have help for that. Relatives and social services need to liaise re: respite home.

21 MARCH

Lucky Tracy, off with her boyfriend for the day, leaving me with this problem ... I suppose she didn't have the time to notify the relatives ... Daughter on holiday, hmm, have to contact the son, but that's no easy matter with his job ... Gosh, she's starting to smell, no point putting clean clothes on her if she doesn't wash ... I'll ask her to take the dirty ones off to put in the laundry basket and then persuade her to have a wash down ...

'You're not Derek's child, L ... Lionel, no, that's the boy, I mean L ...'

'I'm Kelly – you remember me, Mrs Robson!'

'Didn't know I had a grandchild by that name. Where have you been hiding all this time?'

'I've been abroad. I heard you needed some attention, so I came back to see you.'

'Well, chalk it up! At least one member of my family is concerned about me!'

'I'm perfectly capable of washing myself, you just go and get me some fresh clothes ...'

She's been ages in there, she must have finished by now.

'Oh, you've put the dirty clothes back on!'
    'Those are the new ones somebody gave me.'
    'No, it's my fault – I left you to undress and wash and I've been waiting outside the kitchen with the clean clothes. You said you could manage on your own.'
    'And haven't I?'
    'Sorry, just take those dirty things off and pop these fresh ones on.'
    'I've never been so insulted in all my life. Dirty things indeed. Well, I'm not changing again, I'm dog tired. I must have forty winks after all that struggle.'

From the case notes:

Managed to get patient to have a wash, but she put dirty clothes back on by mistake.

22 MARCH

Maybe it won't be long before Sam proposes to me ... unless he gets itchy feet again ... No, I can trust him now, surely?

'You're the one who's dreaming now, Daisy – weren't you and I talking about dreams the other day? I was calling you just now but I got no answer. It'll be that boyfriend of yours, I can see by the look in your eye ...'

She seems on better form today. Memory back? How can

she see my expression without her glasses on, though? I'll try a new tack with clothes.

'Just look at this lovely new dress your daughter bought you, Mrs Robson. Won't you try it on? And here's some new lingerie to go with it ...'

'Linge what? Undies I call them. Why didn't Daphne give the dress to me herself instead of leaving it lying around?'

'Suits you nicely.'

'It's a bit big for me, Daisy.'

'You've been losing weight and Daphne didn't know that – she thought you still took your usual size.'

'Are you sure this is new? I have a feeling I wore it once before – what could it have been for, now?'

'You must be confusing it with another dress.'

'There you go again! I'm always confused, aren't I, silly old fool? Well, it doesn't look so new to me. Besides, I want Daphne to give it to me properly and then I'll wear it. Take the thing off this instant!'

Oh, that backfired badly. She wouldn't wear it. Kelly will say it was unprofessional of me to pretend to Mrs Robson that she had a new dress.

23 MARCH

'They've turned my house upside down already. Why does a man have to come and knock it around again, Derek?'

'It'll only take a week to redecorate upstairs, Mother. Besides, we've found the ideal place for you to spend the week away from all the upheaval.'

'We're going on holiday at last!'

'Not all of us – just you. It's a quiet place in the countryside.'

'What on earth am I going to do there all on my own, Derek?'

'Don't worry, you'll have lots of people around you and folk on hand to look after all of your needs.'

'Sounds like a first-class hotel to me. Just what I deserve for all the hard work I put into your upbringing. The evenings I spent washing those filthy rugby clothes, not to mention your school uniform, and all the ironing and pressing as well ...'

'Yes, I'm sure you'll love it. You're lucky they had vacancies – that's because it's Easter Day today and people have checked out to spend time with their families this week.'

'Don't I have a family to go to then? You're fobbing me off with ...'

'No, Mother, you know how busy Fiona and I are ... Daphne had to go on holiday on her doctor's orders ...'

'What on earth is wrong with her? I'm more than twenty years older than her, and *my* health is sound.'

'She needs a rest ...'

'What from? I'm the one who needs a rest, with all the mess in this house ...'

'Precisely – that's why you're going to have one, Mother.'

'Just a minute. If this is a posh hotel, I can't afford to pay for it. I only get about five pounds a week pension – I'd like to see that minister who looks after our money manage on that paltry amount every week ...'

'It *is* very expensive, but I'm paying for it as a special treat for you.'

'Special treat indeed! About time you did something to repay me.'

'Yes, I did want to speak to the manager, but you'll have to do. The room is satisfactory, but you'll have to move that woman out and find me a different one to share with.'

'Oh, she's the n ...'

'She's the one who's going to look after you, Mother. She won't be here all the time. You pull this cord by your bed when you need something and she'll come running along.'

24 MARCH

They've rearranged my furniture again ... the chest of drawers used to be on the other side ... At least I'm back in my own room again, I can't understand why that Daisy moved me out of it ...

'Breakfast in bed for you today, Mrs Robson.'
    'What happened to Daisy? Who in heaven's name are you, poking your nose into my room?'
    'I'm Mandy, the one who's looking after you this week.'
    'Why the blessed ... do they keep changing these girls over? Did I ask for poached egg? And what's this?'
    'We showed you the menu and you said it was perfectly OK.'
    'I must have been half asleep at the time. I prefer boiled eggs, but never mind, dear – since you've gone to the trouble of cooking it all for me, I'll eat it.'

'Hello, Mr Robson – it's Matron here, from the nursing home. Your mother has settled in really well. I told you that your idea of pretending it was a hotel was unnecessary. In any case, we don't like to hide the truth from our patients. She thinks she's still at home ... No, that's not unusual when they are as confused as she is ... So far, so good, anyway ...'

Somebody has put my light out. It's far too early for me to sleep. They must have moved the switch. I can't get to my

chair in the dark ... I'm not in control of my own home any
more ... This won't do, wait till I speak to Derek ...

25 MARCH

So this is a hotel I'm in. They must have tricked me into
leaving my house. Where is everyone else, then? There must
be other guests in the hotel. I'll go stark staring raving
bonkers if I'm all on my own ... Don't be silly, Amy, you're
always on your own at home, so it makes no difference ...
But then I might as well be in my own house ... Let's take a
look in the other rooms ...

'Come in.'
　'I'm Amy. Are you staying for long?'
　'Can't remember. Enid Burton.'
　'Who's she?'
　'Me, that's my name. How long a stint have they given
you?'
　'No idea ... Oh, I mean, until my son comes to get me.'
　'If you're not careful, he won't, Amy.'
　'Why not?'
　'My children hope I like it here so much that I'll want to
stay for good.'
　'Surely they couldn't afford it. Mark my words, Edith,
we'll be back home before too long.'
　'Don't count on it, Amy.'
　'It's a lovely hotel though, isn't it? ...'
　'Is that what they told you, Amy? Hotel, my foot, it's an
old people's home.'
　'There's no way my children would have sent me here if it
was, they know jolly well I hate those parking bays for old
folk. I would waste away in a place like that ...'
　'That's what I'm doing. I can't get downstairs to the

123

sitting room on my own or even along the corridor, and they don't volunteer to help me very often. You're lucky to have both your legs still working.'

26 MARCH

Mother seems to have remembered that she's not at home, but now she's confused about whether it's really a hotel ... I had to go along with the lie after the invective she poured out about old people's parks ... I'm not sure that it's a good idea for them to put her on the phone to me each evening ... at least before, when she was still at home, I didn't have to hear her dreadful phone calls as she can't use the phone unaided ... Daphne would understand ... though no, she wouldn't admit it ... She won't be back until Saturday ... She has promised to take Mother back with her to her own house for a week or so, but will it work out or will Daphne change her mind? They both ought to be a lot fresher after a break from routine ... Who can I ask to visit Mother in the respite home? The vicar, of course – young Spooner is that energetic kind of priest who quite likes visiting his parishioners – not many of that sort left, I shouldn't think – from what I hear it's a nine-to-five job for most of them today ... anyway, yes, Spooner can look in on her and give me an idea of how she's faring ... Must ring the decorator to see how the work progressed today – it had better be finished some time next week, in case Daphne throws in the sponge ...

27 MARCH

'Are you the day sister?'
   'Well, Mrs Robson, I am the charge nurse ...'

'Just the person I wanted to speak to. Have you taken the medicines round?'

'The morning ones, yes, they were seen to, but ...'

'No buts, get on with it and report to me when you've finished.'

'I beg your pardon?'

'I'll pardon you this time, but if it happens again, you'll be dismissed.'

'What's your name again?'

'Mandy, Mrs Robson.'

'Why isn't this bed made, Mandy?'

'The patient has only just got out of it to have a wash ... You're looking a lot better for the washes we've given you this week.'

'Who on earth are you talking to? Just make sure all patients are washed, bed baths if necessary, you ought to know the routine.'

'Go back to your room and lie down, Edith, you are wearing yourself out.'

'My name's Enid. But you're right, Amy ... I like to see other faces, but it's too ...'

'You should call me by my proper title ...'

'What is your title then?'

'Everybody here knows I'm Matron. No patient has yet taken the liberty of calling me Amy ...'

'Good grief! Well, I never!'

'Yes you did, just now.'

28 MARCH

These young nurses get lazier by the week. In my day, we had to hump the patients around, none of these traptions for lifting them in and out of the bath or on and off the toilet – the nurses don't know they're born, and they don't change the sheets often enough. I must look into that – you'd think they had more time for the patients, but I don't see them chatting much with them – no, they get the work done in a jiffy and sit on their fat backsides ... If I catch that girl lounging about again, I'll send her packing, I'd better check that patients are getting the correct medicine – it'll be my fault if they mix them up or give an overdose, and that tall one needs watching, she comes on duty at a funny time, probably late. I always kept good time, there's no excuse for lateness – of course, she'll go on about her family and this and that – well, I brought up children but I didn't let it interfere with my work ...

'I'm Lizzy, your night nurse, Mrs Robson – I'm just showing you to your room, you shouldn't be wandering around at this hour of night ...'

'Impertinent young hussy, I know where my office is, but how do you expect me to keep an eye on the goings-on here if I stay stuck in there? So, you're the night nurse? Well, you run around and report back to me in my office, because, to tell you the truth, I'm worn out with all the extra work I've had to put in this week.'

'Of course, I'll see to it, while you have a lie-down.'

'I'm not something the cat brought in. Call me by my proper title when you address me. Matron to you. Come on, let me hear it.'

'Yes, Matron.'

'That's better.'

I'm sure she had a cheeky grin on her face as she went away. The standards keep on falling – you can't get young nurses of my cal ... quality any more ... This night is never-ending – how many hours before the day matron relieves me?

29 MARCH

'No, Mr Robson, we're not putting your mother on the phone today, she is fast asleep still ... Well, she was awake virtually the whole night, it appears – she thinks she's the night matron running this place ... So, she was in nursing in her younger days? ... Oh, and a matron of an old people's home? ... Well, that explains it – they often revert to an earlier role in their life ... Quite frankly, the staff are unable to cope with her, we're not specialised enough ... I'm sorry to have to tell you this, Mr Robson, but you'll have to look elsewhere for a respite home next time ...'

Well, that's torn it – Daphne's back tonight and doesn't want to take Mother home with her tomorrow, but the home want to discharge her ... No point in asking them for another week – we only arranged respite for a week, so we can't do anything about it ... But where will Mother go? She can't cope at home now, not even with extra care ...

'No, we don't need your services today, Reverend – nobody has passed away here.'

'It's OK, Mrs Robson, I've just popped in to see how you are.'

'I don't need seeing to, but that old man on the top floor isn't long for this world, mark my words, I can always tell when they're going. Pop up and say a few prayers over him. Then you'd best be getting back to your church for the service.'

'That's tomorrow ... I understand you're leaving here tomorrow, Mrs Robson.'

'I'm not titled to leave for ages yet. I'll take my holiday in August.'

'Your son rang me again just before I came here to say that your daughter was coming to pick you up after all to give you a couple of weeks' holiday at her house.'

127

'That's awfully nice of her, if I can get the time off, that is.'

'Er ... I'm sure she could arrange it for you.'

30 MARCH

You knew it would come to this ... Nobody can put up with Mother, even the trained professionals, you could see the relief on their faces as I put her in the car ... nobody but dear old Daphne – she'll give in and have her for a while, she's too good-natured to resist all the pleading ... Derek's too good at pleading, that's a crucial part of his job, second nature to him ... So, what on earth am I supposed to do with Mother for a fortnight? I'll have to see if I can get some carers in to share the burden ... Ten days, or even just a week, should be enough time to get her back into her own house ... Of course, Derek failed to follow up the decorating work, so they downed tools for almost the whole week ... but I'll make sure Mother's house is ready as soon as possible ...

'I didn't know you had a house, Daphne. What happened to that flat of yours?'

'That was a long time ago, Mother.'

'Well, you might have told me you'd moved. No wonder I haven't seen you for years.'

'Daphne, get rid of that nuisance of a woman ...'

'This is Linda – she's my best friend, Mother.'

'You haven't brought me all this way to spend hours chatting to friends – what about your lonely old mother?'

'Don't you put a tablecloth on your table for meals, Daphne?'

'Yes Mother, but the drawer I keep them in is empty.'

'You're getting like me. My things are never in their proper place ... But your tablecloths were here just a moment ago.'

'Then where did you put them all, Mother? ... Oh, we'll come across them later – you'll have to manage with a few table mats for now.'

31 MARCH

Mother dogs my footsteps and keeps interfering with everything I do ... and criticising ... She always knew better than me, that's why I lack confidence ... If I get angry with her, she makes a scene and it only makes matters worse ... Derek is impervious to it all, I don't think he was listening to what I said on the phone ... The beneficial effect of the holiday has virtually worn off already ... I'll be a bag of nerves again ... I'll have to find a way of calming her down, short of a bottle of sedatives – I don't want it to be in the local headlines that I gave her an overdose ... I'll try looking through the photo albums with her ...

'You remember Uncle Dennis, Mother – Aunt Maddy's husband? He used to come to see us when I was young.'

'I would never let a man like that in my house! He hasn't even shaved, what a ruffian!'

'He had a beard before he took ill ... He died of cancer, horrible death, terrible pain ...'

'They should have put him where I could nurse him, he would have been far better off.'

'And that's Aunt Maddy ... What on earth's the matter, Mother? You'll have the neighbours come rushing in if you scream like that.'

'That Maddy will be turning my house upside down while I'm here, looking for where I've hidden my money.'

'She died of a heart attack two years ago ...'

'How in the Lord's name did she have a heart attack? She never did a stroke of work in her life. I had to do everything for her when she was little ... and for all my other brothers and sisters too, come to that ... Dead, you say? The doctor who wrote the death certificate must have been as blind as a bat – mind you, I've met some dozy doctors in my time as a nurse ... Dead indeed! Then I must keep seeing her ghost. As plain as I see you, I've clapped eyes on her in my house. I wish I had a pound note for every time ...'

'We don't have pound notes any more, Mother.'

'Eeh, Daphne, if I'd known we were so hard up, I wouldn't have lent that money to Maddy the other day.'

1 APRIL

God, I must have slept in – I'd better go and get Mother's breakfast before she breaks everything in the kitchen ... Oh, she's not down here – she must be in the bathroom upstairs ... I'll call her when breakfast is ready and she can sit up in bed with it ...

Well, she's not in the garden either, this is disturbing ...

'No, she's not here, Daphne. Have you tried next door?'

'I've knocked on all the houses in the street, and no one's seen her – though there was no answer at some ...'

'Daphne, just look at that old woman ranting and raving at those young men in the park! They're always there, long-term unemployed you call them, but I must say they don't

130

cause any trouble ... That woman should be locked up! Oh Daphne! That's your mother surely!'

'Your name and address please, madam – we can't have disturbances like this.'

'Look, Officer, these young layabouts told me they don't do any work, they just lounge about here, so I gave them a piece of my mind.'

'And then you hit them with your walking stick ...'

'I'm dreadfully sorry about this, Sergeant – she's my mother, she must have got out of the house without my noticing – she only came here yesterday, and don't worry, she'll be back home in a week or so ...'

'That's all very well, madam, but she was disturbing the peace.'

'She's senile, she can't help it.'

'Who are you calling senile, Daphne? You ought to stick up for your defenceless old mother, but instead you insult me in public ...'

'No, Derek, this isn't an April Fool. It was all I could do – to have the young men drop any charges against Mother and to dissuade the police sergeant from putting it down in his records. Well, they all saw the funny side of it in the end, but that nearly set her off again ... the fact that they seemed to be laughing at her ... What's worse for me, Mother has ruined my local reputation ... because quite a few people witnessed the incident, there was a whole crowd around in the end, and they all saw that it was our mother ... Yes, it's just as well they don't know you and the fact that you are a barrister...'

Typical Derek, thinking of his own reputation first ...

2 APRIL

'No, thank you, I don't need anything today – in fact, I detest people coming round selling at the door ...'

'Mother! That's my next-door neighbour, Alan.'

'I didn't know you had a man friend, Daphne! How long have you known him? Fancy keeping secrets from your mother!'

'Sorry about Mother, Alan, she's a huge embarrassment. She was never able to answer the door at home, yet she seemed to hear the bell here before me. It's my fault for insisting that she wear a hearing aid. We discovered that she had several in a drawer in her bedroom, but wouldn't wear any of them.'

'There's some story going around about her creating a scene in the park ...'

'It's true, unfortunately. She wanders off.'

'Can't you keep the door bolted at the top?'

'Then she has a row with me about being kept a prisoner in her own home ... I think she has started to consider this as her house ... That's not going to happen, I can assure you – I can't even last another ten days with her ...'

'My! You have colour television, Daphne.'

'So do you, Mother.'

'I can't afford a colour set. Derek says the price is high because the colour ones are new, but it will go down in the end ...'

'That was years ago, Mother. You've had a few colour sets since then.'

'Then mine needs seeing to, because I can only see black and white ...'

'You're not colour blind, are you?'

'I can see jolly well that you are wearing a green dress ...'

'No, of course even if you were colour blind you'd be able to see most colours anyway . . .'

'I hope for your sake that when you're my age people don't ask *you* if you're blind . . .'

3 APRIL

Today it's the annual general meeting of the Trust . . . as secretary, I must be present . . . so why haven't they contacted me about providing a carer for Mother for the evening? . . . People have probably heard about the trouble in the park and nobody wants to volunteer – it'd be like putting yourself forward as a German soldier for the Russian front . . . I can't ask Alan – she'd be asking him why he hadn't proposed to me or some such ridiculous question . . . What about Linda, then? No, Mother was rude to her when she came round on Sunday . . . I'll try social services one last time . . .

'Fancy going out for the evening and not inviting me, Daphne!'

'Mother, it's not that sort of an evening out – you remember the work I do, cataloguing the valuable objects in the churches around here? Well, there's a big meeting about it all tonight and I must go as I'm the secretary . . . I have to take notes . . .'

'Couldn't I help you? . . . If you missed something, I could point it out . . .'

'No, it would be far too exhausting for you. Remember you're here for a rest . . .'

'It's no fun to sit all alone at night, Daphne . . .'

'A young lady . . . er, a friend of mine is coming to sit with you. Her name is Claire.'

I'm worn right out after that meeting, must have been the longest we've had ... How badly has Mother been playing that young Claire up? I dread going back ...

I can't believe my ears ... the 'sweetest old woman' Claire has ever met, let alone looked after, 'so kind and pleasant'! ... Are we talking about the same woman? Did she put on a special act because Claire was a stranger? ... She hasn't been so nice to the other people she has met here and they may as well all have been strangers, because she'd forgotten who they were.

4 APRIL

'I thought we were going away on holiday, Daphne.'
   'Um ... the hotel was fully booked ...'
   'That's a poor excuse – book another one then.'
   'There are no others in that area ...'
   'Which country do you mean?'
   'England, of course, Mother.'
   'Why stay in England? What was that beautiful country where Derek went last year on his honeymoon?'
   'That was decades ago, Mother!'
   'Decades? Doesn't sound like the name of the place to me. It began with a B ...'
   'Brazil.'
   'Isn't that the name of a herb I used to put in stews? ... Well, let's go there.'
   'You'd have to catch a plane, and you're not too keen on flying, Mother ...'
   'Nonsense. It'll do me good to get right away.'
   'You are away now. You're at my house.'
   'Oh? What's happening to my house then? ... There'll be burglars! Take me back home immediately!'

134

'We'll go on Sunday when the traffic is quieter.'

Thank goodness the work is completed in Mother's house ... What will Derek say? I was meant to be keeping her here for a fortnight ... But I have to see Dr Devonshire next Friday, so it would be good to see the back of her by then ... No, I shouldn't think like that about her ... she's such a sweet old lady ... huh! ... Then let Derek cope with her ... or Lucy even – Lucy thinks she sounds quite normal to an outsider ... and that's the point, she does appear quite normal to outsiders, but not to her family ... It's when you have to live with them or put up with their problems day after day after day that you see their real predicament.

5 APRIL

'Excuse me, you look like a helpful lady, I'm looking for my house, only it seems to have disappeared. I hope it hasn't been bombed.'

'Do you live around here? I don't recognise you. Perhaps there's somebody else who might know you ...'

'I live somewhere in this street, I'm sure of that ... or perhaps it was that other one I just walked past ...'

'Have you not got something in your pockets with your name on? ... Oh, excuse me ... can you help this old lady? She's lost, and I don't know who she is ... Perhaps we should call the police ...'

'Why, what's the old dear been up to now?'

'So you know her?'

'She's a public menace.'

'She only seems to be a bit absent-minded – she can't help that at her age.'

'You don't know the half of the story. She beat me up with her stick the other day. Thank God she hasn't brought it with her today ... You're living with that Daphne Robson, aren't you?'

'That's right, I'm Amy Robson and Daphne is my daughter.'

'Their house isn't far away ... I'll take her there, if you'll come along with us.'

'There's no point knocking so loud, young man, this Daphne's obviously not in at the moment ... Perhaps she was out walking with her mother and lost sight of her in a shop. Anyway, I have a doctor's appointment, so I must rush. Will you wait here with old Mrs Robson until her daughter gets back? ... Come on, she's harmless really, and besides, you're a strapping young man!'

'I can't understand why my daughter isn't at home. She invited me here today ... You'll be late for work, young man – you run off and I'll just have to wait around.'

'I told you before, I don't have any work.'

'That government is a disgrace. So many people without jobs, while they twiddle their thumbs. How do they think people get by on the pittance they pay them?'

'So, it's the government's fault now, is it? The other day you said it was mine.'

'I can see that you are an honest man who would like to do a hard day's work, but there's not enough to go round. Funny, because my son says almost everybody is doing well – money-wise, I mean. Woe betide us if we fall on hard times, that's all I can say!'

6 APRIL

'Yes, Derek, I'm taking Mother back home today. The work at her house is all done, as you know, and I've arranged for the carers to be back in place – in fact, Tracy is going to rearrange her timetable to be there more often ... Why is she going back? Do you really need to ask? I can't begin to tell you the bother I had yesterday. In a nutshell, she wandered off out of the house and went missing. I was out looking for her when somebody brought her back here ... Hypothermia? I'll hypo you in a minute. She's perfectly all right – it's me who needs seeing to ...'

'This isn't my house, Daphne – why have you brought me here?'

'We had the upstairs redecorated for you, so that it would look nicer. That's your wardrobe, look, with all your clothes in.'

'Who put those strange things in there? I wouldn't be seen dead in some of those clothes.'

'You chose many of them yourself ... and I gave you some of mine you liked ...'

'Am I a beggar to need somebody else's cast-off items? No wonder I didn't recognise the wardrobe ...'

'What's that smell of burning, Mother? You're not cooking, are you?'

'Well, I'll have to get the dinner ready in a minute, but I've put the kettle on for a cup of tea.'

'Oh no! There's no water in it ...'

Obviously Derek didn't put the kettle safely away before he left the house with her. Thank goodness it's still working. I'd better ring that restaurant for dinner – there's nothing in the house. Tracy will have to do some shopping for Mother tomorrow ... Oh, I'd better avoid the place I took her to for a meal in January ...

'Do you like the pork?'

137

'I beg your pardon?'

'That pork you're eating – get them to take it back if it's dry like mine.'

'I'm awfully sorry for the disturbance, sir. Mother! You can't tell other customers what to do. Swap over with me, my beef is perfect.'

'I don't know why you didn't order beef for me as well, Daphne. Why should I have the cheaper food?'

'All roast dinners are the same price, Mother. In any case, you wanted pork.'

'Did you hear that?'

'Er ...'

'My daughter's treating me like a little child ...'

'Mother! Let the other people here eat their dinner in peace.'

I'm still starving. The pork was fine, all that fuss was over nothing, but I couldn't get a bite down with all her antics. At least she knocked back her plateful, so she'll be OK until tomorrow.

7 APRIL

Note from Daphne:

Dear Tracy,
Yes, got groceries and household items. Make sure she has a drink each time you call. Respite home thought that dehydration may have added to her dementia ...

... Well, of all the cheek ... her son probably forgot to give her something to drink before he put her in the home – I'm *always* making her tea ...

'I haven't seen you for donkey's years, D ...'

'Tracy. You've been away, Mrs Robson.'

'*You've* been away, more like. I haven't budged from this chair for days.'

'I've restocked your fridge and larder ... for breakfast and supper, I mean.'

'Don't I get lunch any more, a proper meal?'

'Somebody will bring that in ...'

'Eeh, don't say I've got to eat those meals cooked in the soup kitchen ...'

'No ... er, well ... your daughter has brought some meals that I can warm up for you ...'

From the case notes:

Patient very confused, doesn't remember anything of the last fort-night. Still objects to meals on wheels, so we'll have to pretend that the meals come from her daughter for carers to warm up. All items on shopping list bought.

8 APRIL

'Nice to see you again, Amy. Didn't expect you to open the door, not so promptly, anyway ... Oh, I see you've got your hearing aid in ...'

'Don't know why, Madge. It's starting to irritate me.'

'I spent a few days at Stephen's. He's making good progress on the bridge.'

'What's he doing on a bridge? He wasn't thinking of ending it all, was he?'

'Ending what? Oh, don't be silly, Amy. We've been through this before. He's been building it.'

'He was always playing with his Meccano set. Is he building it for you?'

'No, for everybody – it's taking a major road over a big river.'

'That's jolly good of him. Isn't it costing him a lot?'

'They've given him the money for it, Amy.'

'How wonderful to be able to carry on your hobby at other people's expense.'

'I don't think you get it, Amy, but never mind ... What was it like in the home you were in? ... Only, Stephen thinks it might be suitable for me, should I need it ... I just wanted to check.'

'In Derek's home? I don't think he has paying guests.'

'In the nursing home.'

'I haven't worked there for a while, Madge, so I couldn't tell you if it's OK any more.'

'You were there the week before last, or so your children told me.'

'So they know my rotas better than me, do they?'

'Er ... your garden will need some attention now that spring is here. Our old gardener had a heart attack, so I'm looking for a new one for us both.'

'I don't need any help. I'll be out there as soon as we get a really bright day.'

'In any case, if I find the right sort, I'll send him along to see if you need any help ... Aren't you thirsty, Amy? You haven't drunk that squash there.'

'I need a hot drink.'

'I'll put the kettle on.'

From the case notes:

Patient still disturbed. Doesn't know why carers keep calling. Visit from Mrs Mullins seems to have cheered her up.

9 APRIL

What are these photographs doing here? Maddy has been going through all my things again ... Who on earth took this one? It's all dark, except there's me in my air-raid warden's uniform ... Some joke, perhaps ... What am I doing fiddling with that gas heater? Must be the one in the bathroom ... No, didn't we have to scrap it? And that's one of me in my nurse's uniform ... Did Daphne find these photographs?

'More photos, Mrs Robson? That's a funny one, all in the dark.'

'Blackout, dear, wartime. I could have arrested the person who took that for making a bright light.'

'I didn't know you were an air-raid warden.'

'All the men were away fighting or doing important jobs, but there were some shirkers, of course. I was fit and strong, so they chose me as the one to patrol this street and one or two side streets.'

'Eerie in the dark, wasn't it? Weren't you afraid?'

'No strange men about then, Daisy.'

'Ha ha! ... What was your worst experience as a warden?'

'Bumping into a lamp post and losing my front teeth ... I don't see anything to laugh at!'

'Sorry – I thought you had lost your teeth through old age.'

'My teeth are as strong as a horse's. It took a bad accident to knock them out, Daisy.'

'And this one is odd, Mrs Robson – it seems to be in a different house from this one – did you move here from somewhere else?'

'Been in this house since Derek was born, dear.'

'Well this picture of you fixing a gas heater seems to have been taken somewhere else.'

'My day job. The men weren't around, as I said, so we women had to put our hands to the grinder.'

'Well I never! The things you used to get up to.'

'Just because I spend most of the time sitting in my chair these days, it doesn't mean that I've been an idler all my life, my dear.'

10 APRIL

Must put some food out for the birds, they seem to have flown away from my garden ... These weeds take some pulling up ... the lawn is all lumpy ... Maddy's children have been jumping up and down on it again ... Derek could give me a hand one weekend ... I'd better sit down, not like me to need a rest ...

'What are you doing poking your nose over my fence? If you're thinking of robbing me, it's not worth it. I've nothing of any value left.'

'Mrs Robson? Mrs Mullins has hired me to do her garden and asked me to have a word with you about doing yours.'

'What on earth for? Has she taken leave of her senses?'

'There's my card.'

'I haven't got my glasses on. What does it say?'

'Bill Jackson, gardening services.'

'You're not in league with those Pheasants?'

'Pheasants?'

'The ones who live next to Mrs Mullins.'

'Don't know anything about that.'

'Well, I'll give you a trial. Get weeding this patch and I'll see if you're up to it ... Oh, by the way, how much do you take from a poor old pensioner like me?'

'Reduced hourly rate for you. Just a tenner.'

'Very reasonable. Only ten pence.'

'Mrs Mullins told me you had a wicked sense of humour. Ten pounds, of course.'

'*Ten pounds?* Where do you think I can get that sort of money?'

'Just watch me work for an hour as a trial and then you can decide.'

'There's another weed you've missed, Mr Jackdaw. And you're making a mess of my path, but all in all, not bad, though not up to my standards, of course. I'll have to ask my children if they can pay you for me at your contortionist rates.'

Pheasants, jackdaws? Contortionist? Ten pence an hour! The old dear is round the twist. And she can nag worse than my missus. I'd rather break stones like a convict than work for her.

11 APRIL

I let her down ... . She could have stayed longer ... No, she's coping all right back home, but she needs company ... I know the carers provide that, but it's not the same – as her daughter, I ought to do more ... Stop it! ... Dr Devonshire says that I'll have another nervous breakdown if I go on like I am ... I thought he was a bit abrupt today ... could have been more sympathetic ... says he wants to snap me out of it ... could snap me instead ... Don't ring Mother tonight – she will never understand that I'm not well, so I wouldn't be able to mention the doctor ... But I'd better check if things are still satisfactory at her end ... No, leave it till you're fresh tomorrow ... The seagulls are wading on the field ... Dr Devonshire says I must banish them from my mind ... He finds the image obsessive, perhaps a bad omen ... I pay him an awful lot and I'm not sure he's getting me any better ...

'You seem worn out today, Mrs Robson.'

'Kerry, isn't it?'

'Kelly. You were asleep when I came and I'm just about to leave, but here's your lunch that I made for you ... You did too much gardening yesterday.'

'Did I? How would you know?'

'Mrs Mullins rang the office. She says you wanted to hire her gardener to help you out, but he didn't seem too keen to do more than an hour.'

'What's she doing meddling in my affairs? I'm as fit as a fiddle. As if I can't do a bit of weeding and so on.'

'Your doctor doesn't recommend it. If you fell in the garden, for instance ... .'

'We'll worry about that when it happens, Kerry.'

12 APRIL

The sunlight was streaming through the stained-glass windows casting flickering mosaics on the bare flagstones; the spring warmth was filtering into the cold nave; the scent of the freshly picked flowers was borne up into the very arches; my own choir was raising one harmonious prayer to the bell tower and beyond into the expectant heavens, and a calm of another world was seeping into my mind, as they carried the casket in slowly, respectfully ... Was my mother really inside that wooden box?

That question was what awoke me ... Am I wishing her dead already? ... In reality, the funeral rite would have to be conducted by the Reverend Spooner in my mother's church, not in mine ... And who were the mourners? They all seemed so saddened, yet I felt relief creeping in me, a gradual sense of weightlessness, as if I had been transported into space myself ...

How wicked of you, Daphne ... You've sent your mother back to die deserted in her own house ... No, she *is* taken care of ... She is still alive, even if most of her mind isn't ... You mustn't speak of her as if she were a vegetable ... The dream was a warning ... to make sure that funeral arrangements will be in place ... There you go again, willing her into the grave ... No, it's only fitting for me to approach Reverend Spooner and ask him if he will do the necessary ... when the time comes, of course ... Will he think that I consider Mother as good as dead already?

Already evening ... This self-inquisition can't continue ... I'll go and see Mother tomorrow, take her to church and speak to Spooner. I'll ring her now, and if she doesn't answer, I'll trouble Mrs Mullins to knock on her door and dial my number for her.

13 APRIL

'I wish you'd told me you were coming, Daphne – I would have prepared a roast dinner.'

'Somebody will bring in your dinner, Mother. I've brought some sandwiches for myself.'

'Whoever heard of a child of mine having to exist on sandwiches? I can't have that. The neighbours will think I'm trying to starve you!'

'I would like to go to church with you today, if you're feeling up to it.'

'Do you know, I've forgotten where the church is. I think we'll not get there on foot.'

'Don't worry, we'll go in my car.'

'Well, you've seen and heard it for yourself now, Daphne – the old ladies worship and, indeed, sing in their own way.'

'I did give Mother her glasses, Reverend Spooner, but she can't read well with them – I'm awfully sorry she was singing the wrong hymns.'

'It's OK – most of the others were too – it's not unusual. They set each other off.'

'Mother was starting up the wrong prayers too ...'

'The good Lord hears the intention, even if the words are inappropriate.'

'You must wish sometimes that you had a younger congregation.'

'Daphne, the elderly make up more than half of my flock. Without them the church would be even emptier ... Besides, teenagers have other preoccupations ...'

'Older people like my mother must scare them away.'

'Your mother does complain that there are too many old-stagers here ...'

'But she is the oldest!'

'Yes ... and your mother always chats to the children and young people when she comes – she says they must be encouraged to go to church, that too many of the congregation head straight for the door and their Sunday lunch at the end of the service, which isn't very Christian – as I also try to explain in my sermons ...'

'Ah, that brings me to the ... one of the purposes of my being here today ... Would you be so kind as to preach the sermon ... make the address, whatever it is called ... at my mother's funeral, which I ... the family would like to hold in this church?'

'But of course, I would be delighted – I have known her

well over the years I have been here, but her life stretches much further back. I would be grateful if you could give me some biographical details at some stage ...'

'Yes, Reverend, I realise that it's not something that is going to take place right away, but it's best to be prepared.'

'Hey, you, Spooner!'

'What a rude man!'

'Leave him to me, Daphne.'

'You've broke that agreement we 'ad ... The bloody church bells sounded for two minutes and ten seconds, ten seconds over, don't you deny it, I recorded them ... You should hear the bloody racket in my living room ... And the singing today was 120 decibels ... you didn't even close the doors and windows ... like an army of tortured cats screeching at full pelt, it was ...'

'You shouldn't have stayed to hear all that, Daphne.'

'Why do you put up with him, Reverend?'

'The church is quite small, right in the middle of a row of terraced houses, as you see, and the noise does carry, so it must be aggravating if you are a non-believer ...'

14 APRIL

'Till we meet again one sunny day ...'

'You're singing away there, Mrs Robson.'

'My husband's favourite song, Daisy. Except we didn't meet again, not even on a rainy day. Your generation hasn't had to put up with that kind of parting ... Why are you crying, dear? ... I didn't mean to upset you.'

'My best friend got married a few weeks ago, I was chief bridesmaid ... They didn't have time for a honeymoon ... her husband was called out to Afghanistan soon after the wedding ... and we heard yesterday that he has been killed ...'

'After the Second World War, my mother said that it would be the last, but they said that about the first one, that it would put an end to the lot ... what's the point of all this fighting in the world? I'm too depressed to listen to the news these days, yet my set is still stuck on that news channel ... But poor little soul, what a tragedy – I expect you've known your friend for a long time ...'

'Since we were tiny ... and her husband too, we all grew up together ... I'm sorry, I must pull myself out of this, I'm no use to you blubbering like this, Mrs Robson ...'

'You should have taken the day off, Daisy – in fact, you go home now, I can manage without you for a day.'

'I'm not allowed to take time off just like that ... Anyway, I wouldn't want to let you down.'

15 APRIL

Well, I think the funeral service would be more aesthetically pleasing in Daphne's church ... now, where did I put those notes? ... But burying people is not supposed to be aesthetically pleasing – decorous perhaps ... In court in less than twenty minutes ... Mother would want to be seen off by her friends ... and those who are left in this world have one foot in the next ... A tough brief this one, even Derek Robson won't get him put away, I keep hearing ... Put her away ... You just want to put me away, Derek, she would say ... No, Daphne's right, it will have to be in Mother's church and we'll have to listen to that Spooner – means well, dear chap, will most probably say the right things ... Must make sure I do too ... Her final home ... No other home will take her now, her antics as matron have seen to that ... Suggest maximum sentence ... he'll only do half ... Can't somebody halve our sentence? You mustn't talk like that, my sister would say ... She's frightened of her own skin, is Daphne ... How much longer must we put up with ... ? Fifteen more minutes ... God, I would settle for just fifteen more minutes ... Daphne says it's all right for me, I sit back and let her sweat over Mother, but it's an even greater torment when you have little time to do anything about the situation ... Hardly any time left now, concentrate on the summing up ...

'You're overstretched here, if you don't mind my saying so, Robson. I had a feeling my client wouldn't cop it, but I'm as certain now as I've ever been in my career, after your final effort there. Was that the best you could do? They're muttering that your powers are slipping.'

'Trust you to gloat, Redgrave, but don't count your chickens yet.'

'You can talk! You lay it on thick when you've got the upper hand, but you don't like your own medicine when the tables are turned.'

At least thieves have some honour, Redgrave ...

16 APRIL

'You look worn out, Mrs Robson. Didn't you sleep well?'

'Oh, Daisy ... I think I'll go to bed, I know it's a bit early but ...'

'It's only nine in the morning.'

'Didn't I have bad news yesterday about somebody being killed in a war?'

'Yes, a friend of mine.'

'That's what wore me out, Daisy, I couldn't get to sleep worrying about it.'

'To tell you the truth, I had a bad night too.'

'I'll lie down in my bed upstairs and you can lie on the settee in the best room.'

'Steady on, Mrs Robson, hold on to that banister ... My, it's a struggle for you to get up your stairs.'

'Don't make me out to be a complete invalid – you'll be telling me next to have an escalator or whatever it is that Daphne says I need. Oh, I want to do some cleaning in the house later on after a good rest.'

'There's no need – Kelly and I do light work, and Daphne has arranged for a new cleaner to come in on a Friday, the day Kelly is here.'

'I can't afford to pay cleaners on my pittance of a pension.'

'Your children pay for it.'

'Rightly so. All my money went on their education.'

'We must have a chat about that one day, Mrs Robson.'

From the case notes:

Patient slept much of the day, probably she is staying awake at night.

17 APRIL

'How did you get in here, Madge?'

'Tracy let me in as she was going. Thought I'd better tell you right away, Amy ...'

'What's Stephen been up to then?'

'Stephen?'

'Well, your news is always about your son, isn't it?'

'No, this is about your Derek.'

'He's been honoured by the Queen for counselling her!'

'No, Amy ... but he is in the newspaper today. He ...'

150

'I knew it. I had a dream about him last night.'

'Well I never! Anyway, I'm afraid he lost in his latest case ...'

'Go on, you're joking.'

'No, I'm afraid I'm not – the report says he hasn't lost one for ages, but ...'

'Derek's not a loser, Madge.'

'Come to that, nor is Stephen, but he's dead worried about the new bridge.'

'You didn't come to talk about the bridge?'

'No, just to tell you the news about Derek.'

'Folks around here will be smirking at me. They don't like me having a successful son ...'

'I know what you mean, Amy. Those Partridges keep dropping hints about the delay with the bridge ...'

'It's not just them, my dear. Some people are riddled with jealousy. Their insides are greener than my lawn ... which is just a patch of brown soil with weeds ...'

'You do have the services of that gardener I sent round to you, Amy.'

'Listen, Madge, I don't need anybody coming over here and meddling with my garden – I used to have a garden lovelier than Derek's, it could have gone on that television series ... I can still get out there you know, just wait until the warm weather arrives and you'll see the difference out there.'

'Hmm ... you don't want to overdo it, you know ...'

'It's that gardener you sent me who doesn't want to overdo it – he's much younger than that old one we used to have, yet he hardly moves – he takes all afternoon to cut my lawn and edges and it's no size at all.'

'He doesn't ask for much an hour.'

'That's because he takes twice as many hours as other gardeners, Madge.'

'Well, at least he agreed to work for you in the end, after saying he wouldn't.'

18 APRIL

People come in and out of here as if it was a London station, that one I met Alfred at when he came back from the war, the last time he did come back. Where's that useless twerp Stan? Can't he stop all these people barging in here? Probably out at the bookies again, putting money on a crippled horse ... Wait till I give him a piece of my mind ... What's that woman doing shifting my furniture around? Is it Maddy? She's after my savings, but she won't find where I've tucked them away.

'You call that room cleaned, do you? Well, how about this? Dust on the ledge here ... you are supposed to do all ledges as well.'

'There's only so much I can do in the given time, Mrs Robson.'

'Then Stan will have to pay you for more hours.'

'I knows nothing about no Stan. I picks my wages up at the agency.'

'Clean indeed! I can do a far better job myself.'

'You calls me in here 'cause you can't do it no more.'

'Kelly, I'm gonna tell the agency that I ain't coming here again.'

'Can't you stick it out a bit longer, Joan?'

'I gets it in the neck every minute from the old bat ...'

'Now, now, language, Joan ...'

'She's as deaf as a post ...'

'That's not the point, Joan ... Look, I know she's pretty difficult, but it's hard to replace you.'

'Not surprised, Kelly. I ain't the first to get the skivvy treatment here – the last one warned me ...'

'Just think it over for a day or two.'

19 APRIL

Just read Dr Devonshire's notes again – points to observe ...
'Remain positive, Daphne, think of all the charitable work
you do' ... Could spend more time with my mother instead
... 'Think about what you plan to do each day ... allow only
certain slots each day to think of your mother, then if
anything needs doing for her, act immediately upon it' ...
It's hard to when she doesn't answer her blessed phone ...
'and then banish all thoughts of her' ... How cruel that
sounds ... but harsh medicine is necessary, Dr Devonshire
says ... The tulips are all out – what do the red ones remind
me of? ... 'Don't return to morbid thoughts of the past, for
example, your father's death remember him as a hero' ...
An easy way of dismissing the agony of bereavement in
wartime, make heroes of them ... so Dr Devonshire says I
should dismiss all negative reflections of the past ... That's
it, the red tulips Uncle Stan planted were all in bloom that
day he left us, never to come back ... 'You are not to blame
for the breakdown of your mother's second marriage' ...
He's right, it's not my fault Uncle Stan was making advances
to me, or so I thought at the time – no, I was right to push
him away and threaten to tell Mother ... 'Praise yourself for
your achievements' ... At least I did well in my work ...
though I was educated for something better than a private
secretary ... 'The performances of your choir are something
to be proud of' ... Let's put on that old recording the vicar
made of us ...

'Sorry to disturb you, Daphne, but your mother's cleaner
can't hack it any more ...'

'I can't hack it either, Kelly. What has Mother been up to
now?'

'She was too strict about cleanliness ... Well, it's not
going to be easy to replace Joan, as your mother's

reputation goes before her at the agency. Oh, and you or your brother will have to send another cheque, as the cash is almost all gone ...'

About time Derek went to see Mother ...

20 APRIL

'Derek! What are you doing here? Why aren't you in court?'

'I'm having a bit of time off in between trials, Mother ... Life is all trials ...'

'While you're here, look for your father, he's somewhere in the house but keeps hiding from me.'

'Father passed away some years ago, Mother.'

'Fancy that. He must have banned me in his will from going to his funeral.'

'We both went, Mother. That other woman who you said should remain nameless was there and you had a row with her.'

'*I* had a row! More like *she* started it! Anyway, I can't remember which woman you mean, Stanley had more women than I've had hot dinners – and that's another thing, Derek, my dinner is all cold by the time I eat it.'

'You forget it's there, and only come to it much later, Mother.'

'Your father has come back to haunt me then – I've definitely caught sight of him upstairs. He's wasting his time, as I have a clear conscience, and he won't frighten me.'

'My last case was reported in the national papers, Mother.'

'Naturally, Derek, I would expect it to be. But somebody keeps stealing my papers, so I couldn't read anything about it.'

'The trouble is, the press are likely to be in court the next time to see if I'll lose again.'

'You lose? The judge must have been corrupt like that one in the news a while ago. They ought to replace him with you, there's nobody as clever and shrewd as you ...'

21 APRIL

'Wonderful news, Mrs Robson.'

'Stanley's sent me some money? It's been weeks since he did, Daisy ...'

'No, not that ...'

'Derek has been made a top court judge? I knew it!'

'No, sorry, it's about me. I'm engaged.'

'Somebody else has engaged you, Daisy? That's not good news. What about me? Won't you be coming here any longer?'

'Engaged to be married, I mean.'

'Oh, betrothed, that's what we used to call it.'

'Sam proposed to me on Saturday evening, Mrs Robson.'

'Samuel, that's a name from the Bible, how awful to shorten it to Sam.'

'Everybody calls him Sam. Anyway, we were in this posh restaurant, which is unusual for Sam – we had lobster, then steak – a tournedos, they called it ...'

'Daphne likes those foreign restaurants, all fancy names and paltry portions, and you leave the place starving ...'

'Anyway, we sipped champagne ...'

'And he popped the word, as we used to say?'

'No, then we went to a night club, all dimly lit and romantic ...'

'Dodgy places those, Daisy, you never know what men can get up to in the dark ...'

'Well, Sam got down on his knees ...'

'Make sure he stays there, dear – let him knows who's boss, before it's too late.'

'I thought he had dropped something, but all of a sudden he opened this box and produced this ring – look!'

'He must earn a pretty penny to buy a gem like that. Still, you deserve it, my dear. I think the world of you too. I hope you'll carry on looking after me when you're married.'

'You'll make me cry all over again, Mrs Robson.'

'I must take a look at this Sam to see if he's worthy of you, Daisy.'

Funny woman, she ruined my story ... she made it seem almost trite ... But at least she was affectionate at the end. ... Is she jealous that Sam will have more of my attention than her?

22 APRIL

'You *must* remember us, Amy – we're Elsie and Freda from the church ladies' fellowship – we haven't seen you for months and we heard that you were house-bound, so we thought it was very remiss of us not to have paid you a visit.'

'Elsie? Oh, yes, you used to have a car and bring me home.'

'Sadly no longer, Amy – my son wrote to my doctor some time back to tell him not to sign any more papers for me to renew my driving licence.'

'The cheeky devil!'

'That's what I thought at the time.'

'Don't forget, Elsie, that Amy was in the car when you had that bad accident.'

'So you keep reminding me, Freda, and that you counted your lucky stars not to have come with me that day too ...'

'Was it a bad accident, Elsie?'

'I'm glad *you've* forgotten it, Amy. I ended up with concussion, but you walked away from it uninjured. Of course, it was that young man's fault. The main road was clear when I pulled out onto it – he came like a bolt out of the blue in that flashy car of his.'

'What about the bus and its passengers, Elsie? Wasn't the accident said to be all your fault?'

'Hark at her, Amy – it was through listening to Freda that my son was against me driving any more...'

'Now don't start a row here, you two, I would make you a cup of tea, but they've hidden the teapot and kettle. I have to drink out of that flask there, but the tea in there has gone stale ...'

'We meant to bring you some cake, Amy, but I don't know where I put it – I had it ready near the front door just before I left ...'

'Not to worry, Elsie ... What's the matter, Freda?'

'My handbag has gone ...'

'Those two boys who keep pestering me have probably stolen it!'

'Most likely you left it in the taxi, Freda ... She's always mislaying things, Amy ... Bus fares have gone up so much and the taxi is extortionate, that's why we don't often get over here ...'

'Just a moment, Elsie. Look, there's your handbag, Freda.'

'No, Amy, that's mine. Oh, I had some photos in it from one of our evening dos – look!'

'Who's that then, Elsie?'

'You know the Reverend Spooner. Well, you haven't seen him dancing like *that*, perhaps ...'

'And this lady you are with here, Elsie, she doesn't look that holy to me ... Good God, it's that Pheasant woman!'

'Oh no, it's today, today!'

'What is, Elsie?'

'The appointment for my dentures. The card's been in my handbag all this time! Sorry, Amy – we'll have to get a taxi now and go – maybe they can still fit me in. It might be the same driver who brought us here. If not, he can phone through and ask if your handbag was left in the other taxi, Freda.'

'Good idea, Elsie dear. Sorry to leave you in such a rush, Amy, but we'll come back another day.'

23 APRIL

I'm sure I know those old people in these photographs dancing and partying ... but who left the pictures in my sitting room? That one looks a bit like that Freda – always running people down she was, what a tongue she had in her head – and that could be Elsie, she got too old to drive and would run people down in her car, worse than that Toad in the story I used to read to Derek, how he would laugh at it ... or maybe it's Ivy, the shy one who used to go all red if we mentioned men ... I'll tear that one up – surely it's that Pheasant, hovering over her next victims like a bird of prey. Harpy would be a better name for her ... Long time since I saw any of these friends ... must pop round to the fellow-ship again, but I think it's a long walk, it must be near the church ... or is it in the church hall? I need to find that old map ... What was the name of the road? ... Somebody's trying to break my window – that Pheasant can't wait till I'm in my coffin, she's forcing her way in ...

'Steady on, Amy, it's only me. Put that stick down or you'll do me a mortal injury.'

'Madge! Sorry, come round to the front door – why didn't you ring there in the first place?'

'I did! I practically wore out my finger pressing on that

bell – perhaps your battery has gone again ... I came to tell you that your Derek is appearing at the local court ...'

'They must have mistaken him for somebody else – he's never committed a crime in his life, except neglecting his old mother.'

'No, Amy, he's appearing for the prosecution. They allow the public into the court, you know. I'll arrange for us to have a taxi and go together one day. That's unless Daphne plans to take you.'

'She never takes me anywhere, Madge.'

'Well, I'll have a think about the best day for our visit – the trial will be on for a few weeks, I think. I'll leave this newspaper cutting about it for you to read.'

'Eeh, Derek's here in town, you say? Well, he's hiding from his mother somewhere.'

24 APRIL

'Come on, Mrs Robson, you must eat up your dinner. You hardly had a bite out of yesterday's.'

'I'm excited about something, Daisy.'

'What, Mrs Robson?'

'I only wish I knew, dear. Besides, plastic and cardboard were never favourite items in my diet.'

'Your daughter made this specially for you.'

'You think I'm completely round the twist, don't you? Don't think I haven't seen that van come round just before you bring my dinner to me. The people who make this tripe should hire that young chef from the television, the one who has written those recipes for school meals ... used to be good in my children's school days, until the government economised ... I used to enjoy the cooking programmes, but I can't watch them now that my set's stuck on that news channel ...'

'I left your TV on the right channel for you to watch that programme yesterday, Mrs Robson, you did ask me to ...'

'Then they must have altered the programmes, Daisy.'

'Daphne says you used to be a brilliant cook, you made all kinds of meals, cakes, pastries, jams, marmalades, chutneys.'

'I still could, only some silly idiot has cut my stove off from the mains. I keep asking you to have it seen to, Daisy ... *Daisy!* ... Where has that girl gone to?'

25 APRIL

'Where to, love?'

'I'm not your lover, young man. You'd have to dress a bit smarter than that for me to be interested in you ...'

'Nothing like a sense of humour, that's what I say, but where are you going?'

'To the station.'

'Going somewhere nice?'

'To see my son.'

'Must be a day trip, or have you forgotten your suitcase?'

'Just for the day, I said. Now stop all this chit-chat and get a move on.'

'To the court, please.'

'In which town, madam?'

'Look, it's all in this newspaper cutting I've brought with me.'

'Hmm ... Oh, that's the court that's right here – no need to catch a train ...'

'Let me help the lady ... the court is not far from the station ... You go a hundred yards to the left, then ...'

'Which bus takes me to the court?'

'You don't need a bus. The court is just over there. Follow me, I think I've just got time before my bus comes.'

'It would happen on my day on duty here! Mrs Robson has disappeared. Yes, vanished. Nobody around here has seen her today ... When could she have gone? Well, her bed wasn't slept in last night, but that doesn't mean anything, as Tracy reckons she stays most nights in her chair ... Yes, the police have been alerted ...'

'I must object, Your Honour – the learned counsel for the Crown has, in my humble estimation, overstepped the mark ...'
    'How dare you criticise him? That's my son you are referring to!'
    'Silence in court!'
    'I'm not going to sit back and listen to this upstart criticising my son. What does he know about the law? My son studied like a Trojan for years and has ...'
    'Be silent, madam, or I'll have to ask you to leave the court!'

'That's it, Derek, you tell him – don't let him put one over on you, the shifty little rogue ...'
    'It's that old lady again ... Madam, you can't address the counsel for the defence, and certainly not in that derogatory manner ... See that she is ushered out of the court ...'
    'You've not heard the last of this. Why, the papers will hear how you manhandled a frail old woman ...'
    'The old lady in question seems to have more than a passing acquaintance with the learned counsel for the Crown ...'
    'A madwoman, Your Honour – it's the first time I've set eyes on her.'
    'Silence in the press box! Silence in court!'

161

'Clerk, go and see that she is escorted back to wherever she came from. We don't want to have lunatics like that in here again.'

From the case notes:

Patient eventually brought back home from the court in a taxi.

26 APRIL

Oh, my god! It's in the local headlines: Top barrister denies mother in court. After hearing her call me her son, the press probably found out Mother's address from the taxi driver and made enquiries in Mother's street to verify her identity ... 'Scandal, as court witnesses the worst interruption in years, old lady fuming, ranting and raving at officials ... To make matters worse, in front of all those assembled in court, Derek Robson disowned his own mother in the town he grew up in ... If only he had had the decency to acknowledge her ... His career will surely never recover ...'

What use is a brother like that? It's no use, Daphne, you're all on your own in this ...

All Derek can think of now is how Mother humiliated him. The fact that she could have been found dead in the street eludes him ... Mother was only trying to stick up for him as she used to when he was little ... Have her put away is all he can say ... Perhaps we should send her back to court for him to prosecute her ...

'How is Amy today, Tracy?'

'She can't remember a thing, Mrs Mullins. She has been asking me why she is so worn out after the quiet day she had yesterday.'

'Thank goodness she doesn't get the local paper any more. I'll make sure I don't mention anything. What a to-do! And I blame myself. After all, I gave her the newspaper cutting about the trial in the court here and told her I would book a taxi and go there with her one day ...'

From the case notes:

Patient appears to have spent most of the day sleeping off Friday's experience. Hopefully, she won't be up too much in the night.

27 APRIL

What was the first embarrassment Mother caused me? Yes – well, it wasn't the first, but it was definitely one of the worst I remember – the school uniform, always the best uniform she could buy, always revoltingly clean and horribly well ironed in the eyes of my possibly jealous school chums ... it gave me a priggish look, in the eyes of those other boys ... but that was the least of my worries ... When an evening event took place at the school, such as the school play, of course she always insisted in the first few years on coming with me, so that the rest of my form, sitting together without their parents – and some with girlfriends – whispered and tittered all night at my expense ... Then, when I managed to persuade her to allow me to go on my own, I was still forced to wear school uniform, because I had no other presentable clothes – the others were virtual rags to be worn in the house or when I went out shopping for her ... Endless interrogations from my classmates about my garb, had to persuade them that my mother wouldn't believe that we could wear what we liked, no, she had insisted on my donning the school attire, but naturally I had casual clothes at least as smart as theirs ... And did I manage to pull it off?

Well, that's how I developed my rhetorical powers of persuasion, inventing, rehearsing and perfecting speeches in my own defence ... that's how I came to be counsel for the defence, so perhaps some good came of all that suffering ... Daphne still laughs about all that, not that I have ever explained what went on to her in any detail ... nor have I mentioned my teenage trauma to the children, not even to Lucy, who can take on other people's problems ... And nobody outside the family would believe anything we said about Mother ... she has always presented a delightful front to the world ... Mind you, the mask is falling off now, with her demented, cantankerous antics of late ... Lucy says that dementia doesn't alter a person's character but accentuates the defects. However, my legal voice nags at me that it's not fair to judge her now, as any good points she may have had have been duly diminished ...

28 APRIL

'Tracy, can I have a word with you?'

'Whatever is the matter, Mrs Mullins?'

'Amy has been having loud conversations, often turning into rows, standing outside in her garden most of the night.'

'Who with?'

'It sounded like she was talking to her children.'

'In the middle of the night? I doubt anybody was really with her.'

'Well, in the dark it was hard to tell, but it did all sound very real.'

'What was the subject of these ... er... conversations?'

'All kinds of things – how much she had done for the children, who were now neglecting her, how much trouble she had had with them when they were young ... though I saw Derek grow up and I can't say I noticed much bother from him. Of course, Amy was what they call a single mum these days, so things were tougher, I suppose, with a growing lad ...'

'Yes ... well, Mrs Mullins ... thanks for letting me know about this – I'll ring Derek and Daphne on my mobile before I pop in to see her.'

'Thank you, Derek – Daphne says the same. No, I didn't think for one moment that either of you had visited your mother in the night, but I had to check ...'

'Well, Mrs Robson, Mrs Mullins says you had visitors after I left you yesterday evening. She heard you talking to them in the garden ...'

'What rot! You know jolly well that nobody has been here in a month of Sundays. That woman is seeing and hearing things. They'll soon have her in the loony bin.'

'To get back to practical matters, Mrs Robson, you haven't got your false teeth in to have your breakfast.'

'I'm giving my mouth a rest, if you have no objection.'

'Where are the teeth, though? You do have to eat something today, after all.'

'I think they fell out in the garden.'

29 APRIL

'No, Mr Robson, I can assure you that I'm not from the press, as you can see from my badge, I represent the group lobbying on behalf of people suffering from Alzheimer's.'

'I have only a quarter of an hour to give you, Mr Caldwell, then I must get back to my next brief that has been on the back burner for a while. I suppose the recent events in court prompted your visit ...'

'Well, your predicament didn't go unnoticed.'

'My "predicament", Mr Caldwell?'

'Your mother disrupting one of your cases in the courtroom.'

'Yes, well, what's that got to do with anything?'

'You'll be hearing more and more about Alzheimer's sufferers in the coming weeks and months, Mr Robson. We campaigners feel that they have been neglected ...'

'By whom?'

'Not by their relatives, in our eyes – their relatives suffer along with them ... it's more neglect by the general public, and above all by the government that we are targeting.'

'In my position, I hardly wish to become involved in a political campaign ...'

'Very understandable ... I gather that your mother has been awarded some care in the home?'

'So you have already researched my background, Mr Caldwell?'

'You know only too well how one has to ascertain the true facts of a case, Mr Robson ... Despite the care provided, your mother was able to leave her home and make her way into your courtroom ...'

'Are you suggesting neglect on behalf of the carers?'

'How else could it have happened?'

'Mr Caldwell, my mother is not under military surveillance twenty-four hours a day. There are times when she has to be left to her own devices ...'

'Precisely our point. What we are saying is that she needs greater provision.'

'As her family, we already pay for extra care. The only way to give her even more would be to put her in a home, and she won't hear of being "put away", as she calls it.'

'You don't feel that more could be done for her, Mr Robson? You see, we are trying to persuade the powers that be to increase financial provision. It would help if I could say that you believed that more money would help ...'

'My mother's case would not be altered by increased financial provision, neither from me, nor from any government source – hers is an altogether different predicament, though far from unique, I would imagine. It involves persuading somebody who is increasingly demented to agree to accept what to everybody else is considered rational help.'

'OK, you personally have the financial means to have care provided for your mother, but what about those less fortunate financially, Mr Robson?'

'I would obviously agree that help should be given to them. I'm not sure how much is available to them at present.'

'Not enough, in our estimation. As for your mother, haven't you acquired power of attorney?'

'Very remiss of me, I admit – it would have been so simple for me to arrange it, but I put it off ... I have the forms, but it's got to the situation now where we have to persuade somebody not in their right mind to agree that they are not in their right mind, to understand a legal document, and to sign it. It's far harder than getting a confession out of an old lag, Mr Caldwell. I wish you well with your campaign but I feel that I can be of no real assistance. However, I would say that help is needed not only for sufferers from Alzheimer's but also for relatives who care for them.'

30 APRIL

Just think of what I could do with more money – never had any to speak of, always scrimping and saving to buy what was desperately needed – could hand on some to the grand-children, could go on one of those cruises – there was a

167

brochure that came the other day ... That cat's in the garden again ... That gardener doesn't earn his keep – why, I could beat him into fits – a youngish man, yet with not half the energy that I put into it all those years – I'll have to be out here weeding again ... Time for a bite to eat now though ... Can't find my watch ... Daphne? What are you doing on the wrong side of the fence? You should be in here doing a spot of work for me ...

'Out in the garden again, Mother?'

'That's your voice, Daphne. What are you doing hiding behind the fence in that alley? I hardly have time to do any gardening nowadays. I have to work my fingers to the bone to get the housework done ...'

'Well, I let your carer in as I came in. I thought you were out with one of the neighbours at first, then I heard you out here at the back ...'

'You call them neighbours! The only decent ones are all gone.'

'You still have Mrs Mullins.'

'I never set foot in her house. She's always in mine.'

'Why don't you pop in to see her from time to time?'

'Gave that up years ago. Always had an excuse for not letting me in. I think her place is a pigsty. No surprise, since she's always out gossiping along the street.'

'What are all these leaflets doing here, Tracy?'

'Junk mail keeps coming in, despite the notice on the door.'

'I asked Derek to have this address banned for junk mail. You can do such a thing, you know ... Forms to fill in for loans and suchlike! The sheer waste of it all.'

'Just as well your mother is incapable of filling them in.'

'Did you find her dentures?'

'No luck so far, but she did say they might be in the

garden, although she denied having been out there that night they disappeared.'

'I'll go out there, pretending I'm pulling up a few weeds … I'm staying for a day or two, so we'll see …'

1 MAY

'Get up or you'll be late for school, Daphne.'

'Mother? What time is it?'

'It's already bright daylight.'

'It's May, that doesn't mean anything … five past seven … What did you say when you woke me? School?'

'Don't be silly – just thought it was time you were up. I was going to go down for a paper. They never remember to deliver it. Perhaps you'd pop down for one.'

'I'll open the letters, Mother. Ah, the electricity bill – it's an estimate, so I'll have to read the meter and check it … What's this? Your application for a loan has been granted? What application? Ten thousand pounds! "The cheque will be in the post" … What's all this about?'

'Haven't the faintest, Daphne, but I could do with the money.'

'Did you fill in one of those disgraceful forms that keep coming through the post? No, of course you wouldn't be able to …'

'Can't recall it. Derek may have got me to borrow the money, you know how persuasive he can be …'

'Don't worry, Daphne, I'll write a letter to the loan company on Mother's behalf, with a hint of legal action if necessary. We'll put the application down to her advanced dementia. Like you, I can't imagine how she could have filled in the form correctly. Perhaps that Mrs Partridge was behind it?'

'Quite possibly, but we'll never know for sure ... Oh, Tracy has just come in. I'll mention it to her ... Kelly will be here instead tomorrow, as she always comes on Fridays ...'

2 MAY

'It's not Kelly at the door, Mother, it's that Partridge woman. Open the door to her and pretend you are all alone – I got Mrs Mullins to say I was leaving yesterday evening. My car is parked round the corner, and I'll hide upstairs.'

'Morning, Mrs Robson.'
  'Hello, Mrs P ... What can I do for you, then?'
  'It's what I could do for you, ducky. Well, aren't yer going to let me in? Daphne gone, 'as she?'
  'Afraid so.'
  'Let's 'ave a chat before your young Kelly gets 'ere – should be about 'alf an hour ...'
  'My, you're observant.'
  'Anyway, before she comes, I thought I'd see how things stood with yer ...'
  'I'm still standing, if that's what concerns you ...'
  'Keep up the funny stuff, Amy, it ...'
  'Amy?'
  'Well, I thought we could be on first-name terms ... after all, I did help yer last week.'
  'Why all the winking? Or have you got a twitch, Mrs Pheasant?'
  'Coming all 'ard again, are we? I'll come to the point, ducks. Yer was desperate for more cash and yer got me to help yer with that form. Have yer heard anything yet?'
  'I think they sent a cheque. Was it today?'
  'I can have a look at your mail for yer, dearie.'
  'Why the hurry?'

'I can bank it for yer, Amy ... I mean, I could go to the bank with yer ... Best to do it right now, strike while the iron's 'ot ... then, as a little favour, could yer see yer way to loaning me a little ... ?'

'How much, Mrs Pigeon?'

'Well a few hundred, a grand at the outside, a thousand, I mean ... Course, it will all be paid back in good time, Amy ...'

'What sort of time ... When I'm food for worms?'

'What a cracker! I just ...'

'You can just go back home and leave me in peace.'

'Well, I'm blowed, that's all the thanks I get! Yer wouldn't have that dough if I hadn't helped yer get the loan ... Bangin' the door on me, are yer? ...'

'Well done, Mother. I recorded it all on my Dictaphone, look! ... Yes, the speech is clear enough. The police have got more material on that Partridge woman now ...'

'I don't want to create any trouble, Daphne ...'

'I thought you would be glad to pay that woman back for what she did to Gertie ...'

'Gertie? You'll have to remind me of what happened to her, Daphne ...'

3 MAY

'My mother's not awake yet, Tracy. She got up too early the last two days. She's sleeping less in her chair while I'm here and still going to bed late, so she has to make up for it at some point.'

'Sure she's all right, Daphne?'

'I did check her – she's sleeping soundly, snoring at times. I'll do the shopping today, if you like, but before I do,

I must tell you about a problem concerning my mother and
Mrs Partridge ...'

'No, Derek, neither Tracy nor Kelly knew of what was going
on ... So I'll leave it to you to send a letter to Mrs Partridge
... Are the power of attorney forms ready for Mother to
sign? OK, I'll broach the matter today ... Since the forms
should arrive on Tuesday, after the Bank Holiday, I'll stay
here until then.'

'Daphne, you can talk until you are blue in the face, I'm not
signing my death certificate.'
    'Mother, be reasonable, you would only be allowing
Derek and me to act on your behalf ...'
    'To do what?'
    'Well, sometimes there might be bills to be queried ... or
paid ... I know most things are done by direct debit from
your bank.'
    'So you and Derek would be running my bank account?'
    'In a sense we are already, Mother, as you don't under-
stand the statements the bank sends ...'
    'That's what you think. I look at them every so often.'
    'How can you? I send them all on to Derek.'
    'What? No wonder I couldn't find them ... lately, I mean.
Robbed by my own children!'
    'We're not robbing you ... and the time is coming,
although it's hard for you to accept it, for you to consider
going into a home. We could help you choose one ...'
    'This is the last time I'll tell you, Daphne, I'm not leaving
this house unless it is in a box ...'
    'Don't be so morbid, Mother ...'
    'You're the one who's being morbid, shunting me like an
old railway wagon onto the side ... side track or whatever
it's called ... into a home to rust away ...'

4 MAY

Where am I? ... Eeh, they've put me away! No, that's my wardrobe, isn't it? Better make sure ... don't recognise those clothes ... 'Daphne!' ... Has she gone away? ... 'Daphne! Help! Come quickly and take me back home!'

'What on earth's the matter now, Mother? It's only six o'clock or so, why are you up and shouting?'
    'Where am I?'
    'In your own house, of course.'
    'Of course? You want to push me out of it and sell it. It would fetch you a nice sum right now with all the house prices rocketing. Better sell it now, before a crash in the house money, m ... er, prices.'
    'This is your furniture. Look, your wardrobe is open and you can see your dresses ...'
    'They're not mine!'
    'I told you before, yours were getting too old, so I gave you some of mine ...'
    'You've put my furniture into an old people's park – you can get unfurnished rooms in them now, so I heard ...'
    'Nonsense, look out of the window at your garden ...'
    'Eeh, about time the lawn was cut.'
    'Well, I did weed a bit the other day and found your dentures, you remember, but the gardener will ...'
    'Dentures? I don't leave my false teeth in the garden. You're trying to make me look gaga, to have me sent away ... I bet you tell these stories to Daisy and the neighbours ...'
    'Would you like to go to church, Mother?'
    'That's right, change the subject. No, not on your nelly, you'll be getting all the church folk to agree that I need to be parked in what you call a home. That lot'll be in one before me, they're less compost mentis than me ...'

'This walk is too tiring for me, Daphne, let's get back to your car.'

'Yes, it's hard for you to go anywhere on foot, you need somebody to assist you ... At least you can't go so far now, anyway ...'

'It's nice to get the sea air, Daphne, but that's exhausting as well ... The times on the beach with you playing in the sand or counting pebbles ... I used to take the bus here, not long ago, I think, to watch the little children playing and splashing in the water ... Seeing the very young helps keep us very old-stagers going, they pass on their youthful energy to us in some mysterious way ...'

5 MAY

It's the scent of the irises ... no, the lilac is also in bloom ... I used to adore purple or purply pink ... now it penetrates my pupils like a brad and extorts a response from my heavily protected memory ... the purple dress ... guard against it, Daphne ... move on a few years to anything else ... in my old room here ... Geoff ... trembling hands moving over me ... not knowing what to expect ... then boldness came from somewhere suddenly ... abandon, abandon yourself to it, Daphne, I said ... a few moments more ... then the hammering on the door, Mother's yelling ... futile to protest that I was old enough to do ... Geoff too startled ... shaking again like a nestling before a magpie ... years later she had the same effect on Peter ...

'Daphne, I was calling you then knocking, why did you ignore me? ... Oh, I see, you are in one of those foolish daydreams you used to drift into far too often as a teenager ... Aren't we having lunch in time to go out somewhere?'

'It's a bank holiday today, Mother, too much traffic, and in any case, you were worn out on our outing yesterday ...'

'We never went across the doors yesterday.'

'All right, we'll see.'

The purple dress ... too alluring, Mother said ...

'Mother, why did you remarry, to Uncle Stan, I mean?'

'It was a mistake.'

'But why?'

'If we knew why we made mistakes, we wouldn't have made them in the first place.'

Unexpected logic from her ...

'He left us for good, Mother ...'

'I could never forgive him for what he did to you, Daphne dear ...'

'It wasn't as bad as you made out – besides, I was only fourteen and too innocent to understand what he really intended ... just being over-affectionate, perhaps? After all he *was* my actual uncle, even you tend to forget that – uncles do hug their nieces, don't they?'

'Nonsense. You don't take a girl in your arms like that ... I told him not to darken this door again ...'

'Did you put it as bluntly as that, Mother?'

'What attitude was I supposed to adopt? Turn a blind eye?'

'It was definitely because of me that he left then? ... Or was it, Mother? ... Mother!'

Now she's off in her own world, just when she could have exonerated me ... Or is it deliberate? Making me carry the can?

'Was it my fault, Mother?'

'Stan should be back by now, he just popped out for some cigarettes ... or has he gone away to look for a job? Won't pull a muscle in his search, shyster ...'

Lucid patch over, all sensible conversation gone for today, may as well take her out.

6 MAY

She loves staring out of the window – but at what? At whom, more like. Just as well she finds some pastimes ... The hours I myself would spend gazing into the distant trees looking for hidden adventures when trapped in this place, waiting for some boy to appear and wave to me ...

The postman! The power of attorney forms – at last!

'What am I signing this thing for again, Daphne?'

'I keep telling you ...'

'Don't lose your temper with me!'

'It's so that you can have more care, more time being looked after.'

'Can't you do that for me?'

'I have many commitments where I live ...'

'Then I could live with you.'

'You've tried it, Mother, and you longed to get back to your own home again.'

'Hmm ... care? Then, what's this word – P ... Pow ... *Power* – at the top of this page?'

'You're giving Derek and me the power to organise the care for you.'

'I'm the one to sort that out, not you. How do you know what care I need?'

'Say you are ill, with bad flu, for instance, then we could step in and see you get what you need.'

'Oh, all right, if you really think it's important ... Where do I sign?'

'Practise on this piece of paper first.'

'Don't see why I have to practise, but there you are.'

'That's not your signature, Mother!'

'Then whose is it? ... Ah, I think I changed it recently. Don't you like the new one?'

It'll never work without a recognisable signature ...

7 MAY

'You know only too well where the source of your problems lies, Daphne. They have been exacerbated by the past few days.'

'I can't retrace the past and undo what my mother did, Dr Devonshire. I relive it constantly, embellishing it ... you've no idea how idyllic a childhood I can construct ... but once out of the reverie ...'

'That's not the cure, Daphne. You know what I have been repeating recently. You can change nothing. You must learn to live with it.'

'You're being very abrupt – harsh, in fact ...'

'How long have you been my patient?'

'Longer than I care to remember.'

'Exactly. I can't keep taking your money with no sign of improvement from you. You must find a way of snapping out of it. Tell yourself that you will overcome it. It was a traumatic time, but now at last you can put it behind you, Daphne.'

'So this is your new interrogation technique ... years of gentle sympathy and kind advice fly out of the window and now you turn the screw and make me face the music ... the music ... that's all that is keeping me sane, Dr Devonshire – if I lose that, I lose the last thread of normal life ... already members of the choir are starting to mutter that I'm losing concentration, that the standard is dropping ...'

'Keep on with the new tablets and come and see me next week so that I can pursue ...'

'Yes, and all these tablets are another thing – I'm already a rattling old pill box. They're ruining my health more than all my problems put together.'

'Come, come, Daphne, just for another week ...'

8 MAY

The long idle days by the sea ... Daphne splashing in the water ... that restful sound of paddling as the tide goes out ... ships going out ... tide me over till tomorrow ... rest a bit longer ... water washing under my deckchair ... must put the washing out ... get out of this chair ... take off the wet stockings ... they'll not be long in drying this weather ... weather this storm, be over soon, so much rain, so much water ...

'Mrs Robson, wake up! ... I thought for a moment you were dead.'

'You'll frighten me to death, Daisy.'

'It's all flooded down here – the water's coming through the ceiling.'

'I've not been upstairs to look for where it's coming from, Daisy.'

'Sorry to bother you, Derek, but Daphne's mobile was switched off. Your mother is OK, but there has been a disaster in her house. She's tried to do some washing in the bath, left the tap on and flooded the bathroom. The water didn't do any other damage upstairs, but it found its way down into the kitchen and living room.'

Only one more home to ring, the last on the list.
'Couldn't you please help us out of this situation, just this once? I've tried other nursing homes to no avail ... It will be a week before my mother's house can be made fit for her to live in again ...'

Word must have got round about Mother. No home is prepared to take her. Daphne can't cope. No alternative but to talk to Fiona and beg her to have Mother for a week at our place.

9 MAY

'Your bag is ready, Mrs Robson. Have a nice time at your son's. Here's his car arriving now.'
'That's not Derek, Kerry. Is it a taxi driver?'

'Car and chauffeur laid on for you, madam.'
'About time I had some luxury. I have lived more than ninety years waiting for it.'

'Not so fast, young man. I'm not too keen to give the undertaker my hard-earned money yet. Besides, I want to make this experience last a bit longer. Do you have any music? ... Is that all? Do you think that racket is for people of my age? Haven't you got any Bing Crosby? ...'

'A traffic jam? Well, get out and tell them to move over. You have a VIP in here ... or I'll get out and wave my stick at them.'

'You've arrived in good shape, Mother.'

'What, Freda?'

'Fiona.'

'Just what I said, Fiona.'

'I was just asking if you've had a good journey.'

'The driver said something strange about the car – I think he said it was bent!'

'A Bentley, Mother.'

'I knew it wasn't a Rolls! Next time, tell Derek to make sure it's a Rolls. Fobbing his mother off with second-class vehicles, indeed!'

'I can assure you, Mother, a Bentley is ...'

'I'm starving for a bite to eat.'

'Thank God you're home, Derek. She's been driving me berserk since noon.'

10 MAY

'An estimate for the repairs has arrived here at your mother's house, Derek. I thought that you had requested estimates to be sent to you ...'

'Thank you, Tracy. Yes, I did – who is this one from?'

'Oh, sorry, I'll ring back. Mrs Mullins is at the door and I'll have to explain to her what's happened.'

'Oh, before you go, Mrs Mullins, do you know of the odd-job man whose name is on this estimate?'

'That name rings a bell ... Oh my goodness, yes, it's Mrs Partridge's son-in-law. He once gave me an estimate for some work before I was wise to Mrs P's tricks. I've heard that the Partridges use their bathroom that was done up by their son-in law as a showroom to tout for business for him. Well, I wanted to see it for myself, so some weeks ago I went round to their house supposedly to have a chat and said I needed to go to the loo. I can't tell you how shoddy the bathroom looked, with tacky fittings to boot ... Now I think of it, I did see Mrs P coming in here early yesterday, before young Kelly arrived. She must have brought this bogus estimate with her. She didn't realise that Amy was going to be staying at Derek's. After all, I knew nothing of it myself. Come to that, how did Mrs P get to hear of the flood and not me?'

'So that explains this "estimate", Derek.'
    'It does indeed. Thanks for letting me know, Tracy. Bye.'

So, no need to follow up that estimate back at the house. Life would be so much easier if Mother had signed those blessed forms properly ... well, let's get Fiona to have a crack at getting Mother's real signature ...

11 MAY

Hmmm ... this doesn't look like one of those parking places for old folk, looks more like somebody's house, but why is nobody here? ... They seem to be asleep ... Really! At this hour! ... Creep downstairs ... I was always good at creeping up and down the stairs ... never knew what those children were up to ... and it was handy to tread softly when playing Santa Claus ... They've grown out of that now, but how old *are* they? ... Posh living room ... Don't recognise those people in the photographs ... But isn't that Derek's girl? She must be six or seven years old ...

'Up already, Nan?'
    'You startled me! Who are you anyway?'
    'It's me – Lucy, I'm here for the weekend.'

181

'Visiting, like me? Who are the people who live here anyway?'

'My parents – your son and his wife, Nan.'

'You keep calling me Nan. What was your name again?'

'Lucy.'

'Yes, that's it. Her name is really Lucy.'

'Whose, Nan?'

'The little girl in this photograph. Does she live here too?'

'That's me when I was a little. I'm twenty-seven now.'

'Why have you been hiding away from me all these years, then?'

'I came to visit you a couple of months ago ... at the beginning of March.'

'Isn't it March now, Lucy?'

'Nan's terribly confused today, Dad.'

'You can see how bad she really is now, Lucy. Or maybe it's just that two months have elapsed since you made your earlier appraisal of her, and now she wouldn't even appear plausible to strangers.'

'You need to be with her a while and catch her off-guard to see how she really is. Anyway, if you like, I'll set things in motion for you to have her properly assessed.'

'Just what we need. I don't even know if your mother can hold out for this week while we have Nan's house put right again.'

12 MAY

'Yes, this is my new house. Five bedrooms – or is it six? Some have those sweets with them. Not the ones you suck – you know ... the ones where you can have a wash next to your bedroom ... Lovely stair carpet, takes a lot of tread, not one of those that goes threadbare after a few years ... You haven't seen downstairs ... notice the old chairs in the living room ...'

'How long is this going on for, Barbara? Derek's mother is even more gaga than he lets on!'
   'Shush, George, Fiona said to humour her. Be patient, Fiona will be back in half an hour or so ...'

'You're not paying attention to your guide. I have another tour starting soon, so let's finish off ... This is the newly refitted kitchen – marble worktops, are they? Imitation perhaps ... I bet you don't have a house as fine as this ...'

'We ...'
   'Shut up, George, don't provoke her.'

I think I'll leave the house to that Trust ... the one which looks after splendid old places like this, so everybody can visit it, at a price, of course ... Mind you, they would have to put down some dustsheets so visitors wouldn't ruin the Axminster carpets with their filthy shoes ... And absolutely no dogs, they can do without their business ... I wonder if the Trust has any other houses in this town ... What's their address? ... I'd have to change my will as well ...

13 MAY

Where's Lucy's message? Only half an hour before the court reconvenes ... Our doctor can recommend Mother for assessment ... he can speed up the process ... probably be second week of June ... Defence is making snide remarks about this brief being a bit lowly for me ... all these hints about me coming down in the world of the law ... just as well Mother doesn't comprehend the trouble she caused –

after all, her life's ambition was to see me at the top of the tree – 'All those sacrifices to give you what you needed at school, Derek, they've paid off,' she would say, 'payback for all that hard work of mine and yours, Derek, the neighbours will be as green as the Queen's lawn with envy, it will make my life worth living' ... strange thing to live for, one's children's success – they can hit an iceberg, or turn out plain feckless ... Mrs Mullins is probably sitting in her armchair daydreaming about Stephen, MBE already, wondering when the next trip to the Palace will be ... 'Try to remember, Stephen, what the Queen says to you next time, don't get your nerves in such a tangle, and don't forget what outfit she's wearing' ...

'Ah, Fiona, brilliant! ... I'll have to be back in court in a jiffy ... I never thought we'd ever get Mother's signature on the power of attorney forms! It will at least help us to deal with her financial affairs. Anyway, Lucy is confident that our doctor can recommend Mother for assessment ... yes, she'll arrange an appointment while Mother's with us ... Oh, they're calling me – see you tonight.'

Pyrrhic victory indeed! No expenses perhaps, but the matter has been put to rest ... Must put the other matter to rest too ... Has Fiona made that appointment?

14 MAY

A special clinic in the States? Dr Devonshire seems confident of the benefits for me of the new treatment carried out there ... rather revolutionary, by the sound of it ... No more pills, that would be the reward if the clinic proved to be successful. Ah, he did only say 'if' – though I suppose he can't appear to be too certain ... I don't like the idea of presenting my own case, my life history and problems to a group of similar sufferers ... But Dr Devonshire insists they would be a sympathetic audience ... The remedy doesn't come from the other patients' suggestions, he says, but from the mere fact of having talked it all through in the open to outsiders ... Impossible to go, though, until Mother is in a home ...

'Mother? Yes, it is me – but I thought you were at Derek's.'

'So that's where I am. I just picked up the phone here and pressed any number ...'

'You must have pressed two. Number two on Derek's phone makes a call to me.'

'So he has a phone like mine! Well I never! I'm so glad you answered to tell me where I am.'

'Are you all on your own?'

'Oh! Oh, it's only Fiona – you gave me a start! I'm just phoning Daphne. No, I don't need to talk to her any more, you can have a word with her.'

'I was just out in the garden, Mother, as I told you ...'

'You never told me, Fiona, my memory is still very sharp, at least when people have not long told me something.'

'Hello, Daphne – how did your mother manage to phone you?'

'By accident. She wanted to know where she was!'

'Thank goodness our doctor is seeing her on Friday ... yes, the 16th, to see if he can refer her to a geriatric specialist with a view to committing her ... sounds dreadful, doesn't it?'

Must call Dr Devonshire ... Seagulls settling on the flooded field, leaden skies ...

15 MAY

'Madge! Glad I caught you. Have you any idea when Amy's coming back?'

'No, Ada, but I think they've nearly finished working on her house. How's Nigel?'

'Worse, if anything, Madge ... I keep wondering what will happen to him when I'm too old to look after him ... There's nobody else ... Course, he wants Amy Robson to adopt him, he doesn't realise that she's a good bit older than me ...'

'Reminds me of my niece – you know, my sister's daughter who was severely handicapped.'

'Yes, I use to see your sister pushing her down the street – she wasn't safe on her own in the wheelchair, was she, Madge?'

'No, she wasn't. My sister worried herself sick about her, but as you know, my niece died before my sister, who didn't live too long after that either. We have to accept old age as a blessing, when we consider the ones who never make it as far as us.'

'Blessing? Well, I'm off to the doctor's now, blood pressure ... Nigel doesn't help to bring it down, but it's not his fault, poor ... I almost said boy, but he's over forty ... and still up to boys' tricks ... I fret over what will happen to him after I'm gone, but I couldn't face it if he died before me.'

'The doctor comes to see me now, Ada – what with my rheumatoid arthritis and gammy hips, I can't get about ... At least Nigel is always around to keep you company. Stephen is always too busy.'

'That bridge not finished yet, Madge?'

'Teething problems he says. Talks of it as if it were another child of his ...'

'Nigel is always around all right, but you can't talk to him about problems, he simply doesn't understand. He's very ...

186

vacant – that's the word the specialist used, vacant – I'm not sure what goes on in his head, if anything at all! Well, we have to laugh, not cry, Madge.'

'Amy's had carers helping her for a good while now, and I've started having them too. Why don't you get somebody to look after Nigel while you have a holiday, Ada?'

'A holiday? Nowhere to go ... Besides, Nigel would play strangers up badly ... in the past, Amy used to look after him to give me a break ... Anyway, must be off now. Cheerio, Madge.'

16 MAY

'So, Mrs Robson, what's the date again?'

'Don't worry, Doctor, I always forget it as well. Don't you have it on your desk somewhere?'

'So I do. Now, let's see ...'

'No need to examine me. My headache's gone ... and my backache ...'

'What's your home address?'

'I haven't got it with me.'

'I can write it down if you tell me what it is.'

'It's in my handbag, which I've mislaid.'

'Not to worry, Mrs Robson. What's your current address, where you're staying now?'

'You should have asked that young Lucy, the girl who brought me in.'

'And your age again?'

'Cheeky devil!'

'I need to put it on my form here.'

'Old enough to be your grandmother. I had my eightieth birthday some time ago.'

'So year of birth 1926?'

'Doesn't ring a bell.'

'Earlier, I think ... Hmm ... do you look after yourself when at home?'

'Who else is there to look after me, Doctor? My children are rarely there.'

'No helpers in the home?'

'I used to help a lot of other people, but nobody comes to see me.'

'You don't have a carer called Tracy?'

'Never heard of her. There is a Daisy who comes once in a blue moon.'

Lucy says that Mother couldn't understand why she saw our doctor, but it had the right result. Once he has relayed his findings to Mother's doctor, they'll set up an appointment with the specialist. Wonderful that he can visit her in her own home and see how she really is. Her house is back to normal, so Lucy can take her back tomorrow ...

17 MAY

'Where did you say we were going, Lucy?'

'Back to your house, Nan.'

'I'd forgotten that I had another one.'

'The one we're going to is your real one. You've been staying at my dad's house ... Derek's ...'

'Then why isn't he taking me back?'

'He's at Wembley for the FA Cup Final.'

'He hasn't changed a bit, always putting his pleasures before his poor old mother ... Sport ... football this time, is it? After his studies, it was always sport when he was young. And there was me thinking he'd change when he got older ...'

'He's so busy with his job, he rarely takes time off nowadays ...'

Get lost in the crowd, all our thoughts merge, none of my own remain, wave my flag like a little boy without a care, soak up the spectacle, go dizzy up here looking down at the blue and white banners, become part of the chanting, one voice for tens of thousands, my own lost, no need to think of my next speech, nothing more matters in the world but the outcome of this match, all brain cells focused on that pitch ... A substitution – why is he coming on now? ... Must remember to ring Lucy ... Get back to the match ... we need a goal ... we have to have a goal ... what is my goal now?

'Look, Nan, all those ships in the harbour – Dad used to go on board on Navy Days ... but the ships that he saw must have ended up at the scrapyard since, or been sold off to other countries as museum pieces ...'

'Derek was always careful not to talk about navy ships to me. Alfred ...'

'Sorry, Nan, I forgot.'

'That's the problem – I have never forgotten, can never forget ...'

No call from Dad. Is the match over? Nan's TV still works ... twenty-four-hour news ... Where's the remote? ... Have to change channels on the set ... Ah, here's the game ...

'Gosh, Nan, the Pompey players are going up for the cup.'

'I don't believe it, Lucy. I thought they were a useless team in the tenth division or whatever they call it.'

'They did have a terrible spell, but look, Sol Campbell is holding the cup aloft ... Oh, my phone buzzed ... a text from Dad ... "Goal, Kanu the King 37 mins" ...'

'Don't be silly, we have a queen. And they think I'm losing my marbles.'

'Dad sent the message from Wembley.'

'What? You mean to say he went there today? And left me to come back with you?'

'He did tell you where he was.'

18 MAY

'Sorry I'm late, Lucy. The traffic is nearly at a standstill with the whole area coming to see the cup paraded through the town.'

'Not to worry, Tracy – Nan is still asleep in her chair. She was restless yesterday during and after the journey. She's still a bit confused about time and place.'

'Is your father coming?'

'He's going to see the team display the cup, then coming back here.'

'He'll be lucky to make it.'

People need success – they've been too long ground down by failure, lost matches ... lost trials ... trials and tribulations ... sooner or later lose their money and their homes ... this boom surely can't last, they never do ... back to defeat on dank days ... savour this victory, drink this cup to the last ... when did I ever see such a merry multitude? Coronation Review of the Fleet when I was little ... but there were so few vehicles then, so it was much easier to get here ... and there is a bigger throng today ... Revel in others' glory, it transforms into our glory, we did it, we sitting at home in our armchairs, we willed Nelson to victory ... and countless heroes since were inspired in battle by the propulsion of our passive wills ... we won the cup from our chairs at home, in the pub, in the stands, we kicked that vital goal, we were victorious, that fine delusion, that sacred delirium ... wake up from that and life is purgatory ...

190

'No point in calling in now, Dad, Nan has gone to bed. I'll set off home now myself.'

'Sorry not to get there, Lucy. The traffic has died down now, so it's a good time to make the journey back.'

19 MAY

'You still have a lot of books, Aunty Amy. Do you read any?'

'Well, Norman ...'

'Nigel, I keep telling you it's Nigel. As you're going to adopt me if anything happens to Mum, I reckon you ought to know my proper name, Nigel, Nigel Turner!'

'Don't boil up so, Nigel – what were you saying just now?'

'Your books.'

'They're not mine. They're the ones that Derek and Daphne leave here, supposedly to read when they visit me – fat chance, they don't come that often ...'

'I have some books ... I can read, you know ...'

'Of course you can, N ... Nigel.'

'You got my name right that time, Aunty. You're not like the others. Others think I'm plain stupid. You understand how my brain works ... Funny thing, the brain, nobody can make it bigger or replace it. If my knee was playing up, I could change it, at hospital like, or my hips ... Mrs Mullins ought to have had her hips done, but too late now, she says ... but I haven't heard of a doctor who can repair my brain ... You were a nurse, Aunty ... If you ever get to know about a doctor who can fix brains, be sure to make me the first one to know ...'

'I did see a television programme, Nigel, about some doctors who were watching the insides of a brain, seeing how it works, but it was only on one of those machines, commuters or whatever they're called. They didn't really get inside the brain and stare into it properly ...'

'My books are full of pictures. Mum's really mean, she won't take me to see the places in those pictures ... Perhaps we could go together one day, Aunty ... There's a terrible hammering on your door ... Don't open it – it will be Mum come to take me back to prison ...'

'Don't say that, your mother has doted on you all these years ... I can't leave her shut out ... Come in, Mrs T ... T ... Norman and I were just having a natter ...'

'Nigel, home with me this instant! My blood pressure will bust the gauge.'

What a rude woman! Her son was doing no harm here ... She could have been more civil to me ...

20 MAY

At least Mother has an appointment with the specialist ... Monday the 9th of June ... that was rapid, really ... has to be a foreign doctor, though, as no other is available at such short notice ... we couldn't have put up with a long wait ... I'll have to be there, as Derek, Fiona and Lucy all have other commitments ... committing your mother to the insane asylum, the person who has looked after you since the womb ... stop it, it's that voice from my nightmares again ... play some music ... this disc ... no, not opera, I can't stand the torture of the emotions ... Mother as Agrippina ... Derek as Britannicus ... I should be there as her daughter instead ... Lear's Cordelia suffered less ... when I am as dead as earth, perhaps the woman of stone will howl ... If I should die before her ... no, do your duty, Daphne, you are the chosen one to look after her ...

21 MAY

'You ought to be ashamed – look at your uniform, straighten your shirt, tighten up your tie, and you could give those shoes a better polish ...'

'Ah, there's the old lady in question haranguing a pupil ...'

'Excuse me, could you take me to the headmaster? I know his office is somewhere above these old arches.'

'I am the headmaster, madam. What can I do for you?'

'My son's homework hasn't been up to scratch recently, and as we haven't had a parents' evening for a while I wanted to discuss matters with you.'

'Your grandson or perhaps your great-grandson, you mean?'

'No, my son, Derek.'

'Derek ... ?'

'Derek Robson. Surely you know him.'

'I pride myself on knowing the names of all my pupils, but that name eludes me ...'

'Well, your knowledge is rather shaky, isn't it?'

'Ah, here's my deputy, Mr Smythe. He was a pupil here himself and has taught here all his working life. I'm sure he'll be able to help us ... Roy, this lady is looking for a Derek Robson. Does the name ring a bell?'

'Why, certainly.'

'There you are. At least this deputy of yours is on the ball.'

'A word in your ear, Tony ... I was at school with Derek Robson and recognise his mother here. Unfortunately she's suffering from ...'

'So you've enjoyed your little tour of the school, Mrs Robson?'

'Yes, thank you ... er ... Smithers ... quite a lot of changes, as you say ...'

'There wasn't anybody you wished to see in particular, was there?'

'No, no, my son was here a few years ago ... but I'm quite worn out now and I have to find my way home ...'

'Oh, don't worry, I'll order a taxi and pay for it myself. Your son Derek is an old friend of mine, you know ...'

'Well I never! But then he *is* famous and so many people know him.'

From the case notes

Patient was missing in the morning but returned home by taxi before lunch. She wasn't able to say where she had been. Taxi driver left before I could ask him where he had brought her from.

22 MAY

Yes, Father, your clothes have to be ready for work tomorrow. Don't see the point of fussing over them too much, they'll be filthy dirty from the pit by tomorrow night ... I know, you never see daylight for most of the year, down to hell before sunrise and up to this purgatory we live in after sunset ... The trouble with your washing is that our washer seems to have gone and somebody has put something strange over the bath taps so I can't put the mucky clothes in the bath ... probably my brother Bertie up to his silly tricks again ... Yes, of course, we should be able to carry the bath tub around, but it's got too heavy, I can't remember it being as big as it is now ... Yes, Mother can see to things when she gets back ...

'Who are you chatting to, Mrs Robson?'

'Oh, Daisy, you startled me! ... I wasn't saying anything, I was just reflecting a little.'

'I sometimes think aloud as well ... I see you've been looking at the photos of your parents and brothers and sisters that Lucy brought when she drove you back here ... Mrs Robson, I wanted to tell you that Sam and I were making our wedding plans yesterday ...'

'What? You ought to be betrothed first! The things that go on today! When I was your age ...'

'We got engaged a month ago yesterday. That's why I encouraged Sam to think of a date and a venue ... You know what men are like when it comes to getting married, they put everything off as long as you let them ...'

'Feckless lot, none of them any better than that Stanley I had the misfortune of putting up with ...'

'Well, it's going to be on the 31st of August.'

'So soon? That's next month!'

'Not quite. We didn't want anywhere too expensive, so it wasn't too hard to fix it up for a few months' time. I'll tell you more about it as the time gets nearer.'

'Time! Where did it all go? That's what puzzles me. He'll make a fortune, the man who discovers how to hold up time. They only know how to hold up banks right now. I'm not surprised they do. The money that must be in them. Look – isn't this piece of paper here offering me piles of money?'

'Ooh, I'd better tear that up right away.'

23 MAY

What is this silly little girl doing here? Fiddling around, poking her nose into all my cupboards and drawers ... She's worse than my sister Maddy ... I expect Maddy will be back here soon ... Just as well I told her off for stealing my things, otherwise she'd still be here ... Well, she did find me that job in the factory ... too young we were for that drudgery ... at fourteen we started ... she had survived it for eighteen months, so why shouldn't I, that's what she said ... survivor, that's what I am ... Girls of that age today would be in their coffins by the end of the week's work that we had to put in ... What's that dozy ha'p'orth up to now? ... She should be polishing my nice furniture so I could see my face in it, like I had to polish my mother's on my day off ... time off was sheer idleness and that led to mischief, my father used to say ... no time off for those girls, make sure they knuckle down to it ... I can still hear his voice now ... perhaps he's calling me ...

'Who in God's name are you?'

'I'm Kelly, Mrs Robson, your carer!'

'I don't have a Kelly coming in here. Just a Daisy. Why hasn't she turned up today?'

'It's her day off. Don't you remember that I always replace her on Fridays?'

'That's it, just like my children, always instigating that I've lost my memory. Pity I can't tell where I dumped it. Did I bury it in the garden?'

'Now, now, Mrs Robson, nobody's insinuating anything. We all have spells of forgetfulness.'

'Then perhaps you will remember one day that I don't like people rattling through my drawers.'

'I was just searching for your dentures – they've gone missing again. Your dinner will be here soon, and you'll need them ...'

'Eeh! I clearly told them not to post that stuff to me, it's just cardboard.'

'They don't post it, they deliver it in a van.'

'That's what parcels come in. What's the difference? Why do I have to rely on food parcels?'

'Because there's nobody to cook for you here ... Mrs Robson, it will be hard to chew, like it was yesterday, without your dentures.'

24 MAY

The garden is too much work in the heat ... Alfred wasn't much of a gardener ... Stan had green fingers but they were mostly in other people's soil ... The grass should be greener ... We spend our time longing for greener grass ... It's always somewhere else ... Madge Mullins can't see to her lawn either ... That gardener could do a better job here ... He seems to do Madge's better than mine ... I'll give him the sack and do my own gardening until I find a proper gardener ... Derek has a son, doesn't he? He used to be good for a turn in the garden ... What's he up to now? He must have finished studying ... *Aaah!*'

'No need to scream. Mrs Robson – it's only me, Andy Spooner.'

'Ah, the Reverend. You used to poke your nose over the fence, but I haven't spotted you for ages.'

'That would be the old vicar who used to do that, when your son was small. I've heard tell that he used to like doing such things ... I believe your fence was lower in those days. It's just as well I'm tall enough to see over this one. Since you don't feel well enough to come to church, I thought I'd pay you a visit, and when there was no answer to my knocking, I decided to come round the side way – like my predecessor we were just speaking about ...'

'Pre ... deceased? He's dead then?'

'Oh, possibly ... he'd be getting on a bit, like you, Mrs Robson.'

'Have you come for tea and cakes, Vicar? You used to like that.'

'Er ... my wife has given me strict orders to limit my intake, even of your splendid cakes – *especially* of your cakes, I should say, because they put on the calories – awfully sorry.'

'You take orders from your wife? I thought vicars took them from God.'

'Ha, ha ... oh, holy ones, you mean?'

'I could never get Stanley to take orders. Alfred was much more of the bliging kind.'

'Bliging? ... ah, yes ... willing to go along with others' wishes ... I ought to know, I have to oblige so many parishioners ...'

'You sound tired, Vicar. Come into the garden and we'll sit down for a chat. It's too hot for gardening anyway.'

25 MAY

'You mentioned not having visits from your carers on Sundays, Mrs Robson, so I arranged to come today instead of yesterday.'

'Did you enjoy your day off yesterday, Daisy?'

'Yes, thanks – I was making more plans for my wedding.'

'*You* were making plans, Daisy?'

'With Sam ... my fiancé, of course.'

'In my day, our parents made the plans.'

'Sam couldn't see the need for many flowers, Mrs Robson ...'

'My mother chose those, pretty cheap I think they were...'

'You can remember it all well then?'

'Better than what I did yesterday. Yesterday seems further away ...'

'We probably won't have such a choice of flowers at the end of August as we would now.'

'August ... Am I invited, Daisy? I've lost my diary, so I don't know whether I'll be here in August.'

'Wouldn't it be too tiring for you, such a long day?'

'My first wedding went by like a flash. Come to think of it, the second one was even quicker – just as well! You can never bring those things back again. My mother used to say that there's more bad than good in life, so we shouldn't want to be able to relive any of it.'

'Hmm ... Sam and I will be able to relive ours in a way with a video.'

'What's one of those?'

'You used to have some here ... films of events in your family ... where are they? You know, the things you used to put in that machine under the telly.'

'I couldn't get the constraption to work any longer, Daisy.'

'Your ninetieth birthday party was on one. I'll have to ask your children where it is. We could watch some of it one day.'

26 MAY

I bet Mother is still in the cupboard under the stairs ... Nasty air raid, deadly patrol ... This air-raid-warden business is taking its toll on me, I'm worn out ... Mrs Wilshaw's house has gone down – thank God she was in the air-raid shelter ... I'll have to see if Father has come out of ours ... To think that Mother insisted on coming here to avoid the London Blitz ...

'Mother! Mother, what are you doing under the stairs? ... We've told you it's the most dangerous place to be when bombs are dropping ... Come out this instant! ... The raid is over ... Why do you insist on staying in that dark, damp cupboard? ... I can hear Father walking in the garden – you see, he's come out of the shelter, there's nothing more to fear ... Mother!'

'What are you looking for in that cupboard, Mrs Robson? Let me find it for you.'

'Who's that? My eyes can't cope with all this light. Don't you know there's meant to be a blackout? Why have you lit up my house like the luminations? Here's me telling the whole street to put out all the lights and ...'

'Mrs Robson! It's me, Tracy. It's bright daylight, the war ended more that sixty years ago. Sit down in your chair and I'll make you a cup of tea. You've gone all white.'

'Won't you need your dentures in to eat that cake, Mrs Robson? Thank goodness Kelly found them yet again, on Friday.'

'My gums are rock hard, dear. I must have eaten a thousand times without any teeth. Besides, if it was my home-made cake, it would melt in the mouth – not sure who made this one.'

'Your daughter-in-law.'

'My daughter's not in the law, it's my son Derek who is.'

'I mean Fiona, Derek's wife.'

'What did you say I was doing when you came in, Daisy?'

'Looking in that cupboard under the stairs.'

'Can't think what it was I wanted ...'

'Not to worry, Mrs Robson.'

27 MAY

Who has left this album lying around? Don't recognise him ... but that's that woman from church ... and that's another one, I think ... maybe not ... That's me, and there's Daphne ... When were all these pictures taken? Can't understand this writing on the cover ... looks like a party of mine ... I never liked that busybody, who asked her to come? Why is that Spoon man there? It wasn't a wedding, was it? Or perhaps a funeral?

'So, Mrs Robson, you've had a good look at the album I found?'

'Where was it, Daisy?'

'In the shed, behind the garden tools.'

'That'll be my interfering sister, always hiding my things away so I can't find them – she's jealous that I had a party and she didn't, it was the same when we were children ... Now, what party was this anyway?'

'It was your ninetieth birthday party, of course. No luck in locating the video of it yet.'

'Never! I'm not really ninety, am I?'

'Ninety-five, actually.'

'Get away! Only a few years and I'll be hearing from the Queen. All the neighbours will be eaten up with envy. Poor old Amy Robson, they say to themselves, good for nothing any longer, then whoosh, a message from Her Majesty!'

28 MAY

'Amy, it's only me, Madge ...!'

'What a fright you gave me, Madge, banging on my door so early in the morning.'

'Early? It's past lunchtime ...'

'I must have dozed off again ... I was shattered ... all that decorating ...'

'Hmm ... Are you feeling well, Amy?'

'Right as rain really. You've been keeping yourself away from me, you know.'

'I can only get around now with my mobility machine, as I call it. I've left it outside your door. I was on my way back from visiting Mrs Turner.'

'That thing? Don't say you can't get around without that, Madge!'

'You're lucky, Amy. OK, you don't break the record for the Olympic speed walk, as you used to in your heyday, but you can still move those legs about.'

'Who did you say you visited?'

'Mrs Turner. That Nigel locked them both out and a locksmith was helping them get back in, so I went in with them for a chat. If Nigel has any screws left, they'll all be loose.'

'That's a nasty way of talking about a poor boy, Madge.'

'That's the trouble, he's not a boy any more. Mind you, he's company. My Stephen is using that bridge as an excuse not to come and see me.'

'Never have just one child, I say. An only child is spoilt and takes all you do for them for granted. All your eggs go into the one basket, not a good insurance policy.'

'You don't see your two that often though, do you? Is Derek still hoping to become a judge?'

'Hoping? Why, he has been made one already ... can't remember when.'

'In your dreams.'

'Why are you muttering, Madge? ... I would make you a cup of tea, except I stick to water or juice these days. If you can find my kettle ... it's gone missing ... you can make yourself one.'

'It's OK – I had one at Mrs Turner's with a bite of lunch, thanks.'

29 MAY

'Oh dear, you've torn a page out of your album, Mrs Robson.'

'Me? Are you accusing *me*, Daisy, of dec ... decimalising

my own book? It was my sister again. She flew into an insanely jealous rage when I showed her the album. Didn't I tell you how she would behave?'

'I can stick the page back in when I get a moment.'

'Don't bother. I didn't invite the people on that page, couldn't stand them, hoity-toity lot.'

'You keep leaving quite a bit of your meals, Mrs Robson. You need to eat more to keep your strength up.'

'Eating on your own is a trial, Daisy. Just shoving food into your mouth, what's the point?'

'I do sit and talk to you while you're eating.'

'But you don't eat with me, do you? Oh, I don't blame you. A pig would struggle to get that stuff down.'

'The meals are well prepared in the firm's kitchens ...'

'Eeh, so I'm having to rely on soup kitchens now, am I?'

'It's nothing like that, Mrs Robson, I can assure you ... Look, I'll go and get my lunchbox and – eat with you while you have your meal.'

From the case notes:

Patient has no appetite for cooked food, wanted to swap her lunch for my sandwiches.

30 MAY

Father's birthday ... how old would he have been? Mustn't mention it to Mother ... 'You should have banished all thoughts of him, Derek, as I have,' I can hear her saying ... He came back once for his birthday when I was small ... Mother wouldn't let him take her out ... She eventually let me go with him ... We ended up at the funfair and amusement arcade ... Mother was outraged ... squandering

what little money he had instead of passing it on to her ...
'Derek needs clothes,' she told him ... 'Teaching a little boy
to gamble and throw money down the drain ... dressed like
a hobo, Stanley, what will the neighbours think of you
coming back to the house so dishevelled?' ... Well it was a
hot day ... Mother attributed Father's hobo look to his spell
in the States, and his happy-go-lucky approach to money to
that as well ... He must have had to save up for weeks to pay
for his birthday treat, and Mother wanted the money for
everyday necessities instead ... The marriage was doomed to
failure, they were poles apart ... 'The lad's had a good time
for once,' Father said. 'You keep him cooped up, he'll wilt
away without fresh air' ... 'That's it, go on about the out-
door life, that's where you idled most of your time away,
Stanley, in America, Australia' ... Father's work was all out
in the open in Aussie, as he called it – construction worker,
gardener, lumberjack, jack of all trades ... 'Master of none,'
I hear Mother nagging ... 'If only you hadn't stopped
ashore, Stanley, you ought to have been back on that boat
doing your proper job, earning good money to keep me
and your child' ... After that day, it was prohibited to as
much as mention Father's birthday ... I had to buy, write
and post the card in secret ... I remember the dreadful year
when she discovered the card hidden in my schoolbag and
shredded it in white rage ... Daphne thinks she was hard
done by ... Was it better to have a dead father to haunt you,
like Hamlet, or a living anathema?

31 MAY

Derek has gone into his shell, always does around his
father's birthday, nobody's phoning Mother except for me
... Monday week can't come quickly enough, all my hopes
are pinned on that ... It's that 'Gaslight' film, she'll say,

you're trying to prove I'm round the twist, Daphne, to have me put in an asylum ... Mother is for ever on her guard for that, she'll find some way of proving that she's still *compos mentis,* she'll defy us again, by hook or by crook ... Derek believes it's me who's around the bend, he makes a pitiful job of hiding it ... The specialist will tick all the correct boxes on the 9th of June, Derek is cocksure of that ... just as Mother was of his becoming a High Court judge – fat chance of that now, I reckon ... Mother's to blame for it all, she has stifled the living daylights out of us ... I struggle for air, some days I feel as if I'm choking ... Mother has her hands on my throat, every day her grip is tighter ... People wonder why I keep touching my neck ... it's to see if the noose can be loosened ... One day my neck will snap ... Will some smart detective ever trace the identity of the executioner?

1 JUNE

Day in, day out the same ... what's the use of getting up? Empty house, just me drifting around from room to room ... No, my sister what's-her-name is hiding somewhere from me ... at least she calls in to see me, bad as she is ...

What are those two old women doing outside my house? Are they looking for somebody? They're glancing at my front windows ... I'll have to open one and call out to ask their business.

'Don't you recall us, Amy? You know us – from the church ... Fanny and Dotty.'

They both look dotty to me, but I'll let them in to pass the time of day.

'There. A nice cup of tea. Dotty's just made it for you, Amy.'

'Thank you, er ...'

'Fanny.'

'Ooh, those delicious cakes you used to make for us, Amy, when we used to call on Sunday afternoons. I don't expect you use that beautiful bone china tea set nowadays.'

'Yes, Fanny, on each plate there'd be a little doily, and all on that handy tea trolley.'

'Trolley, er ... Dotty... Well, the television is on the trolley and it's too heavy to shift.'

'Goodness, Amy, you ought to have one of those big television screens that stand on those glass tables, like Fanny. We love to go round to Fanny's to watch TV in the evenings when something good is on.'

'Most nights a load of tripe is on, that girl who comes in shows me what's on all those blessed channels ... just as well my set keeps getting stuck on the news channel, Finney.'

'Fanny. Finney was that nursing colleague of yours, Amy. Everybody used surnames in those days, of course. Put the sugar spoon back for me please, Dotty.'

'How's Reverend Spoon these days?'

'Spooner, Amy ... oh, the same as ever. He doesn't take us old folk too seriously, if you ask me.'

'Nobody was asking you, Dotty. I think he puts up with us all rather well. We're a dying breed. Weren't there thirty or so of us? Only ten of us left and some like you, Amy, unable to get across the doors.'

'Nice of you all to call on me, Fanny. Didn't you two call a week or two ago?'

'No, but Elsie and Freda popped in to see you some weeks ago, they said.'

2 JUNE

This one's lasting a long time, I can still hear the rumbling of explosions not too far away ... getting nearer and nearer ... must have lost the gas mask ... or did I give it to old Mrs Wilshaw? ... It must have been torn to shreds when her house went up in splinters ... That one dropped only a few houses away, surely ... Gertie could have copped that one ... You either suffocate in the heat with the mask on or risk being choked to death with poison gas ... Just as well Mother's not here, her nerves would have been worn to a frazzle with all this ... Now that bang was fainter ... Not a time for faint spirits ... Just as well I made sure all lights were out before the raid started, otherwise the whole street would have disappeared in a ball of flame ...

'Is that you in the shed, Mrs Robson? I've been looking all over for you.'

'Who's that?'

'Tracy. I thought I heard a voice coming from out here.'

'Come into the shelter, or is it all over?'

'The thunderstorm has passed now, Mrs Robson. I didn't think of searching for you outdoors in that deluge.'

'Thunder? Don't be friv ... frilly. You can't argue with Nazi bombers.'

'The shed wouldn't be much good in an air raid.'

'Shed? Oh! Well, the air-raid shelter was blasted away in the last attack, so I had to make do with the shed. I'll have to send for one of those apply forms to have a new shelter put up.'

'Come on in, Mrs Robson. It's past your supper time. You look done in. I'll make you something to eat and put you to bed.'

'Night night. You're Daisy, aren't you? Where did you say I was when you came tonight?'

'In your shed.'

'Of course. I was looking for some tool or other to do ... well, I've forgotten what.'

3 JUNE

Mother's driving us all up the wall again, phoning me and Derek in the middle of the night to see if we survived the bombing. I won't survive bearing this burden ... Lionel had a call too, serves him right, he's kept well away from his grandmother ...

'Mrs Mullins? Whatever is it? What's happened to Mother?'

'Don't panic, Daphne, but I think I ought to let you know that Amy phoned me at three a.m. to ask if my house was still standing. Something about bombers.'

'Bonkers, you mean. She's gone stark raving bonkers!'

'Don't get so worked up. I'm sure she's settled down again. That storm yesterday must have disturbed old memories.'

She continually disturbs old memories that I have buried deeper than the dead at sea ... Father, are you listening from that salt grave, the salt of tears, countless useless tears, listen when I cry unto you, only you have the power to understand ...

'Derek? Sorry I sound so startled. I was ... well, I was thinking about something ...'

'No need to tell me what, Daphne – Reverend Spooner had a frightening call from Mother at around 3.30 this morning. He couldn't make anything out of her rambling until he seemed to get through to her about who he was, and then the call got worse.'

'What was worse about it?'

'She told him to make house visits in the parish to see how many funerals he would need to conduct.'

'Mrs Mullins has explained to me that Mother thought there had been an air raid. She must have pressed every stored-number button on her phone.'

'Yes, one after the other at random. Lucy had two calls from her, for a start.'

4 JUNE

If he were my boy, I'd make sure Lionel went to see to Mother's needs from time to time ... the way Mother used to spoil him, all the silly toys and sweets, the pampered golden boy he was, well, perhaps his halo has dropped off now ... Lucy is reluctant to be there on the day the specialist visits Mother – quite understandable after what happened when she did her pre-assessment. Anyway, I've a good mind to persuade Derek to force Lionel to go instead ... Somebody needs to tell us what went on, whatever the outcome ... Perhaps I'll contact Lionel myself ...

'Yes, Aunt Daphne? ... Very busy actually ... with a book I'm writing about ... No, it doesn't have to be finished right now, but the deadline is in August ... Me see Nan? Is it urgent? ... Point taken – it *has* been a while ... March was my last visit, when she flooded the place ... Oh, yes, the guy who is going to see if she is mentally fit enough to stay on in her own house – are you sure it's a good idea for me to go along then? ... Well, supposing Nan fails ... I said supposing because Lucy found that she has plausible moments ... OK, Lucy has seen a worse side of her since ... But if she does fail the test, won't she want you or Mum and Dad to look after her? ... I was only trying to look at it in terms of how she would see it, not from our point of view ... No, no, it's not a case of siding with her ... The fact that she thought or maybe thinks the world of me doesn't cloud my judgement, Aunt Daphne ... Really, be reasonable ... Look, I'll go down to see her on Sunday and wait until the interview or test or whatever it's called is over on Monday before returning to work ... Yes, I'll have to rearrange a lecture or two, but don't worry about it ...'

Lionel thinks he's doing us all a great favour ... Have I done the right thing? He sounds as though he wants Mother to stay put ... He might try to influence events ... But what could he do to alter the course of things anyway? ... Hope I don't live to regret this ...

5 JUNE

Of course little brother Bertie didn't do it ... always innocent ... Amy should have been looking after him anyway ... blame Amy ... let her get it in the neck ... a clip round my ear ... or my father's belt ... Where's Bertie now? ... He's up to mischief somewhere ... Oh, you startled me, Bertie ... What's all this money in your bag, Bertie? Father couldn't give you that much ... Where did it come from? We could do with it, that's for sure ... You've been out of work for weeks, so where did you get all this cash? ... No, I didn't see anybody following you ... Who? Policemen? ... Nobody else has come into the house ... All the notes from the till? ... It's not the man's fault for leaving the till open, Bertie, it's yours for stealing it ... What can we do now? ... Hide the money ... Someone's knocking on the door! ... Yes, let's tear the notes up and burn them on the fire ... The knocking has stopped ... No, there it is again ... I'd better get some matches ... Where are those matches? ... Keep ripping up the money, while I hunt for matches ...

'Mrs Robson! What on earth are you doing? That's your money you're destroying!'

'Stolen, all stolen!'

'No, here's the special delivery envelope Derek uses to sends cash for you when he can't come to see you ... I know we should insist on cheques, but it takes a while to process them. I'm to blame for this. The cash seemed so handy, but look at it now, all torn to shreds. I should have waited for Lionel to bring it on Saturday.'

'Don't take on so, Daisy. You didn't steal it. It was my brother Bertie here.'

'Nobody's here but us.'

'The sly little devil – he must have slipped out as you came in. The police will be after him, as he is sure to have taken some bank notes with him. They were banging on the door just now.'

'That was Mrs Turner. I saw her going out of your gate as I came down the street.'

From the case notes:

Patient very distressed. She has destroyed the cash sent by her son. Some story about the money having been stolen by her (dead) brother.

6 JUNE

Who was I thinking of? ... Something like tie tie? Ah, poor Gertie, fancy being a cripple, not able to get around, probably can't come down to open the door ... I was crippled when Stanley deserted me, that's the only word for it ... Gertie knows how unreliable he is, she'll listen to me, Daphne shuts her ears ... The curtains in the front bedroom are closed, so Gertie's resting ... Her face lights up when she sees me ... She'll need some shopping done ... Better go out and knock at her door ... I heard some knocking in my dream ...

'You, of all people! It's Amy Robson, Ivan.'

'You're that Pheasant ... and your husband's Ivan, is he? Ivan the Terrible.'

'She can't even remember our name. Partridge, ducks.'

'Ducks? Is that your name?'

'What's the old bird on about, Ag? Let me deal with her. Your son sends us threatening letters and you turn up on our doorstep?'

'Derek would only send letters to criminals.'

'She's calling us criminals now, Ag! We were only assisting you in your hour of need.'

'What need?'

'Money, you old goat. You were always on about needing more of it.'

'Insulting me as well, are you?'

'What did you call *me* just now?'

'Well, you called your own wife a hag. You're right, she's a witch.'

'Ag – it's 'er name – Agatha, you demented ...'

'Leave off, Ivan, she has no idea what we're talking about.'

'You've been warned not to have any more to do with Mrs Robson. Leave her alone immediately.'

'Yer bodyguard's arrived, ducks. Look, the old goat came here without an invitation and started insulting us.'

'Come on, Mrs Robson, I'll take you back to your house.'

'I was looking for an old friend, Kerry ...'

'Kelly.'

'My friend Gertie must have moved without telling me or been taken to hospital. Those ghastly creatures from that horror film have taken over her house.'

7 JUNE

To think that nobody has bothered about that old church, so few parishioners, not enough income to keep it going, stone starting to crumble and needing urgent repair ... but containing hidden treasures – that old painting, artist not yet known, the statues beginning to be eaten by time, the ornate chalice, the silver, I adore silver, I could polish it for days ... Now we've catalogued these items, how long before they're auctioned off to meet the cost of renovation? ... At least it took my mind off Mother this week ... well, apart from her spate of phone calls ... And now the crypt has revealed unspeakable horrors – I can still see Mother emerging from a coffin down there, asking why I had buried her alive, why I couldn't wait for her to die of natural causes ... My shrieks have delayed our work, they think the crypt must be haunted ... well, yes it is, but they'll never guess who the ghost is ... Destroying her money – well, Derek was a fool to send cash when he can just write a cheque on Mother's account now we have power of attorney ... But if she can do that to money, what else can she destroy? She wanted to burn the money, according to Kelly ... That's it, Mother will burn the house down and the great legacy she is so proud of being able to pass on to us will go up in flames ... A terrible inheritance anyway, nasty memories ... and as urgently needing renovation as much as that church ... Monday! On Monday all will be put to rest ... It wasn't me, Mother, we all agreed you had to be put away ... the doctor pronounced you dead … dead to us … Mother, are you sure you are not dead to yourself?

8 JUNE

'Who did you say you were again?'

'Lionel, Nan – Derek's son.'

'Why are you here today? Is it a special day?'

'Tomorrow is a special day. You have an important visitor coming, Nan. I'll be there to help you … er … entertain him.'

'Sounds a grand person. I must be honoured, I suppose. Why hasn't your father been honoured … by the Queen, I mean, L … ?'

'Lionel. Don't know, Nan, you'd have to ask him.'

'Do you work in the law profession too?'

'No, I'm a university lecturer.'

'I always knew you were very bright – des … designed for a good job.'

'The man will ask you lots of questions tomorrow, Nan.'

'What sort of questions?'

'Your date of birth, age, details of your family, maybe what you think of items in the news …'

'I must be famous, then! Are you helping him write a book about me?'

'Er … not exactly …'

'What then?'

'Er … maybe an article in a magazine.'

'Then you must rehearse the answers with me. I don't want to look daft for the magazine readers, do I?

'Er … no.'

The boy's hiding something. More likely it's somebody sent to have me put away.

9 JUNE

'Are you sure I'm nearly ninety-six, Lionel?'

'Yes, Nan.'

'Born in 1912?'

'Yes.'

'I remember hearing about the Great War as a child, must tell the man about that. If he's young, he'll know precious little about it. And I can fill him in about the last world war, when I lost my only true husband, yes, he'll need to know about my two husbands. How old are you and Lucy again?'

'It's not going to plan, Dad ... I've been cornered into a quiz game with Nan ... She has been rehearsing all the likely questions this fellow is going to ask ... I try not to answer, but she is so insistent ...'

'Hello, Mrs Robson, I'm Dr Gudenov.'

'Good enough? I hope you are.'

'Ah yes, joke, good English humour sense. Not worry, if you see me write. This big form to complete. Your grandson explained this ... interview?'

'Yes, it's good of you to come.'

'So, all details of you and family written here, Mrs Robson ... What you think of your President?'

'My, I can tell you are a foreigner. You haven't been here long enough to know we have a Queen.'

'Ah, it was ... how you say? Slip of tongue.'

'America has a President, for instance. I was just watching the news with my grandson Lionel and it seems as though there could be a coloured man as President there.'

'Ah, yes, you mean Obama.'

'What is your country?'

'Russia.'

'Oh, Russia suffered terribly during the last world war ...
Now, I can tell you a thing or two about that war ... and
about the Great War when I was a little girl. I grew up
afterwards with everybody talking about it ...'

'Yes, Mrs Robson, suffering very great in Russia, very much
in last war. English talk about their suffering. Not many
people realise Russia suffer most, Russia always a country of
great suffering ...'

'So, what is your opinion of my grandmother, Doctor?'
'My report, it confidential, but her memory no worse,
maybe better than most old people. Very intelligent lady. I
not having such interesting conversation since arrival in
England. She survivor, like Russians. What a life!'

10 JUNE

Daphne blames Lionel for the fiasco of the Russian doctor's
visit. I'm flabbergasted that we have Russian doctors prac-
tising in this country. Lionel is my flesh and blood but I'm
the first to admit he is a bit naïve at times – needs to get out
into the real world, says Daphne ... mind, she can talk ...
Lionel must have thought he was preparing his students for
an examination, he pretty well rehearsed all the answers
with Mother over and over again, so that they stuck in her
mind. Lionel thinks Mother would still have good cognitive
skills if she had constant company, says that being on her
own with nobody to talk to has caused her decline ... He
should try staying with her! Or having her to stay with him –
Daphne could tell him what that might be like! Of course,
Lionel is right that regular mental stimulus would keep
Mother's mind more alert and her memory more active.

The problem is that nobody can put up with her for even twenty-four hours, let alone days on end.

11 JUNE

'Well, you'll never believe this, Madge, but a man came here to write a book about me ...'

'Something to do with your son, Derek, probably.'

'There you go again, belittling me. Why shouldn't somebody want to write about me? You may think you've had an interesting life, Madge, but your life pales into insig ... into nothing compared with mine.'

'I've never wanted an exciting life, Amy. When Doug dropped down dead at work with that massive heart attack, my one aim was to raise Stephen properly, make sure he had a good education and career ...'

'I always put the education of my children first, spent all my hard-earned money on their school uniform and sports equipment and ...'

'Stephen wasn't one for sport, he was always making things with his Meccano set or building models, and all that cost a bit, I can tell you. He ...'

'Derek could have taken his sport further, but he wanted to concentrate on his qualifications for ...'

'Stephen has a string of qualifications ... Anyway, what I wanted to tell you today, Amy, before I forget ...'

'Are you starting to lose your memory, Madge?'

'Mine's in better shape than yours, Amy.'

'Is it, indeed? Well, we can put that to the test. When was the Queen's coronation?'

'I can remember that from the big street party outside here.'

'Not what happened, I mean the actual date.'

'Amy, it was in June 1952 ...'

'But the day of the month?'

'Look, Amy, I must tell you this and go, because I'm about to have my buggy checked for a fault ...'

'What kind of bug have you caught?'

'My *buggy*, it's a kind of motorised wheelchair.'

'Eeh, you need a wheelchair to get around? Thank goodness I have full use of all my limbs ...'

'Stephen's bridge is finished and they're going to open it officially on Sunday. A government minister, no less, is going to cut the ribbon.'

'On the Lord's Day? Why?'

'Because there's less traffic to redirect on Sundays. It'll be on the news. Watch out for it. Or maybe you can come and watch it with me. Must be off now, though. Bye, Amy.'

12 JUNE

'Did I tell you how many bridesmaids I was having, Mrs Robson?'

'I had five for my first wedding, Daisy, but only Daphne for my second.'

'I'm having three – my sister and my two best friends.'

'Didn't know you had a sister.'

'She's four years younger than me.'

'With a brother in between, Daisy?'

'Yes.'

'My mother kept having them at intervals like that, sometimes shorter, steps of a ladder they called us.'

'Sam thinks three is too many, with the price of the dresses. He's always thinking about cost – not that he and his family are contributing much.'

'Be careful there, Daisy my dear, as men begin, they always go on. Your Sam sounds like a penny-pincher. Even Stanley was generous, but money ran through his fingers like the sand on that Isle of Wight beach where we spent one of our only breaks away together.'

'Sam has agreed to my flower arrangements now, though. It'll be expensive to get good flowers.'

'Make sure he keeps buying you flowers. Stanley only gave me the ones he picked out of the garden. He was a better gardener than Alfred, I'll grant him that.'

'The wedding is only seven weeks away. We're in June already, Mrs Robson.'

The garden colours in late June with the roses and the sweet peas, the scents to drive you madder than the raging heat ... We had proper summer weather then, not this damp dankness ... Stanley kept cutting the sweat peas, to make them grow more, he claimed ... more likely to make a bouquet without having to fork out for it ...

13 JUNE

Dr Devonshire is refusing to put me back on medication ... though I suppose I was the one who wanted to come off it in the first place ... This clinic in the States ... I just have to give him a date and he'll arrange to find me a place on the programme ... I don't think I can face making myself into a showcase though ... with all those ghoulish eyes and ears sucking in my every word and gesture ... perhaps they only go to cast off the burden of their own distress and sit like dummies when others spout forth ... Mother lingers on in her house ... 'Why can't you do something to make your mother's life easier?' I sense them thinking, those acquaintances who haven't had a lot to do with her when she was here ... I should have drawn more attention to her antics when she was here at the beginning of April and not hushed them up out of shame ... But none of this is my fault, so why should I feel ashamed ... or guilty? ... It's not your fault, Daphne ... keep repeating Derek's words ...

14 JUNE

Why can't Daphne show a little patience? ... It's my problem as well as hers, after all ... Lucy reckons we'll have to wait until Mother falls down the stairs and breaks some bones – that's the only way we'll get her out of the house ... But how long will that be? ... Anyway, then she'll have to accept that she has to go into an 'old people's park' ... what a phobia she has of those ... 'I worked in them, Derek, I should know what terrors await me in one of those,' she has said ... And now I have decided to defend the owner of one who's being charged with neglect ... Should I be taking this on? Why switch suddenly back to defence counsel? The case might colour my judgement of these places ... or my ability to defend might be compromised as I'm hoping my mother will go into one, which could allow Prosecution to insinuate that I am prejudiced in favour of such homes ... But Mother's outrageous behaviour in the court is still a vivid memory in legal circles, and surely will also be in the minds of the jury if they read the newspapers at the time ... Many will know she is gaga and understand why I am having to place her in a home ... They'll understand my remarks for the defence in that light, surely ...

15 JUNE

'I've never been in your house before, Madge – to sit down, I mean.'

'Don't be silly, Amy, you must have been here a hundred times.'

'No I haven't – you're always in mine. In the days when you could get around easily, you were never in your own home, you were in everybody else's house having a good gossip, not to mention gallons of tea and slabs of cake.'

'What impression would people have of me if they listened to you, Amy?'

'Ask Ada Turner, she'll tell you the same.'

'Just sit down and I'll turn on the telly.'

'There's nothing on at this time of day, especially on a Sunday. You did say it was Sunday, Madge?'

'Yes. I invited you in because it's the ... oh, what do they call it again? ... I've written it on this piece of paper ... inguration, no in ... au ... guration day for Stephen's bridge.'

'Augur? That sounds like a bad omen.'

'No, nothing about augurs, Amy.'

'Well, you could knock me down with a feather!'

'You'd need something a damned sight heavier than that to budge you, Madge.'

'Stephen has waited all this time to get his bridge open, and now that stupid woman is dangling off it.'

'Perhaps she's doing a final test, Madge.'

'More like a suicide case or somebody drawing attention to themselves ... Go on, get on with it, jump, you silly cow!'

'That's a cruel thing to say, Madge.'

'They're focusing on her when they should be getting a close-up of Stephen. You're taking the limelight off my son – go on, dive into the river!'

'As the viewers can see, the woman has climbed onto the parapet. She won't hear calls to come down, so I'm afraid the bridge opening is going to be delayed ... I'm just hearing from the studio that we're staying with this ... er... incident for the time being.'

'My god, Amy! Isn't that woman your Daphne?'

'What's got into you, Madge? Daphne would never do such a daft thing ... Eeh, it *is*! ... It's Daphne! Daphne, come down this instant! Did you hear me? I told you to come down.'

'It's no use screaming at her from my sitting room, Amy.'

'Think of yourself, Daphne, even if you are not bothered about me!'

'Amy, I always thought your Derek would outshine my Stephen, but it's a bit rich that it should be your daughter Daphne who is taking the country's attention away from him. She has literally ruined Stephen's big day!'

'My daughter is in peril and that's all you can say? ... Daphne! Don't jump! ...'

16 JUNE

'It's all over the front pages, Mrs Robson.'

'What is, Daisy?'

'The story and pictures of Daphne.'

'I had a bad dream about her. What's happened?'

'She wanted to jump off the bridge, the one built by Mrs Mullins's son ...'

'What on earth for?'

'"The elderly woman ..."'

'Daphne's not elderly like me!'

'I'm reading from the paper ... "The elderly woman named Daphne Robson claims she was in a trance. She said that she didn't know where she was, and denied that it was a suicide attempt ..."'

'Suicide? Daphne has had a wonderful life. Why would she want to do away with herself, Daisy?'

'Apparently, she didn't ...'

'What? Is everybody instigating that Daphne didn't have a good life?'

'No, I mean, she didn't want to commit suicide. She had kind of lost her senses or something.'

'Ring her up for me, Daisy.'

'She's in hospital under observation, according to the paper. They're saying she might have to be sectioned.'

'That sounds nasty. What kind of operation is that?'

'It's not an op. It's when they have to put you into a mental institution in case you harm yourself or others.'

'Eeh, and I thought that was what she wanted to do with me!'

17 JUNE

From the case notes:

Patient telling strange stories. She claims to have seen young men entering Mrs Mullins's house, thinks it has become a brothel. Patient probably saw members of the press. Patient also maintains that a young couple were almost naked and were having sexual relations in a car parked outside her house. Tracy's boyfriend did pick her up yesterday evening, so patient could have imagined something from that. Of even greater concern is that she believes her (dead) husband Stanley tries to enter the house at night to rape her. She doesn't want any more children, so she sits up in the chair afraid to go to sleep. Patient's granddaughter informed of above.

18 JUNE

Lucy says that fantasies are common in us all! Old people lead boring lives and have to fill them with something enticing, much as the tabloids do with their pages, she says. In some forms of dementia, she states in her email to me, the patient actually sees people who are not there as if they are real flesh and blood, moving about … She considers that as an explanation for Mother's belief that her sister visits her repeatedly, that her brother was there with stolen money, and that urchins, sometimes confused with her nephews, frequently appear in her garden … But why fantasise about Mrs Mullins? … And why am I thinking of Mother, instead of worrying about Daphne? … I must visit her in the mental clinic … Mother must not hear tell of Daphne's state … Hopefully, she will have forgotten about seeing Daphne on the bridge during the TV coverage … I'll ring all the neighbours and friends who still visit Mother to tell them not to bring up the subject …

19 JUNE

Come on down into the waters, Daphne, they will cradle you … rock you gently … the river will bear you down gracefully to the sea, the never-ending sea, where your father is waiting to recover his little girl … we will be joined together again by the water which parted us … Have no fear, Daphne, I shall banish all seagulls from our special pond, a deep, private pond for my small Daphne within the wild ocean … just float on your back and let all cares drift away …

'The patient is still talking to herself as if in a trance, Mr Robson. No visits are allowed, I'm afraid, until we stabilise her properly. We are attempting to avoid medication as she took too much during her illness … Yes, Dr Devonshire has seen her, but she is in our care now …'

Perhaps Lucy should be the first to visit Daphne anyway, not me?

20 JUNE

My dreams are all about water, terrifying drowning ... must be Alfred ... somebody calling out to me in total distress ... that bridge keeps popping up ... don't recognise it ...

'Why doesn't the television work, Daisy? No, you're not Daisy, are you?'

'Kelly, Mrs Robson. Your television needs to be repaired. You'll have to do without it for a while.'

'Then put the radio on.'

'Tracy told me that you couldn't understand how to get it to work, so your son took it away.'

'Well, of all the brazen cheek! He might have asked me first.'

'There's a little alarm clock radio by your bed, Mrs Robson.'

'Then I'll just have to lie in bed whenever I want to listen to the news or some music.'

'Stay in your chair for a bit. You'll be having your lunch soon.'

From the case notes:

Patient at a loose end without her television, keeps asking for a radio. It will be difficult to keep up this media blackout.

21 JUNE

'They fully understand that I am her niece, Dad, but they don't want either family or professional visits until they notify us otherwise.'

'Did they say how she is?'

'No change.'

'Which means?'

'She's still rambling on about the river, water, the sea, her dead father.'

'Oh, my dear sister. How can we get her out of this? It's my fault for not taking Daphne's problems more seriously.'

'Don't blame yourself, you didn't cause them.'

'Cause them? What *do* you think caused them?'

'It's the sudden loss of her father when she was young and, even more, her troubled relationship with Nan. Nobody other than Dr Devonshire could have got to the bottom of that.'

'That quack! They pretend to do good and in fact only do more harm.'

'Steady on, Dad. Have you forgotten what I do for a living? I could have spent time with Aunt Daphne, but it's impossible to do a proper professional job with a close member of your family ...'

'Sorry, Lucy, I was getting carried away ... No, I didn't want you to get entangled in it.'

22 JUNE

'How long has it been, Stephen, since you came to see me?'

'Can't remember, Mother. Now the bridge has been opened, I can come more often, I hope.'

'You've no idea what a terrible job I've had getting rid of those reporters and photographers this last week. Once I opened the door, they flooded in. I had to ask the policeman guarding Amy Robson's house to come over and shoo them away.'

'Why was she protected and not you?'

'She's older and more vulnerable for a start, and the reason for hounding her was an ugly one – there's no pride in having a daughter who tries to commit suicide on the telly, whereas I could, if I was that sort of person, brag to the journalists of your achievement in constructing the bridge.'

'Are you sure you didn't encourage the press, Mother?'

'What gives you that daft idea?'

'Well, some of the statements I read in the papers, which are said to have come from you ...'

'Naturally, Stephen, I did tell them what a great designer and engineer you are, and ...'

'Yes, Mother, well, at least the whole matter has died down now for Mrs Robson.'

'Not for me, though – I have all the cuttings and photos from the *Daily* ...'

'Yes, yes, I saw them on the table. It's good that you have them to remember my success, but you absolutely mustn't let dear old Mrs Robson see them.'

'To think that Daphne used to babysit you, Stephen ... She used to say what a cherub you were – by far the handsomest baby in town you were, though Amy used to claim that her Derek was more bouncy, but I still maintain ...'

'Aunt Daphne, as I used to call her, was always very kind to me ...'

'Yes, but what a to-do! She must have gone really loony to do a thing like that – stealing the big occasion away from you, Stephen.'

'We shouldn't talk about what happened like that, Mother. Poor woman – and I feel sorry for her poor old mother too – Mrs Robson. She was so kind to me as well, always offering me more cake and ...'

'That's because she thought I didn't feed you properly. That's what I heard from all the neighbours at any rate.'

'Really, Mother, you do like to gossip. It would be best if you said no more to the press.'

My one chance to get recognition for Stephen, and Amy's child steals the limelight yet again.

23 JUNE

Where did I buy that Minton teapot ... or did somebody give it to me? ... Whose present was it? ... That dinner service was brought back by Stanley from China ... Who broke one of the plates? ... One's missing ... My sister Maddy could have taken that ... the envious look on her face when she had dinner off it, she could have broken a camera with her scowl ... The old settee and chairs that Alfred and I scrimped and scraped for have gone ... These modern ones are ugly – where did I buy them? Couldn't afford anything better ... It's a struggle to get up these stairs, too steep, they must have put another set in, the old ones were easier to climb ... Still the same bedroom furniture, you don't get mother-of-pearl inlay like that now, Alfred's wedding present, he did without cigarettes and alcohol for a few years before we were married to give me the matching wardrobe, dressing table and bed ... I'd like to see the young ones of today making such sacrifices – they buy everything in the house and more besides on borrowed money, it'll have to come to a sticky end ... Why should I leave all these possessions behind just so that they can park me in one of those waiting rooms for the graveyard?

'Are you upstairs, Mrs Robson?'

'I'm coming down, Daisy.'

'Mind you don't fall.'

'I take each step one foot at a time.'

'Even so, you shouldn't really be using stairs. Your stair-lift will soon be installed ...'

'Eeh, they're altering my house without my permission. What about my banisters?'

'Oh, they'll have to go, I'm afraid.'

'Are you indeed? Those beautiful mahogany banisters were installed by Alfred on his last leave, the last job he did in this house, and my family want to throw them on the scrapheap. Not on your nelly!'

24 JUNE

How do my family imagine my day, or my night, for that matter? Do they bother about what I do hour after hour all on my tod without any entertainment? ... No visitors ... Tod Sloan alone, Stanley used to say – he was one for his cockney rhyming slang, he had all the cheek of a cockney too ... better to be alone than have him about me ... if he hadn't followed me up the apples and pears that night he came back on the last train, there wouldn't have been any Derek – I could swear that's when it happened, must have done, for Stanley didn't come back for weeks after that, looking for work he said, more like gambling on those wretched horses, don't you worry, I'll have a big winner on Saturday and see you all right, you won't nag me about going down the betting shop after that, he said ... well Saturday came and went a thousand times ...

'Don't live past ninety, Daisy.'

'Why not, Mrs Robson?'

'What's the point? I'm not up to doing anything that needs any energy. I could go and stay with Daphne or Derek, but do you know, I'm always grateful to be back home after visiting them. I go into every room in my house and look at all the wonderful belongings I have and I think I must be mad to leave my house.'

'You're not as free in other people's houses, Mrs Robson. I feel like that living with my parents – I'll be glad to get a place of my own with Sam.'

25 JUNE

'Good morning – Derek Robson here. I'm ringing about my sister Daphne.'

'Ah, Mr Robson, we need to consult you as next of kin.'

'Next of kin?'

'We understand that you and Daphne have power of attorney for your mother, which rules your mother out, and as Daphne has no children ...'

'Yes, of course, sorry, I wasn't with it ... How long do you think you might be keeping Daphne in the clinic?'

'That's what we need to discuss with you. We would like to keep her on a temporary ward for a fortnight from Sunday before we decide whether we will be able to discharge her or move her to a permanent place here.'

'Permanent? Let's hope it doesn't come to that ... Er, yes, by all means, keep her there for a couple of weeks. Can I visit her?'

'Hopefully you can by the weekend, then you can sign the papers – for the extra stay, I mean.'

Good God! I might have to face signing her away ... though it's Mother who really needs to be away ... away from that house ...

26 JUNE

'In the garden, Aunty Amy? You shouldn't be overdoing it at your age.'

'N ...'

'Nigel. I'll give you a hand ... Can you could unlock the gate?'

'It's completely stuck. Better that way, against burglars. No, don't climb over the fence. I know you like climbing,

230

but you'll ruin my new fence. Go round to the front door and I'll open up.'

'We've done enough out here now, Aunty, let's go in and have a drink ... Oh how's Daphne? She used to babysit me when Mum and Dad went out of a night. I always liked Daphne. She had a lovely pink dress and pink ribbons in her hair, so pretty she was ...'

'I haven't seen Daphne for a good while, so I can't tell you how she is, Nigel.'

'But she was on the telly. Didn't you see her?'

'My Daphne on the television? Get away! More like Derek was.'

'No, Mum recognised her too. She didn't jump into that river though, did she? I kept the telly on until they got her down. I gave a big cheer when they saved her, a bigger cheer than when Pompey won the cup.'

'That was before the last world war surely ... you weren't even born then.'

'No, Aunty, they won it again last month.'

This poor boy has lost any marbles he had left, wittering on about Daphne and bridges and cup wins ...

27 JUNE

'I just phoned yer on the off chance that yer paper was still interested in the story ... Only too pleased to 'elp yer, ducky – I'm not surprised yer didn't get any gen from folks around here, they closed ranks around 'er ... Yes, Partridge is the name ... Mrs Amy Robson? Gor blimey, she's right off 'er rocker, 'as been for some time ... She's always refused our 'elp ... gone and refused it again, I said to Ivan ... Ivan, 'e's my husband ... always willing to help old folks in distress is

Ivan, a heart of pure gold 'e 'as ... Yes, Mrs Robson lives all on 'er own ... abandoned, she is, by kith and kin ... They scarcely visit 'er ... As I sees it, there's always been something peculiar about 'er daughter Daphne ... From what I've picked up around 'ere, she's never really got on with 'er mother ... Yes, yer'd think she would take 'er mother to live with 'er – after all's said and done she lives on 'er own, this Daphne, I mean, what bother would it be to look after yer poor old mother what's cared for yer night and day when yer was a nipper and beyond ... Just by the way like, is there a fee for all this info? ... Oh – can't yer up that a bit? Ivan has medical complications and 'e can't work any more, 'e wouldn't say nothing about neighbours of course, old softy that he is, so I reckoned that I oughter ... That's more like it! That'll tide us through for a bit with 'im out er work and that ... Yer've got me number, 'aven't yer ducks, in case yer need to know more? ...'

'Top notcher, yer are, Ag. Couldn't've done better meself.'

28 JUNE

Not too long before my wedding, and there are still the bridesmaids' dresses to sort out ... but more important, what will happen to Mrs Robson for the three weeks I'm away? Kelly has a full workload ... Would Mrs Robson take to a new major carer? She's not the easiest person in the world to get along with ... but since I've got to know her better, we've managed all right ... In fact, I think she has some sort of soft spot for me, like she would for a grandchild who is close to her ... Her grandchildren are so busy, as happens in all these cases ... these old women live on so long and become lonelier and lonelier ...

'Hello, Tracy here, can I help you?'

'It's Lucy, Tracy. I wanted to tell you that I shall be coming to see my nan on Thursday the 3rd of July to coincide with a visit from the head occupational therapist of your area. We need to decide what to do about Nan. My father has found a home that is prepared to take her.'

'Two problems there, Lucy. One, your nan won't want to go into it, and two, she would cause so much trouble if she did that they would want you to take her out almost immediately.'

'The first problem is the stumbling block – we all realise that. As for the second, Nan would have a private en-suite room with a secure lock on the door, so she couldn't wander around to disturb anybody else.'

'She would need to have a nurse constantly checking on her.'

'She would have that as well, Tracy. There's a bell and also an intercom, should she need to call for help.'

'She won't be able to work the intercom, Lucy.'

'That would be just as well for the staff! Anyway, we would have to take Nan to see the place first.'

'It'll cost your family a packet.'

'Dad is going to pay for it.'

'Well, it's up to all of you ... See you on Thursday then. And good luck, Lucy!'

29 JUNE

Clinically clean, all physical germs eradicated, but the mental ones remain, more virulent than superbugs ... rows of identical rooms ... still the stench of urine – incontinence? Loss of will? ...

233

'No, I'm not the doctor – I'm Mr Robson, and I'm visiting a patient. I can't take the buzzing out of your head, sorry.'

Poor woman ...

'No, I can't take you out ... No, I've no idea where your room is either.'

Quite young, that man ...

Thank goodness – this is Daphne's section. Now, what was the code again? ...

What a terrible din, what's the matter with that man? ... Oh – Daphne's door is shut ...

'Daphne!'

'Derek!'

'I'm sorry I couldn't see you before today – I came on Sunday, but they said you still needed rest.'

'Well they should have let you in. They did say you were coming today, but I wasn't expecting you just yet – it's quite early.'

'Not really. Perhaps you're still tired? ... Are you feeling more settled?'

'Settled? How can one settle in this place?'

'I hope they're looking after you well.'

'As well as can be expected. How's Fiona?'

'Oh, OK – she'll come with me next time.'

'Next time? I'm not planning to stay here that long.'

'Sorry, Daphne.'

'Sorry about what? It's not your fault ... not your fault my father died and Mother remarried ... not your fault you came into the world ... you were a lovely baby, I was so happy to look after you, I was sure I would have a baby boy as bubbly as you ... It wasn't my fault that I came into the world either ... it was a sin ...'

'It's nobody's fault, neither yours nor Mother's ... Conceiving within wedlock isn't a sin, if you're thinking along church lines.'

'It is a mortal sin to neglect your child.'

'Daphne, I don't think you were neglected.'

'Not physically – Mother was obsessed with good nourishment and cleanliness, spotless clothes ... and mine were not shabby, as yours were – Father had more money, or at least gave Mother more than Uncle Stan did ... No, it's the emotional deprivation that I resented ... that sounds cold, I've become frozen ... Mother wasn't cold, no, she was obsessed with her dead husband, enough to make me hate my own father ... dear Father, taken away in the prime of life, who could fault you? I'm sorry if I have sinned against you in thought or word ... Mother could only see him, his idealised image ... No, he became more real to her than your father, more real than the man who was absent most of the time ... So Father lived on in Mother's manic possessive world ... Are you listening, Derek?'

'Yes, yes – I apologised earlier because I couldn't find the words, but it's better you talk anyway.'

'Mr Robson, a word outside the room, please ... I'm sorry, Mr Robson, we can't allow a longer visit – the patient is becoming extremely emotional ...'

'Isn't it good, Doctor, that she should talk to her next of kin? We were getting to the bottom of her troubles.'

'That could be dangerous outside a controlled environment.'

30 JUNE

'Fiona? ... Yes, they've postponed the trial for the day, so I'm going back to the clinic ... Yes, love ... speak to you afterwards. Bye.'

Daphne looks a bit dazed – I hope they haven't doped her ... Maybe at last she is resting. I'll see if I can wait here until she wakes up properly ...

'Ah, Daphne ...'

'Why did you abandon me yesterday, Derek?'

'The doctor forced me to go.'

'You shouldn't have listened to him.'

'I have to respect professional judgement. In my job I like people to respect mine ...'

'Profession ... respect ... those words sum up the grown-up Derek ...'

'OK, let's play make-believe then, as you used to do with me when I was little ... I'm a small boy again ... You find Mummy possessive?'

'Possessive? With you, Derek?'

'With you, Daphne.'

'She was determined to hold on to me, not to allow me to marry – she drove away all suitors by one means or another ... I've told Dr Devonshire the long, tragic story ...'

'Do you still resent the emotional deprivation?'

'Derek, you're not playing the little-boy role any more, you're interrogating a witness or a suspect. I'll do what people can't do to you in court – I'll turn the question on you. Do *you* resent it?'

'I've felt very sharply that that deprivation existed, but I've replaced Mother with Fiona so that I could accept it, hard as it was ...'

'You're just rubbing in the fact that I'm a spinster!'

'Don't shout like that, Daphne!'

'Mr Robson! Time to go again.'

'Take me with you, Derek!'

'I can't, Daphne, I can't!'

They eavesdrop like the Stasi in there ...

236

1 JULY

They threw me out before I could explain to Daphne that the deprivation was firmly in the past ... Since I grew up, Mother has become more affectionate towards me ... although it took her a while to accept Fiona ... and a little jealousy still exists perhaps ... Just as well they called a halt to our conversation – Daphne clearly feels that Mother still has no affection for her ... never has had, to her mind ... But why? Why this coldness between them? ... It has become mutual, now that I really think of it ... My work thrives on my ability to weigh up others' relationships in court, but I have failed to analyse the inner workings of my own family ... Ring Mother tonight ... but for now, back to the trial.

'No, Daphne can't visit you, Mother. I keep telling you she is ill ... Not physically, no ... she's depressed, severely depressed ... Why? I can't explain on the phone ... I just can't. Wait until I see you ... Not sure when that will be, I've just started on another brief ... Of course I'll make sure I win it ... This time I'm acting for the defence ... No, I'm not defending the country, just somebody in court ... No, I'm not actually counselling the Queen, even though I'm called a Queen's Counsel ... No, they haven't made me a top judge yet, Mother ...'

2 JULY

Don't know why Mrs Turner always believes her son is here with me, he only comes now and then – in fact I haven't seen him for weeks – not as if I encouraged him ... I think she's getting jealous of me, he likes his Aunty Amy more than his mother, she was always too strict with him – he gets up to a few tricks but he can't be expected to be an angel all of the time ... Those two nephews of mine can be little devils most of the time – they've hidden my wool, my knitting needles are useless without it, I'll never finish this pullover for Derek's birthday ... Did I post his card? ... Eeh I didn't buy one, I must get that Daisy to pop out for me ... but she won't know the type to choose – hard to buy a card for a man, unless you want some sports picture on it, or a fast car, or a boat ... Derek doesn't have time for those daft things these days, too busy with his job, and good for him too ... I remember that voice that was on the phone just now, it was that doddery old woman from the church, Winny or Fanny or some such name ... why that Daisy said they can't come to see me tomorrow I'll never know, though Friday afternoon is better perhaps – I used to like something to happen on Friday afternoons or evenings, all the men in the street were handing their fat pay packets over to their wives – if Stanley had a pay packet it was more than half spent at the pub or the bookies before he brought it back here ... I could never understand why the men meekly put the lot in their wives' hands and timidly asked for a bit of pocket money for the week ... You'll be lucky to get more than a few pence with all our expenses, Madge Mullins used to say to her big softie ... What she could have spent it all on, I'll never know, she had only the one child ...

3 JULY

'I'm Mrs Rawlinson – I did show you my badge ... Look, Mrs Robson, here it is again, it says Head Occupational ...'

'I'm not a little child, I can read. Why are you here? That's what I want to know.'

'We need to see if the care you are receiving in your own home is adequate.'

'That young Daisy is doing a good job. I must put a good word in for her, if you're checking up on her.'

'No, we're not doing that, Mrs Robson.'

'So, Mrs Rollings, you've really come to say that I'm not managing here even with her help and so I have to be shoved into what you call a home ...'

'Let's talk things through, Nan ...'

'Eeh, my two children can't even be bothered to come with you and so instead they send this little girl who has not long finished her studies, the most junior member of my family.'

'Lucy is a professional person like me – she's a psychiatrist and works with a lot of old people.'

'It's my daughter who loves seeing those psych ... psychic people, not me, there's nothing wrong with my brain ... You both might as well go back to your other work, you're wasting your time here with me.'

'Well, as you want so keenly to stay in your own house ...'

'Wouldn't you, Mrs Rollings? I'm the one who had to put my nose to the grindstone for donkey's years to pay for this place – my rotten husband failed to send enough money, any money at all most of the time. Ask this Lucy here, her father ought to have told her all about it ...'

'Yes, yes, Nan, I do know about all that, but what Mrs Rawlinson was about to say was that you need to have the stair-lift installed, otherwise you'll fall down them and break your ...'

'Neck, I hope. That way, it'll all be over. There's no point whatsoever in spending all my time alone unable to get out and do things, and when I try to, I'm told off like a naughty little girl. Would you like to lead such a life? Go on, answer me! Would you?'

'Your life would be better if you had other people around you, Nan ...'

'In the old people's park, Lucy, I know, I can tell what you're getting at. Why don't my family come to see me? Some churchgoers are coming to visit me soon. I don't have many friends left, but they think more about me than my family ...'

'That's not true, Nan. We ...'

'All right, Lucy ... Your family members are all busy or have their own problems, Mrs Robson. Look, your son has found you an excellent care home, you must have a look at it at least ...'

'God! Mrs Rollings, how many times do I have to say this? I'll not go out of here unless it's in a box!'

4 JULY

Mother was quite impossible yesterday – what an ordeal for poor Lucy! I was going to get Lucy to see Daphne too, but that would be too much right now ... Anyway, focus on the brief ... The charges of neglect in the nursing home go back so far that I can suggest that the witnesses' recollections are faulty, that they were reacting to suggestions from the police, who were anxious to get corroboration of other accusations ... Fortunately there's nothing in writing from relatives ... except that letter from an old lady's son ... Supposing I have to write a similar letter if Mother decides to go into a home? ... Nonsense, keep your mind riveted on this brief, where that elderly daughter who has initiated all this is probably having spasms of guilt about ceasing to look after her mother and putting her in the home in the first place ... Must ring to see how Daphne is ... Who will visit her this weekend? Fiona? Lionel? ... Still, the high number of complaints about the nursing staff will be hard to argue away ... Just as well Mother doesn't know what I'm working on right now ... Ought to give her a call, maybe leave it until another day and speak to Tracy too ... Well, may as well put the dossier away now until early tomorrow morning ... Better ring the clinic.

'So, Doctor, you're saying that Daphne's more settled, but more depressed? Much more? ... Highs and lows, yes, of course ... Another week? Yes – well, we agreed on a fortnight before we decide, so that would be next Wednesday, according to my diary ... OK, make it next Friday ...'

5 JULY

Nice of Mrs Turner to drop the paper in for me – her Nigel must have told her that my children have stopped them, thinking I can't read any more ... Good of her to spot Derek's name in it ... Now, where *is* his name? ... Ah, that's a picture of the nursing home – that's been on the television news recently, where they've been polishing off all the old patients ... doesn't surprise me really – at the best they neglect you and you starve to death ... What? I don't believe that my Derek is trying to defend the people who run it! What on earth is there for him to defend? ... Oh, of course – he thinks the world of such places, and he'd love to stick me in one ... he'll most likely tell me that this horror home is fine, fit for me to go into ...

'All right, Mrs Robson, I'll be off now – see you tomorrow.'
    'All right, Daisy? How can I be all right? My children and grandchildren are plotting to put me away and you can see from this paper what sort of place Derek thinks would suit me ...'
    'They're only thinking about what's best for you ...'
    'So you're siding with them now? You think that sort of hell hole is best for me too?'

'They've chosen a much nicer place than that, I can assure you. We'll talk about it tomorrow – I really must go.'

Tracy's advising me not to call Mother until she forgets about our plan to put her in a home ... Can I wait that long, especially now that she knows about my part in this trial? ... It'll be in the headlines for quite a while and keep refuelling Mother's wrath ...

6 JULY

'How did you get here, Daphne?'
'You're a nurse, you ought to know. You people brought me in here a few days ago.'
'No, I meant through to this section?'
'Oh, you mean I'm a prisoner here? I'm not even allowed to stray from the room they've put me in?'
'No, no, but let me take you back there.'

Trapped like an experimental mouse in a little room ... why am I always kept in this room? I need to walk through the fields, hide in the long grass, let Daddy find me – he'll pretend not to see me for so long that I can't contain my giggles any longer and have to say 'Boo!' I need to return to the flowing waters, let them wash over me, cleanse the deep pit inside me ... Mother's obsession with washing clothes – it's me who needed the rinsing and rinsing ... Derek can't face up to my illness ... You're not ill, only needing some rest, oh yes, Brother, the rest that does not confront the stab in the heart of dawn, that does not witness the great black-headed gulls hovering overhead ... the only thing not black is their head, their white head and throat, luring you with their horrid squawks, enticing you, swirling over the dark pools, awaiting the final collapse of their defenceless prey ...

'Fiona? It *is* you ... Why are you visiting me?'

'I ought to have come before, Daphne.'

'Where is my brother? Is there a friend that sticketh closer than a brother? Ha! Do you know what came between us? No, not what, *who*?'

'Nobody, Daphne, nothing. Derek is so distraught ...'

'Then he should be here, getting me out of here. Can't he see that it's this place that's the cause of my insanity? I am mad, hopelessly mad, aren't I? Your eyes have answered for you, Fiona. But I'm not as loopy as the others in here – I've just seen them, not one brain cell left, any of them, frothing at the mouth on their beds or wandering with holes for eyes like Lady Macbeth ... What lies in those holes?'

'Daphne, I didn't see anyone like that on my way through to you ...'

'No, no, you wouldn't have, they brought you a different way, they hide the other cells ... If normal people outside could see them, just for one minute, they'd make sure all these places were closed ...'

'But what would those sick people do, if they were left on their own at home or out in the streets?'

'Sick people like me, you mean, all putrid inside – complete invalids like that can't be released for all to see, it would turn sane people's stomachs – I understand, Fiona ...'

7 JULY

'What on earth's the matter, Norman?'

'I'm Nigel, not Norman, Aunty Amy. Anyway, come

quickly, something is happening to my mum's heart, she says. I came to you because you were a nurse, you'll know what to do.'

'I can't remember where I put my nursing books and things about illnesses ... You'd better phone for an ambulance.'

'Well, it might not be as bad as that. I heard on the telly that too many idiots were making 999 calls and I don't want them to call me an idiot. People are always whispering that I'm an idiot, Aunty. You don't think I'm an idiot, do you?'

'Of course not, Nigel. You'll have to grow a thick skin like me and let all those evil comments wash off it. Ring 999 on my phone for me and I'll speak to them. I have mislaid my glasses.'

'Yes, and get the ambulance there this minute, do you hear? Yes, I've just told you that's where she lives ... Look, her son is right next to me, he ...'

'No, Aunty, don't mention me, they'll blame me ...'

'Thank you, you've been *so, so* obliging!'

'Why did you talk to them like that, Aunty?'

'All those stupid questions, as if I'm off my rocker! Well, the ambulance is on its way. We'd better go and see your mother.'

'I wish I could be like that, Aunty, when I hear people say things about me. Can you teach me?'

8 JULY

'Nigel!'

'Yes? You're Tracy, aren't you?'

'Yes, that's right. How's your mother?'

'Oh, you know about Mum?'

'Yes, I looked all over for Mrs Robson yesterday until I

found her outside your house. She told me your mother had had a heart attack and you had gone with your mother in an ambulance. Thank goodness they wouldn't let Mrs Robson go as well. She's not up to those things, you know, Nigel.'

'Isn't she? Oh ... but who's going to look after me now? Mum has to have an operation to go past her heart ... How do they get past it? ... I can't look after myself – least I've never tried ... They'll put me away! Aunty! ... Aunty Amy can look after me.'

'You know jolly well she can't, Nigel.'

'Oh, can't I? And why not? I'll look after whoever I choose, Daisy!'

'I can't phone your son or daughter right now, Mrs Robson, but ...'

'Them! They're never around when you want them!'

'But I'll phone Mrs Mullins and get her to come along here to have a firm word with you about this.'

'Mrs Mullins? I don't like her, least nowhere near as much as I like Aunty Amy. She'd not look after me properly.'

'I don't mean that, Nigel – she's an invalid herself. I just want Mrs Mullins to have a word with Mrs Robson.'

'Eeh, Nigel, if only your mother had let me sign those papers to become your guard, they couldn't have stopped me adopting you now, could they?'

'No. And Aunty, you just remembered to call me Nigel – that's made me feel better already.'

9 JULY

Things become more absurd with every new day ... The sudden death last night of Mrs Turner, and Mother wanting this morning to adopt Nigel. She's obsessed with his problems and doesn't understand what's wrong with Daphne. Perhaps I should tell Mother more about Daphne's illness? No, Mother's doctor won't allow me to do it – it would be the final nudge over the edge for her, according to him ... Indeed, Fiona herself hasn't recovered from seeing Daphne in that appalling state, so what effect might it have on Mother? ... Is there a cure for Daphne? ... There certainly isn't for Mother ... One day she's a little more with it, and then the next few days she declines ... On and on and on it goes ... Most of the time she seems unaware that her quality of life is deteriorating ... yet sometimes she wishes she hadn't lived so long ... To go like Mrs Turner with a heart attack at 70-odd or to linger on well into your nineties like Mother? ... Just as well we're not given the choice ...

'Derek! We're being called back into court.'

10 JULY

'It's only me, Aunty – Nigel. You can open the door safely – I've come to say goodbye. Goodbye until Mum's funeral, that is.'

'Where are you going, Nigel?'

'They've found a place for me, for the time being like. I'll have my own room and there's somebody to see to me if I need them ...'

'Don't cry, Nigel. It's more than I can stand to see a grown man crying. It reminds me of my father when I went to tell him the news that Alfred had died ... I'm so sorry I couldn't look after you ...'

'It's all right, Aunty, I was really crying for Mum ...'

'If we only knew when that scythe was chopping ... My mother used to dread the scythe ... It struck her unawares too ... So sudden ... You need time to come to terms with it, Nigel ...'

'You will be at the funeral, Aunty?'

'Nothing, neither hell nor high water, will stop me, Nigel.'

From the case notes:

Patient extremely upset about Mrs Turner's death and her son Nigel's predicament. She insists on going to Mrs Turner's funeral. Her doctor advises strongly against it.

11 JULY

The air is so balmy, warm enough to transport me, up and up and out of here ... I must find a way to reach the garden, smell those lilies ... these slow-witted nurses will think I'm inebriated as I reel from their scent, then I'll float over the garden wall, over and beyond, to the country of beyond ... Why haven't I visited it before, where everything is so sedate, so composed? ... Compose some music for the choir, they'll need a piece or two for the concert ... They're missing their rehearsals ... no, I heard their voices a moment ago, they've come to intone a prayer for me ... The harmonisation was wrong, they weren't in unison ... It wasn't them, it was the sirens singing to lure me ... Only one has a really beautiful voice, the others soothe with false words or brainwash you, then tie you up in a straitjacket ... Out and beyond before the bell tolls ... it's ringing now, Daphne, they've come to seize you ...

'Daphne! There's nothing to be afraid of – it's your vicar, he has come to see how you are.'

'You look very nervous, Vicar ...'
  'Oh ... er ... do I? Are they ... looking after you well?'
  'As well as could be expected.'
  'I'm glad to hear it, Daphne ...'

'Sorry, Daphne – I'm not usually so tongue-tied ... The parishioners would love to have me like this when I launch into one of my rambling sermons.'
  'I like your sermons, Vicar, they take my mind off ... other things ...'
  'Quite so ...'

'Well, Daphne, everyone has asked me to pass on their very best wishes for a speedy recovery – we hope to have you ... back with us soon.'
  'Yes, the choir needs me ...'
  'Ah!'
  'Why "ah"?'
  'Er ... well ... Daphne ... I've had to engage a temporary choirmaster ... He wouldn't take the job on unless I specified a term ... so six months is what we agreed ...'
  'Six months! So you expect me to linger here for that long?'
  'No, not at all ... but you would need to have some convalescence ... a holiday ... Of *course* it wouldn't take six months ... Maybe you could work alongside him for a time before you took over again ... He insisted on some sort of a contract and we needed him desperately for the concert – we've sold almost all the tickets and some important people are coming ... important for the parish, that is ... and with money being so badly needed for the restoration work ...'

'That visit must have bucked you up a bit, Daphne.'
  'Don't let him come again ... Did you hear me? He's not to come again, that Judas!'

12 JULY

'What a terrible to-do with Mrs Turner, Amy.'

'Yes, Madge.'

'I wouldn't want to go struck down like that, it's like being struck by lightning.'

'A good way to go, if you ask me, Madge, before you can't walk or talk any more or remember who you are or where you are ...'

'You always had a morbid streak, Amy. I can only get around in my buggy but I don't want to drop down dead.'

'You'll be a burden soon like me. Then how will Stephen cope with you?'

'Your children don't see you as a burden, Amy, surely? ... As for Stephen, heart of gold he has, he'll most probably ask me to come and live with him if I get any worse ...'

'What? With that wife of his? Mark my words, Madge, he's got one of those old people's parks lined up for you, your name's top of the list ...'

'Don't go on like that, Amy ... By the way, Nigel wants you to visit him in his new place – perhaps we could take a taxi there together? How about Wednesday? Cheer him up before the funeral.'

'When's the funeral?'

'Friday. We ought to allow him a day of proper mourning on Thursday.'

'Mourning. Now you're the morbid one. I've done enough mourning.'

You can't mourn when you still cling to the hope that your loved one is still alive, and when you know that the death is final, you can't mourn without the body ... They're bringing the soldiers' bodies back from those pointless wars so that families can mourn, be proud of their bravery and put them to rest ... Those killed at sea can't come back in a coffin, they return only as spirits never to be put out of your mind ... The war memorial helped, though they took too long to build it ... Alfred's name was on it, I thought of him as lying underneath it, but that didn't last for long, I knew he was somewhere drifting on that turbulent ocean calling me for help, and I couldn't come to him, but soon I will come to him ...

13 JULY

'So, ladies, are you going to see Amy Robson today?'

'Well, Reverend ... she behaved very strangely last time we went.'

'Really, Dotty? I thought you had one of those splendid teas with her – you told me all about it.'

'That was the time before last. No, last time she seemed greatly ... how can I put it? ... irritated by us, and we only stayed with her for a few minutes.'

'Is that so, Fanny?'

'She said something to us indicating that she thought we were ... well ... a little past it ... as if she was a sprightly youngster entertaining us ...'

'How extraordinary. Well, well ...'

'There's nothing amusing about it, Reverend ... We were just discussing this, as a matter of fact, and we both feel that it is your duty as vicar to go and see her.'

'Yes, well ... you see, I can't possibly visit *all* my parishioners ...'

'You've hardly got any of us left, and some of us are a dying breed, soon to become extinct ...'

'Well, I promised my family an outing today – such splendid weather, I can't disappoint them.'

'Oh!'

'Yes ... well, I'll call on Mrs Robson before Ada Turner's funeral.'

'Ah Ada Turner – we were going to mention that as well ... she wasn't in our congregation, Reverend ...'

'No, Fanny, but her funeral is here. You don't have to have a membership card for such an occasion as that!'

14 JULY

'Why are all those things out in the garden, Mrs Robson?'

'What things, Daisy?'

'Clothes, books, a chair ...'

'Let me see .... Oh, those things. Get rid of them for me, Daisy.'

'I can't. Anyway, why don't you want them any more?'

'I'll let you into a little secret. Do you want to know it?'

'What's that, Mrs Robson?'

'My sister brought those things when she first came to stay with me and I'm adam ... determined that she's not going to put a foot over the threshold again. We had a terrible row yesterday – she still owes me a lot of money and wouldn't help pay the rent, so I threw her out with her things.'

'That's your best cardigan and skirt lying out there on the lawn ... and some of Derek's books he left here ... I'd best fetch them back in.'

'Oh no you won't. I defy you. They're all for the scrapheap.'

From the case notes:

Patient threw a number of her belongings into the garden yesterday. When she was asleep in her chair, I brought them back in and sent the clothes to be washed. Patient under delusion that the items

*belonged to her sister with whom she was still living and who had
rowed with her.*

15 JULY

'What a surprise to see you on a weekday, Stephen.'

'I came to make a preliminary inspection of my new
construction project just outside the city, Mother, so I
thought I'd pop in and see you while I was here.'

'Oh, I thought you'd come all this way especially to see
me, but I'm ever so pleased you have a new project under
way ...'

'Thanks, Mother. Actually, though, I did come to see how
you were faring. You're becoming less and less mobile, you
know.'

'With the stair-lift, the walking stick and the buggy, I can
still get about, and what with meals on wheels, I can
cope ...'

'But for how long, Mother? Jackie and I were just discussing this ...'

'Amy Robson, you never spoke a truer word!'

'What has she got to do with anything, Mother? You
aren't thinking of staying on in this house to keep Mrs
Robson company from time to time, are you? She'll be in a
home soon – I had a chat with Derek a little while back and
he has found an ideal place for her ...'

'She's refusing to go into it ...'

'Well, she was always an unreasonable, intractable woman
– not like you, Mother.'

'Oh, so I'm docile, am I, Stephen? Do what you want with
me, can you? Not feisty like Amy, no, so you can walk right
over me ... I suppose this lovely home that Derek found
appealed to you and your scheming wife too? ...'

'You should visit it, Mother ...'

'Just what Derek Robson said to Amy!'

'We're not planning to put you into it now, it would just be in reserve, ready ...'

'For the day you want to cart me off like old Steptoe. I remember you watching that episode with me and you said how callous that son of his was, you would never put me away like that ...'

'Circumstances change, Mother.'

'No, *children* change, Stephen ... I never thought I'd be like Amy.'

'In what way, Mother?'

'Wishing my children had never grown up.'

'You've moved from *Steptoe and Son* to the Christmas pantomime now!'

16 JULY

'Didn't I tell you, Madge? You thought Stephen was made of burnished gold, but he's the same as all of them.'

'Let's not say any more about it, Amy, except that we'll make a pact that neither of us is going into a home and we'll stick up for each other.'

'Yes, provided you don't weaken, Madge.'

'Hello, Nigel. What a nice place you have!'

'Oh, Aunty Amy ... and Mrs Mullins – hello! We'll have some tea. I can't make cakes, but they took me down to the shops to buy some ...'

'I thought you could shop on your own, Nigel.'

'Yes, Aunty, but sometimes I forgot what Mum wanted me to buy or they swindled me, so Mum said ... Anyway, I didn't know where the shops here were ...'

'Have you chosen your mum's coffin, ordered the flowers and so on, Nigel?'

'The people here helped me, Mrs Mullins. I chose oak, rather expensive, but Mum loved oak. When Mr Watson was buried in that oak coffin, I heard her say that was what she would like, under her breath like, but I remembered it. Wasn't that good of me, Aunty?'

'Yes, you always were a good son, Nigel.'

'More than some I can think of, Amy ...'

'Shush, Madge ...'

'You always say kind things about me, Aunty. I heard some neighbours whispering that the funeral would be a disaster, because I wouldn't be able to sort it out proper like ...'

'Well, just ignore them, Nigel. So do you like it here? Do you think you can settle in here?'

'They're very helpful here ... but then they said it was only for a while ... Maybe if I like it I can stay ... but I don't know who would pay for it ...'

'Oh, you're Mrs Robson's vicar, aren't you?'

'Yes, and you're Tracy, I believe?'

'That's right. I'm afraid Mrs Robson is visiting Nigel Turner and I don't know when she'll be back.'

'Not to worry. Just say I called on her and that I'll see her at Mrs Turner's funeral ... Oh, she will be going, won't she?'

'Yes, my colleague Kelly is taking her, as Friday's my day off.'

17 JULY

Now Mother is threatening to change her will and cut us out. She claims we don't need the money, and says that in any case we don't deserve it, we neglect her, we take her for granted, and so on ... All of a sudden she wants to bequeath her estate to Nigel Turner, whom she calls her adopted son ... If she does, he will need somebody to look after it for him ... the Partridges will probably put themselves forward for it ... But his late mother, Mrs Turner must have made some provision for him, surely? ... Anyway, Tracy has told me that Mother wants to find her will ... Well, we can say she has mislaid it if necessary ... She won't think of the solicitor's as a likely place of storage ... Let's hope Tracy warns Kelly to plead ignorance about this ... Oh, surely Mother will have forgotten all about this tomorrow, so no need to bother Daphne with it ... Mother still doesn't understand why Daphne doesn't phone her, Daphne can't be really ill to her way of thinking – not that she would remember if Daphne did contact her ...

'Struck upon the same idea as us, ducks, 'ave we? We was about to alter our will a bit to leave poor old Nigel a little cash, wasn't we, Ivan?'

'How did you get to know about my plans?'

'Madge mentioned it in passing like, Mrs Robson.'

'To you?'

'No, but as she 'as so loud a voice, we couldn't 'elp over'earing it just as she was passing outside our door ...'

'Well, I can't leave him anything, as my will is all made up and I've no idea where I put it even if I did want to change it.'

'Want any 'elp looking for it, ducky?'

'No point. I've searched my house from top to bottom.'

'Then it's gotter be at your solicitor's office in 'is vaults.'

18 JULY

I wonder how many will turn out for *my* funeral ... not many neighbours from the old days left ... can't remember how many of my brothers and sisters are still alive ... The same old dodderers from the church are sure to come as are here today for Ada Turner ... That's how I'm departing from my house ... in a posh box like that ... Peaceful here in the churchyard, I could lie here meditating ... No, my soul wouldn't rest, good job I'm going to be cremated ... Some people will be glad to see me burned so I can't come back to haunt them, those Pheasants for a start ... My mother said cremation was surer, so you wouldn't toss for ever in your grave, grieving over things ... Not that I have anything to feel guilty about ... I've always done my best for people ... I can't understand why Daphne is so peculiar, towards me at any rate ... She had a lovely childhood, she would always be dancing and singing ...

'It wasn't my fault, was it, Aunty?'

'What wasn't your fault, Nigel?'

'Not ringing for the ambulance straight away. I heard some people whispering that it was too late when I called it for Mum, and that any normal son would have phoned from his house ... they touch their foreheads, you know, like this, to say I'm not altogether there like ... they reckon I shouldn't have gone to your house first, Aunty ...'

'They're not Christian people if they're saying that, Nigel ...'

'I don't know if it's people from your church, Aunty, because I haven't gone there since I was little ...'

'Not to worry about them, whoever they are, Nigel. You did what you thought best for your mum. She'll be very proud of you.'

'If only they could open up her coffin so she could just tell me so ... and tell me that she didn't mean it when.... you know, Mum used to complain herself to people about what a nuisance I was to her, that I'd be the death of her ...'

'She was feeling tired then, Nigel. Of course she didn't

mean it. After all, she carried on looking after you, didn't she?'

19 JULY

'What a mess, Mrs Robson! All these drawers emptied out – whatever were you looking for?'

'None of your business, Daisy.'

'Well, it is my business, as I'll have to put everything back for you.'

'You will not, not unless I tell you where to put everything.'

'I think I'll ask for somebody in your family to come and sort it all out instead.'

'No you won't, because they'll hide the thing I'm looking for if they come across it.'

'Why would they do that, Mrs Robson?'

'Because it's something they want to get their hands on before I die.'

'What on earth is it, then?'

'I can't remember exactly, but I wouldn't tell you if I could, Daisy. That Pheasant woman told me where I might find it ... now, where did she say? ...'

From the case notes:

Patient searching for missing item, probably her will (following my telephone conversation with her son on Thursday). Have contacted son to get a family member to sort out the mess in the house. Ominously, the Partridges seem to know what patient is looking for and where it is.

20 JULY

How can I have a brother? Daddy has just died, so I can never have a brother now. Mummy won't marry again – we'll live together and comfort each other, just the two of us, just as it was when Daddy was away at sea, only us two, only we know the depths of the grief ... Friends and neighbours who try to console you only stab clumsily at the wound like voyeuristic ghouls ... I wanted to bring Daddy back but I couldn't alter the dream – some dreams you can alter, you realise somehow you're dreaming and you decide you don't like what has happened, so you go back on it and make things go the way you want ... then you wake up ... but I can't make Daddy stand in front of me now ... I'm not dreaming now ... just Mummy and me, I don't need a brother, we'll pull through, just the two of us – inseparable, we'll be ...

'Doctor, I insist on knowing what medication my sister is on.'

'None, Mr Robson. Except the odd tranquilliser.'

'Then how do you account for her sudden inability to recognise me?'

'I'm afraid, Mr Robson, that this is another symptom of her mental illness, which is worsening. Indeed, Dr Thompson, who specialises in dementia, considers that your sister is showing clear signs of premature dementia in addition to her ongoing illness. There may have been earlier signs which were not diagnosed.'

'Ah ... ah ... I see. What is the next step now, then?'

'Well, we have drawn up a document for you to sign to allow us to keep Daphne here for an extra fortnight. I'm afraid that a final decision will have to be made then. We need to consider Daphne's long-term treatment urgently.'

21 JULY

From the case notes:

Result of today's visit from doctor: Patient showing increasing signs of incontinence. Hydration is a related problem. Doctor concerned that patient is not taking in enough fluids. One reason could be a fear of passing urine. Another is that the patient may forget to have the drinks left for her. The wetting of the carpet could also be spilt drinks. If these problems worsen, doctor may push for patient to be placed in a home for (physical) medical reasons. Patient's son informed.

Ought I to be distressed that Mother has worsening physical health, or rejoicing that it might help us to put her in a home ... for her own good, of course ... but for our good too?

'So I maintain, Your Honour, that this particular accusation of neglect against the nursing home is not proven.'

22 JULY

'Sam and I went through all the brochures again over the weekend, Mrs Robson, and we decided yesterday on where to go for our honeymoon.'
    'Are you getting married then, Daisy?'
    'On the 31st of August. Sam's going to book the honeymoon today. We're going to Florida.'
    'I think I went there once ... with Daphne ... maybe she has some pictures ... something to do with Glades ... a kind of whatsitcalled ... a place where a lot of water collects and they have those ... those long animals with rows of terrifying teeth ... Daphne had nightmares afterwards ...'

'Was she very young?'

'Oh no, quite grown up ... she paid for the holiday as a break for both of us ...'

'Sam wants to visit the Everglades – they look really exotic in the brochures – but I'm mostly looking forward to going to Disneyland.'

'That's for children, isn't it? ... My granddaughter ... oh, what's her name? ...'

'Lucy?'

'Yes, Lucy. She went to the Disney place when she was a teenager ... not in America though. They built another one somewhere else.'

Have another look out of the window to pass the time away ... That family is going off for a while with their car all loaded up ... Everybody's going on holiday except me, poor old Amy, stuck here in this ... well, it's a lovely home, but it has become a jail with a life sentence, might as well call it a death sentence, because I'm not getting out until I pop off.

23 JULY

'Where's this coach going again?'

'I told you – it's a mystery tour, er ... what did you say your name was?'

'I didn't, but you might as well know it. It's Mrs Robson.'

'Hello, Mrs Robson – I'm Edith Jackson. Didn't you realise it was a mystery tour when you booked it?'

'I had only just jumped out of my taxi when I saw this coach about to leave, so I just asked for a ticket for it.'

'Double mystery tour then! Anyway, I'm none the wiser myself. Here we are, thrilled to be going into the unknown, just like little kids again. It's like that old radio series, *Journey into Space*, I think it was called. I used to try to imagine what things were like in outer space ...'

'No better than here, I'm sure, Enid ...'

'Edith. There's got to be a better place somewhere ... What's your Christian name, Mrs Robson?'

'Amy, dear.'

'Well, Amy, just imagine that this tunnel is a black hole.'

'I've had enough of those in my life, thank you.'

From the case notes:

Patient finally returned to the house at 8.15 p.m. in a taxi. The driver was going round in circles on patient's directions until he stopped to find patient's address in her handbag. Patient not sure where she has been all day, something about a surprise trip. Family unaware of anything planned for her. Patient had wet herself, her clothes smelled badly. Police alert called off.

24 JULY

I can't just put off writing this book any longer. It has to be published by October ... I'm meant to have published one last year, according to my job description, so it's well over-due ... But how many people will ever read it? Well, the few specialists in the field find the subject fascinating enough, so it might make a name for me ... 'Lionel Robson, you must have heard of him, the author of that distinguished book' ... Could get a promotion at another uni ... It's absurd to think that I should take Nan out one weekend ... Where on earth would she want to go? She can hardly walk twenty yards without wanting to sit down ... Just because she took herself off somewhere on her own, or so Dad thinks ... When I phoned Nan, she had no recollection of having had a day out ... All the more reason to take her somewhere,

Lucy says ... Well, why doesn't *she* think of some place to go with Nan? Why me? Can't they all see I'm too busy? ... And all those things to sort and put back in her drawers ... Will Nan even let me do it?

25 JULY

I can't believe what this girl says – she can't have possibly paid that much for a few items of shopping ... Why, I could buy all of those things and have change left from a pound note ... Perhaps she's taking some of my money to save up for her wedding ...

'No, Mrs Robson, I'm not getting married – it's Tracy who is ... I'm Kelly. As for the cost of things today, you should know – you spent a lot on your day out on Wednesday. What did you do with it all?'

'Pooh! Me have a day out? *That* would be something.'

'Anyway, I bought these things for you with my money until Derek ...'

'That's very kind of you, dear, people don't usually give me things. But if you need to buy anything else, don't take it out of your own pocket, I'll go and draw my pension at the post office. My sister said she would fetch my pension for me last week – I bet she kept the cash, that's why I'm short. Eeh, and she didn't give me back my pension book. Wait till I get my hands on her ...'

26 JULY

I never imagined Daphne's house to be in such a muddle ... all these newspapers, magazines, books and letters, all lying around in haphazard piles ... Here are the photographs of that holiday that Daphne spent with Mother in Florida ... Can't see why Tracy thought they would be useful ... Is it sensible to revive old memories? Tracy might like to discuss some of Daphne's photo collection with Mother, but Daphne would prefer that any photos that involve Mother remain buried in this drawer ... Or perhaps they would help the specialist talk Daphne through all her problems. Did Dr Devonshire ever refer to any of them? Probably not, as they are hidden away here ... Think I'll take a selection of different eras and people, some for Daphne's specialist and some for Tracy ... Maybe these of me and my family would serve as a prompt to Mother's memory ... It would be also be something for me to talk to her about, as I struggle sometimes to start up a sensible conversation with her ... Lionel could take some with him ... whenever the boy eventually gets around to visiting his nan ... Daphne's clothes are all tossed just anywhere as well ... These need washing ... I know Daphne wanted to be the opposite to Mother, who was over-zealous with cleanliness, but not to this extent, I'm sure ... Come to think of it, the first sign we had of Mother's mental decline was her neglect of her belongings, followed by an insane desire to tidy the mess away into all the wrong places ... These photographs stuffed under towels in a bottom drawer remind me of that ...

27 JULY

'The rock gardens are just here, Nan, I parked just by them.'

'Thank you, Lionel. You're a good boy.'

'Boy, Nan?'

'Well, you are grown up now, I suppose. About time you found a nice young lady friend.'

263

'No time at the moment, Nan. I have to finish writing my book. Let's sit on this bench in the shade. You can see quite a few shrubs and flowers from here.'

'Your book? Is it about me?'

'It's a book for academics at university.'

'Very few people had the chance of going to university in my day, Lionel. In fact, we hardly had any schooling. I don't know how I learned to read and write.'

'And now, Nan, a lot of young people stay on at school too long and still haven't learned to do that properly. Indeed, many even go to university just because they go along with the powers that be who think they ought to be there. Some of those I am supposed to teach need to go back to school and learn the basics first ... Anyway, I'm not here to talk about myself ... Are you happy just to sit here, Nan?'

'I could sit here all day every day, but there's nobody to take me here.'

'You won't want to have a little stroll along the promenade then, Nan? The sea brings back bad memories for you, Dad says.'

'Oh, I got over that a long time ago. You can't let those things destroy you, Lionel.'

'Destroy you? Aunt Daphne has some disturbing ideas about the sea ...'

'Does she? Now, somebody told me she can't come to see me, she's unwell ...'

'She can't visit you just yet, Nan ...'

'What do they call the illness? I was a nurse, so I would understand what is wrong with her, if you told me what the dia ... dia ... is.'

'Er ... well ... it's a new disease, rather complicated ...'

'She's not going to die, is she?'

'Oh, no ... they will cure her soon ... I hope.'

28 JULY

Lionel claims Mother wouldn't let him rearrange her things. I bet he gave up easily. And how on earth did he forget to take the photographs down with him? He always was absent-minded. I suppose his mind is on his book. At least he took her out of the house for a bit, as she's always moaning about being a prisoner in it.

'Oh, hello, Mrs Mullins ... Are you all right? ... Oh, I see – my mother wants to speak to me from your phone? ... Ah, of course, she has forgotten how to use hers ... Yes, put her on ...'

'That man hasn't come to see me yet today, Derek.'

'What man, Mother? You haven't hired somebody to do any work for you, I hope ...'

'And why shouldn't I? This place will fall down if nobody sees to it. But that's beside the point. A man was going to write a book about me but he hasn't come back.'

'A book about you, Mother?'

'What's so extraordinary about that? People write books about those blackguards of politicians who never did anybody any good ... Politicians even write books about themselves, but don't ask me who buys them ...'

'Mother, who was this man? ... What did the man look like?'

'Young, good-looking, well-spoken ... can't remember his name ...'

'He came today?'

'Maybe it was yesterday.'

'Oh ... you are thinking of Lionel, Mother.'

'How is Lionel? I haven't seen him in ages ...'

'Don't worry, he'll come back soon ... in a few days.'

'Lionel? Or the man who's writing the book?'

'Both of them.'

'I don't know why you sound so sure, but I'll expect them tomorrow perhaps. Mrs Mullins needs to use her phone, so I'd better say bye bye, Derek.'

29 JULY

'Come in Madge, but wipe those dirty shoes first.'

'It's all the rain we've been having.'

'It has been a good while since I saw you.'

'No, Amy, you were talking to Derek yesterday on my phone about a man that you were expecting ...'

'I spent too much of my life expecting a man, but he never showed up.'

'I don't mean your Stanley.'

'I don't think he ever was *my* Stanley. He called more on my neighbours than on me, especially when their husbands were out ... Evil witches, they were, preying on other people's husbands, as if their own were not enough for them ...'

'You've never mentioned this before, Amy.'

'Kept it in the family, Madge, in the cupboard, like all filthy secrets ...'

'Amy, I think you were talking yesterday about that man who was writing a book ...'

'What book? What man? Just because he has called on you, it doesn't mean to say he has been to see me as well ...'

30 JULY

'To save you going upstairs, I could make a bed up for you down here, Mrs Robson, just like I did when you had a flood up above.'

'Flood? Sleep down here? You haven't got your head

266

screwed on, Daisy. What would happen if I wanted to go to the toilet? There isn't one downstairs.'

'You could use one of those special sanitary toilets and I could empty it in the morning.'

'What? And have that mess stinking the house out all night?'

'Well, Mrs Robson, you keep refusing to have a stair-lift put in, and you can only just about struggle up the stairs.'

'So long as I can still struggle up them, I shall.'

'You're likely to fall right down them, as we all keep telling you.'

'My family wouldn't mind if I did. They'd come into my money quicker.'

'What a terrible thing to say, Mrs Robson ... Anyway, I have to be going now, but when I come back tonight I expect you to have eaten up all your dinner. The last couple of days you have only half eaten it.'

'Only half of it was any good. I'm being treated like a child at school dinners. You'll be force-feeding me next.'

31 JULY

Daisy keeps saying she's getting married – so who's going to look after me when that happens? She's more than a daughter or a granddaughter to me, I see her most days – she does everything for me ... Oh, that cat's preying on the birds in the garden again ... Shooooh! ... That's scared it ... I can't get dressed unless she's there – course, I *can* still dress myself, but the clothes are harder to put on and I can never find where they are ... That ruddy fly has got in again, I told that Daisy to shut all the windows ... Take that, you germ-spreader ... Eeh, that's the vase that Derek bought me, I think, smashed to smithereens – I'll have to glue it back together ... Daisy encourages me to eat, not that there's much point, not as if I needed the energy for anything ... but I might as well eat the rest of that meal ... But that fly has been on it, I bet – I'll have to throw it away ... She changes the TV channels for me, not that it's worth switching on, but Derek says I don't have to pay to watch it – huh! They should be paying me to watch it ... She does all my shopping ... and hasn't the cost of living gone up ridiculously too? Not that she can help it, she tries to get me bargains ... And there's my washing – I don't want to have to do that any more, it's too heavy to lift those wet things and put them on the line ... Starlings on the line, haven't seen a flock of them for ages, hideous birds, scavenge all the food away from the others, they remind me of that Pigeon couple, or is it the Pheasants? ...

'What's your dinner doing in the garden, Mrs Robson? Some seagulls are eating it ...'

1 AUGUST

The trial is not going too well – the weight of accusations against the home is too great ... The press have highlighted my new role as counsel for the defence, hoping that the public will draw their own conclusions about my private interest in securing the good name of such institutions ... What tack should I take next? ...

'Yes, it's Derek here ... Oh, hello Tracy – why are you calling me on your day off?'
  'Because I need to talk to you about arrangements for your mother.'
  'Well, OK, but I have only a few minutes.'
  'As you know, your son couldn't really sort out Mrs Robson's things to put them back into the correct drawers.

I've done my best, but you'll have to send Lucy down or come yourself to put things back properly.'

'Is there much point, Tracy? Mother is sure to mess everything up again ... Well, I'll have to see ...'

'Apparently they came to fit a stair-lift on the day your mother had her strange outing, so nobody was there to open the door. I'll see if they'll tell me the appointment time next time so that I can make sure I'm at your mother's house to supervise the installation.'

'Our problem there, Tracy, is that she might create such a scene that they won't be able to install it. I think I'll have to arrange for her not to be there at the time of the appointment, even if it means getting Mrs Mullins to take her in for a couple of hours.'

'My main reason for calling, though, Mr Robson, is to discuss what will happen when I get married at the end of this month. I had hoped that Kelly would take over from me, but they don't want to disturb her timetable and other patients, so your mother will have a totally new temporary carer.'

'That could be disastrous, as she may not take to that person at all.'

'That's what I'm worried about too, as I have built up a very good relationship with your mother. But it has been very difficult for me at times and I'm sure it will be very tough for the new carer.'

'Oh dear ... Well, there's nothing we can really do about it. I'll have to monitor the situation carefully in September. Thanks for the call, Tracy, and my sincere thanks for all you have done for Mother.'

2 AUGUST

'Ah, Mr Robson – we need you to sign the papers.'

'Just a moment ... you mean that you wish to detain my sister? ...'

'We merely want to keep her in a safe environment ...'

'So, you're saying that she wouldn't be safe if you released her?'

'Daphne has almost no memory of current events at times. She behaves in an extremely irrational way and wouldn't be able to cope on her own.'

'Let me see her first and then we'll talk further about it.'

'Very well, Mr Robson, but I must warn you to prepare yourself for a shock. She has declined rapidly.'

'My brother, you say ...'

'Yes, Daphne, I am your brother.'

'I had a brother once. His name was Derek.'

'That's me. I'm Derek.'

'A clever young man he was, and studying to be ... what was it now? ... Is it time to go down for lunch? Is that why you've come? Take this dirty cup with you and shut the door on the way out.'

'I'm not a nurse – I'm your brother.'

'If that were true, you'd be able to tell me how my mother died.'

'Our mother isn't dead.'

'See! You're a rotten liar! ... Nurse! Nurse! ...'

'Whatever is the matter, Daphne?'

'Who is this man, nurse?'

'Why, he's your brother.'

'So you're in on the plot too. Well, you can't fool me. Get out, both of you!'

I had no option but to sign the papers allowing them to detain her ... She's better off in there with people to look after her ... Or is that place merely making her worse? ... People rely on my professional judgement, so likewise I'll have to rely on the doctor's advice ... I suppose I can go back on my decision later, if necessary ... I'll have to visit Daphne again soon – she might just have had a bad day today ...

3 AUGUST

'Yes, this is Madge Mullins here. Oh, hello, Derek ... No, I haven't seen your mother for a while, not since she came here to phone you almost a week ago ... I don't mind your mother coming here, of course not, but when is the stair-lift going to be installed? ... Well, you'll have to ring me again when you have a date ... No, the fact is that I may have left the house altogether by then – Stephen wants me to go into an old people's home ... No, I don't really want to, but I don't want to be a burden on him and on others ... By the bye, Derek, I've been reading about that awful place you're defending in court ... No, I've not mentioned it to your mother – but why are you sticking up for such dreadful people? They've neglected their patients something terrible ... No, I grant you that they haven't been found guilty yet, but when they are, and sure to God they will be, things won't look very good for you then ...'

Thought it might be Stephen, but he'll only ring when he's found a suitable place ... or park, as Amy would say ... and Derek only phones when he wants me to do something for his mother. You would think that he could find it in himself to make a social call to me to enquire about my health from time to time ... Don't know why I couldn't manage to stay in my own house like Amy with a few more calls from carers ... But when I think of all the crises she has had this year, perhaps I'd be better off out of here ... No use trying any more to get Stephen to take me in ... He's right, he wouldn't be able to do his job properly – and a difficult, responsible job it is – with me causing upsets in his house ...

4 AUGUST

What did they want to do again? ... Take my stairs away? ... And how would I get up to bed then? ... Have to keep an eye on that new gardener ... Look at him sitting down, I'm not paying him for that. Ooh-ooh ... yes, you – you're not finished already, are you? ... So, you've done an hour's work, so what? I used to do three or four hours non-stop, I don't know what you young people are made of ... Go and prune those bushes at the bottom of the garden, they're stopping the sunlight from reaching my flowers ...

You'd think that a member of my family could come and see to the garden – they could take it in turns ... I'm feeling rather hungry ... Did I have my lunch? ... Where's that Daisy? ... Nobody's bothered about me sitting here all day long, day after day ... Madge has made herself scarce of late, don't know what's got into her ... I'd even be grateful for another visit from my sister Maddy ... Looks like rain, that dismal darkening cloud ... That lad had better get a move on before it pours ... Maddy must be sulking ... Why do I want her back anyway? She's always rowing with me ...

'Yes, this is Derek Robson ... David who? Oh, my mother's gardener? Sorry not to remember who you were, but she has had a few gardeners ... Ah, you haven't been working for her for long. So are you calling me about the arrangements for paying you? ... Rude, was she? Well, you have to make allowances for her advanced age, they get cantankerous ... Yes, you're right, a little criticism is justified ... Oh, she keeps tearing you off a strip? ... I'd be very grateful if you could put up with it for another few weeks until the summer is over ... Say a further pound an hour ... Two pounds then ... OK, that's settled, fifteen pounds an hour ... You have my address from Tracy, do you? So send me your invoice monthly and I'll post a cheque to you ... No, cash is not possible, I'm afraid ... Thank you ... Goodbye.'

That David will be the most expensive gardener in the country if Mother keeps playing him up ...

5 AUGUST

'Your garden is looking really tidy, Mrs Robson.'

'Yes, Daisy, I was out there all day yesterday working away ... Did you make me a drink?'

'You've just drunk it. You don't want to have too much fluid or you'll be having to go up to the loo.'

'You're right – in fact, I need to go right now.'

'You went only half an hour ago, Mrs Robson. Hang on a bit longer.'

'I only wish the weather was better so that I could sit outside and appreciate my garden ... Who's that staring over my fence, Daisy?'

'I can't see anybody, Mrs Robson.'

'Right there just past the shed.'

'It's probably a shadow or something.'

'I could have sworn it was somebody, but it probably was a shadow or spirit come back to call me to the afterworld.'

'No need to be so morbid, Mrs Robson.'

'It's not morbid. When you get to my age, you'll be hoping that one of your deceased nearest and dearest is going to come to accompany you into the next world – you don't want to be leaving on your own.'

6 AUGUST

'Who's that on the line? If you're a friend of Derek's, he's not at home at the moment.'

'You remember me, Aunty Amy. You must do … I'm Nigel … Nigel Turner …'

'Turner?'

'Yes, I used to live just up the road from you.'

'Why did you move?'

'My mum died.'

'Mrs Turner? She isn't dead – I saw her the other day.'

'No, I'm afraid she is dead and there are still some who say that it was all my fault, Aunty.'

'Don't be silly, Norman …'

'Nigel.'

'It couldn't have been your fault.'

'Did you know that I'm able to go out of my new place without supervision now?'

'Of course you can, you're a teenager now, Nigel.'

'I'm older than that, Aunty – I'm a grown-up. Anyway, I can call on you tomorrow, if you'd like.'

'That would be lovely. Come in the morning, as I get too tired in the afternoon.'

7 AUGUST

Who is that man at the door? If he's a thief, he's wasting his time, I've got no money left. Is he the vicar? Perhaps it's Sunday and I'm late for church … Better not open up in case he's up to no good …

'It's only me, Aunty Amy … Nigel … I told you I was going to visit you today … Please open the door, as I've sent the taxi driver away because I couldn't afford to keep him waiting for me ...'

'No need to shout as loud as that, the whole neighbourhood'll be popping out to spy on who's come to see me. Let me shut the window and go down to open the door.'

'Are you sure you're all right, Aunty? That sounded like a nasty fall – I heard you bumping down the stairs.'

'Just a few bruises, Norman ...'

'Nigel.'

'I only missed the last step or so ... Anyway, what brings you here to see me? Did you sneak out when your mother wasn't looking?'

'My mum's ... never mind about my mum now, she's ... Aunty, how are you?'

'Keeping myself to myself, that's all. Rarely do I have a visitor. I'd offer you some tea, but I don't know how to make it any more.'

'Oh, I've learned to make tea, Aunty – in fact, I can cook a few meals for myself now, so I'll go into your kitchen and see what I can rustle up.'

'It has done me good, Aunty, living in my own little flat. When I was at home, Mum did everything and I didn't know how to look after myself ...'

'You've left home, Norman? I mean N ...'

'Nigel. Yes, I have – my mum meant the best for me, but the people who keep an eye on me now say that she over-protected me, but I know it was just that she didn't want me to come to any harm when I used to wander off ... She never thought I would be given a place all for myself like where I am now. Perhaps I wouldn't have had one if Mum hadn't died ...'

'Eeh, your mother's dead and nobody invited me to the funeral!'

'You were there, Aunty, and I'm glad you were, as I don't think I could have gone through it without you.'

'Well I never! How could I forget that your mother had died?'

8 AUGUST

They say they'll have time to put Amy's stair-lift in while I'm visiting the old people's home with her today ... I want to get Amy's opinion about this place – Stephen is acting too hastily for my liking, he's bullying me into accepting somewhere I haven't even seen yet ... If there's any fault to be found with the place, Amy's the person to find it – after all, she worked in a few herself, and was matron in one of them ...

'Oh, you're not ready, Amy.'

'Ready for what, Madge? To meet my end? I've had enough time to prepare for that, if that's what you're worried about.'

'We were going together to visit an old people's home ...'

'Why, Madge? Do we know anybody in there who needs a visit?'

'We're going to see if it's a suitable place for ...'

'So you're in on the plot as well, Madge! Derek has put you up to this, hasn't he?'

'No, no, Amy, it's a home that Stephen has chosen for *me*.'

'I'll soon put a stop to that – you're too docile. What's Stephen's number? I'll give him a piece of my mind.'

'Oh, here's Kelly. Kelly, love, please get Mrs Robson ready to go out with me. It's urgent.'

'Sorry I'm late, delayed by my last client. Come on then, Mrs Robson, let's get you smart to go out.'

Rushed out by that silly girl just to please Madge, all to see this dump ... Old drivellers slumped in armchairs, stinking in their faeces until they're cleaned up, no conversation, just the odd babble, some drifters swaying from room to room looking for a way out – and who'd blame them? This place is not fit for Madge – she's not that far gone yet ...

'You, young man, order a taxi for us right now! I'll go out of my mind if I stay here a minute longer.'

'You shouldn't have been so abrupt in rejecting the home, Amy – the other section we looked at had a few people in it like me – I mean, still with some faculties. Stephen will be annoyed that I'm saying no to it without giving it enough consideration.'

'You're frightened out of your skin by your own son. Pull yourself together, Madge. Tell Stephen to have a word with me ...'

9 AUGUST

Fancy having this stair constraption cluttering my front room! To think that they would have put it on my stairs if I hadn't got back too quickly for them ... when? Was it yesterday ... or a few days ago? Anyway, the thing can't stop here ... I'll get them to take it away ... They haven't put my banister back very well either – that's dangerous, and they've scratched it badly ... It has been there for sixty years, and I've looked after it, polished it regularly, for most of that time, only for those hoodlums from the council to wreck it like this ... If only I had their number, I'd ... I bet it's them banging on the door now ...

'About time too! Do you want to damage my door as well as my banister rail? Oh – it's you, Madge.'

'I've got Stephen on the phone getting very angry with me about that business with the old people's home … Come and have a word with him, would you, Amy?'

'Remind me, Madge.'

'You saw the home he wanted to put me in …'

'No, I didn't, but I know what those old people's parks are like …'

Oh, dear, Amy's only made the matter worse. She was far too dismissive of the home, and now Stephen thinks I'm in league with Amy, so that we can both stay on in our own homes. That'll not be good for her either, as Stephen will talk to Derek about it all. How do I get Stephen to realise that I *can* manage here? … But then, perhaps I can't … I'm not as confident about my abilities as Amy is, even though I have more of my faculties left than she has … And I don't want to cause Stephen all the trouble that Amy has caused her children …

10 AUGUST

'I like you – you're a kind nurse. What did you say your name was?'

'Derek.'

'There is one more thing you can do for me, Derek.'

'What would that be, Daphne?'

'Tell them not to feed the seagulls.'

'The seagulls?'

'Yes, they shouldn't encourage them. Swarms of them swoop down on the lawn.'

'I can't see any now, Daphne.'

'No, they're cunning, they hide when you want to catch

them. But at night they wake me with their insistent squawks.'

'Perhaps it is a kind of nightmare?'

'I can go off people, you know. Until now you've been understanding, but you're starting to disbelieve me.'

'No, no, Daphne, I'm not ... So the gulls are noisy at night? ... I'll make enquiries and see what can be done.'

'You can go now. I'm exhausted and need to have a nap.'

'Of course. See you next ...'

'Next what? Are you taking some leave, Desmond?'

'No. See you *soon*, I mean.'

The matron thought I too had a screw loose when I asked about the seagulls ... So it looks like Daphne is sinking more and more into her own ever-closing-in imaginary world ...

11 AUGUST

I've put the washing out ... I must get a new washing machine, that old one is giving me too much work ... It looks like rain, I might have to bring the clothes back in ... What can you do on these dank days when you're all on your own? ... Derek will be back from school soon and he'll want his tea, but I think the kippers have gone off ... That Stanley should see how I manage on a few pounds a week ... When did he last write to me? ... Gertie was supposed to call on me if she needed anything – she's getting too unstable on her feet to go shopping ... I wish Daphne would get married, but not to that last young man of hers, too happy-go-lucky for my liking ... she's not good at choosing boyfriends ... For a moment I thought I was dreaming and trying to wake up ...

'Help! Police!'

'It's all right, Mrs Robson, it's only me, Tracy. I had to wake you up because I have to be going in a few minutes ...'

'Why, you've done a vanishing act in general of late – this is the first time I've seen you here for a long time.'

'No, I'm still coming every day bar Fridays, but you're always sound asleep in your chair. I only managed to get the odd word out of you last week, so I was getting worried ...'

'What about? I'm fit as a fiddle. Remind me why you call every day – not that I remember seeing you that often.'

'I do more things than I'd care to mention, Mrs Robson, but right now I need to see that you've been to the toilet before I go.'

'For goodness' sake, I know where it is – and that means I can go any time I like.'

'No, my orders are to see that you go each time I call.'

'Sounds as though I'm in a concen ... one of those camps where they put people away during the war, what with being made to do things at your command ...'

From the case notes:

Patient still sleeping in chair most of the day and becoming obstreperous about going to the toilet, but this is the first day that I only had to change her underclothing once.

12 AUGUST

How does one compare these two impairments? Mother's is more natural, the result of very advanced age, while Daphne's is untimely and perhaps not directly caused by premature senility ... no, it's a mental illness ... So, what's the difference? ... Could I have a more sensible conversation with Mother than I could with Daphne? Both sets of conversations soon drift into the absurd, yet they are very real despite their surreal aspects ... My own mind has suffered as a result – my concentration constantly wavers, the trial was a fiasco, and what will the other partners have to say at the meeting? I must prepare myself ... my defence will have to be more cogent than their prosecution ... Or should I just accept that it was yet another embarrassing defeat?

'We're not questioning your role as senior partner, Derek, but even as junior partners we have the right to ask you to review your performance. We did warn you that it was inadvisable to take on that brief on a private basis, that you should have kept to our prosecution remit ... er ... and we feel that it was not as well handled as it should have been. We're sorry for the damage to your reputation, but we also have to consider our own. So what we all think, Derek, is that you need to take a holiday ... to have a good rest ... in order that you can come to terms with your family problems, sort things out in your mind, as it were, and return refreshed to the next brief ...'

Did I do the right thing in agreeing to take a week off next week? They're pleased that I'm following their advice, but won't it be even harder to restart? ... I shall sink further and further into the morass while on leave, and half of myself will then be stuck in the sinking mess when I resume work ...

13 AUGUST

'Is this the right stop for the town centre?'
'I've told you at least three times, my dear, I'll let you know when we get there. Besides, most of the passengers

will be getting off there as well. Sit back down, please, or you'll fall and I'll most likely get the blame.'

'This isn't the centre. We haven't passed that writer's house, the one that's on the main road into town.'

'If you mean Dickens's birthplace, that hasn't been on the main road for ages.'

'Fancy moving that! Nothing's sacred today. They'll be pulling that church down next.'

'The road moved, not the house. Are you sure you're all right to walk on your own, love?'

'Do I look as though I'm handicapped? Why didn't the bus stop outside the shops? Where are they?'

'Just up there. No vehicles are allowed in the precinct. You don't live here, then?'

'Course I do, but they've messed the town up so badly, I can't recognise anything. Where's the Guildhall? I know that building at least – you can see it from anywhere.'

'Not any more, you can't, love. It's hidden behind other council offices now.'

People darting around with loaded bags, buy now pay later, I couldn't afford all these things, pushing past you as well, no manners ... The counter is moving away, so I can't pay for this, don't really want another cardigan ... I need a seat ... Those people are drunk, they're swaying about ... no air in here ... need to get out ...

'She's wearing rather old clothes and she's quite an age. How long has she been lying here?'

'Just a couple of minutes. We didn't want to move her, in case anything was broken. Just as well it's the precinct and there's no traffic.'

From the case notes:

Patient went missing, apparently took bus to town, returned home via hospital in an ambulance. She had collapsed but check-up showed no signs of stroke or heart failure or injuries. She was washed and put to bed.

14 AUGUST

Where am I? ... They've kept me in that hospital, that smell of disease smothered with disinfectant, I'll catch a deadly illness in here, the ward is like a transit camp to the graveyard, a transit camp just like in the war, death always sneering around the next corner, must get out of here ...

'Mrs Robson, why are you dashing out of your bedroom like that? You'll have another fall.'

'Oh ... Daisy ... I need to go to the toilet.'

'Sorry about the strong smell – I've just put some bleach down the loo. You must have a stomach bug.'

'Isn't that what you go to hospital for these days?'

'So you remember being there yesterday?'

'You still think I'm completely gone up here, don't you, Daisy?'

She's tetchy today, not a good time to talk about what happens while I'm on leave. Only two weeks left.

From the case notes:

Patient had a difficult day following yesterday's trauma, up late, then sitting in chair but restless and often muttering to herself, grumbling about this and that. Complaints became louder when I

283

put the news channel on! Stomach was upset but seems to have settled.

15 AUGUST

Is this going to be a day I can sit in my garden? Not much point keeping it in shape just to look at it from the window. Derek would play ball here and annoy the neighbours – what were they called? Happy times … Huh! No money … but at least I wasn't on my own …

'Thank goodness I can hear you in the garden, Amy.'
'Madge?'
'I'll come round to your house. Open the front door for me, I've got Nigel Turner with me. He has come to visit us.'

'I tried phoning but your phone is off the hook – see? I'll put it back on the receiver.'
'Most unusual for me. I must have knocked it when dusting.'
'Derek often phones me to say you've got it off the hook. What with the bother of getting in my buggy for such a short distance, I can't always get round to tell you nowadays, and besides, when I do, you can't hear me banging on the door.'
'That's just Derek's excuse for not phoning me.'
'No, I've tried myself and there's that funny tone …'
'Look, you two, I haven't come to hear you arguing.'
'Nigel, bless his soul – he wanted to come round to see you…'
'What's kept you from visiting me, Nigel? You used to be a regular here.'
'I have to come quite a way now, Aunty Amy. I don't live just up the road any more.'

'So you've moved! Perhaps I can come to visit your new place and maybe stay a couple of days. They're going to leave me in this house all on my own soon, so they tell me.'

'I only have one room, so I can't have any staying guests, Aunty. I really like it there and I don't miss my old home so much now ...'

I forgot to ask after his mother. I'm surprised he moved away from her. I used to envy her with her son at home all the time at her beck and call ...

16 AUGUST

Never see those children of mine ... what's the point of having them if they can't be bothered with you? Don't even know what Daphne is doing, perhaps she has gone abroad ... and I haven't heard a sausage about Derek's law business for months ... and as for those grandchildren, well, they live in another world today, don't have to graft for their living like I had to ... no time for folks out of the ark like me ...

'Derek, is that really you? I was just dreaming about you ... How did you get in here?'

'With my key, Mother.'

'I thought you gave me that back when you left home.'

'How are you today, Mother?'

'Daft question. Fighting fit and raring to go!'

'Seriously, Mother, we need to talk about what's going to happen when T ... Daisy has a few weeks off to get married and go on honeymoon ...'

'So that's why you've come – not to see how your poor old mother is faring, but just to shove her into an old people's park.'

'No, I can see that we'll never see eye to eye about those places ...'

'I worked in them and ...'

'Please, Mother, we don't need to go over it all again. You can stay in your house here.'

'Most c ... descending of you. Do I have to go on my knees and thank you, Derek?'

'Really, Mother ... Anyway, you'll have a new carer ...'

'That K ... Kerry will do, not a patch on Daisy, mind, but I'll get by.'

'No, it will be somebody else, a young lady you don't know.'

'You're just trying to scare me into going into one of those parks, Derek, I know what you're up to. I refuse to discuss it further.'

'Going, Derek? Aren't you staying the night?'

'No, I have to see Daphne tomorrow. Er ... she has just got back from holiday and ...'

'For goodness' sake, go and tell her to get down here and see her abandoned mother.'

17 AUGUST

'You've been away, haven't you?'

'Yes, Daphne.'

'I thought I'd seen you before, but it was months or years ago. Your name is ... is ...'

'Derek.'

'It *is* you, Derek!'

'Yes, Daphne, your brother Derek.'

'You're not one of those religious people ... you're just a nurse ... so you can't call yourself a brother.'

'Well, now I'm back, is there anything you need, Daphne?'

'When you're next on night duty, tell my mother not to come any more at night. I need her to visit me in the day-time ... There's so much we need to talk about ...'

'Mother visits you in the night?'

'Yes, Derek ... you did say Derek? ... She stands by my bed staring down at me.'

'What does she say?'

'I ask her what she wants, but I must fall asleep before I hear her answer. She looks very disturbed. I need to know what the matter is with her, though, so ask her to come during the day, when I'm awake. I'm quite often awake in the day ...'

'Yes, Daphne, I'll bring her in with me if I can.'

'Unless she's dead, of course ... I might be seeing her ghost.'

18 AUGUST

At last Lionel has finished writing his book. He has timed it just right, before he goes on holiday. He's right, Dad doesn't want us to visit Aunt Daphne in her present state and he recently saw Nan, so there is nothing to keep him in the country. I suppose he needs a break ... He couldn't understand why Dad was only half delighted about his book – he doesn't seem to realise the stress Dad is going through. He ought to spend a weekend with Dad when he gets back, but meanwhile I'll have to bear the brunt of it ... That won't be much different from usual, really – Dad is mostly on the phone to his compassionate Lucy anyway, as Lionel hasn't been in the right frame of mind to talk to, obsessed as he was by his writing ... Dad's career has suffered badly ... I reckon he'll retire early – this leave that he's on now will be extended and then ... I must get from Tracy the date she is going to introduce the replacement carer to Nan, I'll make sure I'm there to persuade Nan that the new one is a lovely person – some hope! I can hear her now: 'I don't give a damn for what you say, Lucy, I'll judge her for myself.'

19 AUGUST

'I'm sorry, Daphne, but Mother is ... unable to come to see you at the moment.'

'Don't try to humour me, I'm not insane. I know my mother's dead. Who are you anyway?'

'Derek, your ... nurse.'

'Can't they get staff to stay here more than a day or two? I can't stand any more of this changing around.'

'Daphne, I need to talk to you about Mother.'

'*My* mother?'

'Yes ... and mine too.'

'Mine was enough to worry about, Derek.'

'When Mother lost her first husband – Alfred, that is ...'

'Alfred? Wasn't that my father's name?'

'Yes ... Anyway, she found it impossible to forget him, the loss was so sudden, and there wasn't any grave ...'

'Don't talk about graves – I know they're getting one ready for me, I can see them digging every night, but they're wasting their time, I'm going to be cremated ...'

'Yes, I know ...'

'You've seen them digging too?'

'No, I know you will be cremated. Listen, Daphne ... Well, what I wanted to say is that Mother married Stanley – *my* father, that is, Alfred's brother, your uncle – in the hope that a new husband would help her to forget the dead one ... but it didn't work, Stanley wasn't at all like his brother Alfred in character, much more assertive, so he clashed with

Mother, they had frequent rows ... and Stanley, my father, left her ... Are you following me? Are you listening, Daphne?'

'I had a relative called Stanley once ...'

'It was the same Stanley ... Well, Mother wanted to obliterate all memories of Stanley, only each time she looked at me, I reminded her of Stanley ... the resemblance was too strong, and Mother therefore showed hardly any affection for me, or so it seemed to me as a small child ... You used to take pity on me, take me in your arms and play with me ... You used to try to arouse some maternal feelings in Mother towards me ...'

'I had a little brother once, just like the child you are describing.'

'That was me, that *is* me, Daphne.'

'My mother didn't like that Stanley, so he didn't come to see us very often .... Ah, there, see there!'

'What are you staring at down there, Daphne? Daphne?'

'I'm sure that was my mother walking across the lawn. You'd better go now. I want to talk to her on my own. Oh, bring me a clean towel ... quickly, before she comes. My mother hates to see dirty things. You ought to be doing your duty instead of standing around chatting about your private matters.'

20 AUGUST

Why did I leave it so late, until Daphne was unable to understand? ... No, she knew it all before ... before even I did ... But I had never talked it through with her ... Would talking about it have been for her benefit? ... She would have realised that she wasn't on her own in having problems with Mother ... Or for my benefit? ... It has always been clawing away at the back of my mind ... And yesterday it was good to bring it out into the open ... Or it would have been, had Daphne been able to respond ... We could have struck up a better understanding ... of her illness ... of each other ... I should have broached the subject earlier ... No, it was impossible to have discussed it on previous visits, as Daphne seemed to reject me ... No, she just didn't recognise me any more ... But why didn't I at least hint at it before Daphne became ill? ... Mother is still fighting tooth and nail not to have a stair-lift ... but, although she doesn't know it, one is going to be installed – so who is going to take her out while it's fitted? ... And what will be her reaction when she returns to the house and sees it there? ... That's why Daphne and I didn't discuss deeper issues – we have been bogged down in the day to day minutiae of Mother's troubles ... Poor Mrs Mullins might be put in a home soon, yet she appears to be in a better state to cope in her house than Mother ... Stop this! You are about to accuse Stephen of acting prematurely ... And God knows what he has been thinking about me ...

21 AUGUST

'Well, Mrs Robson, that's it for today. It's my day off tomorrow and I'm going to London to see some of my relatives before my wedding. Then on Saturday I'm bringing with me the carer who is going to replace me for three weeks while I'm on honeymoon and ...'

'Don't go on that honeymoon, Daisy. I had a nasty dream about you going away somewhere and having a terrible accident. Besides, I need you here. I can't cope without you.'

'I'm sure you'll manage with Sophie, the new carer, she's very sweet.'

'Sweet and good for nothing, I bet. She couldn't possibly

understand me like you do. I realise that I'm not always the easiest person to get along with, that's what old age does to you ... And I bet she doesn't have as much experience as you.'

'Sophie has been with us for a year now, Mrs Robson, she has been learning how to do things by standing in for other carers, getting to know lots of different clients and their needs.'

'There, you see! A new one and still wet behind the ears.'

'No, no, you'll see, she's very good. Besides, I'll be back before the end of September.'

'Mark my words, Daisy, I'll be gone by then.'

'Into a home?'

'Don't you dare mention that word again! Sorry, Daisy, I didn't mean to lose my temper with you, you're a good soul, the only person I have left who cares for me. No, I meant I'll be done for if you go ... When you come back you'll find me in the cemetery.'

22 AUGUST

Just the same dreadful news channel, nothing but wars and knifings and shootings. Where's that thing to change the channel? They've hidden it again ... Another shooting in London ... outside a pub ... mistaken identity, my foot, those thugs have victims lined up to be popped off ... A young woman ... What would they want to kill her for? ... Jesus Christ save us from destruction! ... That's Daisy's photo they're showing ... Is she in London? Why are they calling her Tracy? ... She looks after elderly people ... Tell me, God, it's not her, not my Daisy ... Who would want to gun down that poor girl full of goodness and kindness?

Is that the phone? Somebody told me I never have it on the hook ... Well, it's certainly ringing now ...

'Hello Amy, it's Madge here ...'

'You sound as though you're shaking like a leaf, Madge.'

'Aren't you, Amy? Or haven't you heard the news about your carer Tracy?'

'So it *is* her? I know her as Daisy – isn't that her real name? I can't bear it. You might as well call the undertakers, Madge.'

'Tracy's family will see to that ...'

'I don't mean for her – it'll be a double funeral, with me in the other coffin.'

'Don't go on like that, Amy. Look, I know you're upset. I'll come round to see you in the buggy ... Be there in a minute or so ...'

From the case notes:

Patient in terrible state owing to Tracy's tragic death. I was too distraught to comfort her properly. Will call tomorrow to introduce Sophie, the replacement carer, who will start on Sunday, a week earlier than foreseen. Kelly.

23 AUGUST

I don't go much on my coffin, rather thin-looking wood ... and those ugly handles ... surely my children could have dug into their pockets for something more elegant ... Are they putting me in that plot next to my parents? I haven't been to their grave for years ... A good job somebody has weeded and tidied it ... Who are those mourners? That's not my family ... Couldn't they even turn out to pay their last respects? ... Are they burying somebody else? ...

Besides, I'm to be cremated ... Who's in that coffin? Open the lid! ... It can't be ... it's young Daisy ...

'Sorry to wake you, Nan, but I've come to see you.'

'You're a good-looking young lady, but who are you?'

'Lucy, your granddaughter. Kelly has also come with a new person to look after you.'

'Mrs Robson, here's Sophie, who is replacing our ... dear lost ... Tracy ...'

'Kerry? You're here as well? You look so sad! Where did Tracy get lost? Oh, Tracy ... Why do I call her Daisy? I thought her death must have been a dream ... I did dream about it, you know, before it even happened, I mean ...'

'It was a tragic, stupid murder, Nan. My nan is always having these portentous dreams. Dad calls her a sibyl.'

'Call me an old witch if you like, Lucy, but I say we might as well call a halt to this world, it has descended into madness ... I'm the lucky one, I'll soon escape from it, but you poor young people ...'

'We must think of the good events in the world, Nan ...'

'Which ones, for instance?'

'Let's just think for a while of Tracy and all her kind deeds, Mrs Robson.'

'That's right, Sophie – I'll leave you to get to know Mrs Robson and call back here when you're visiting her later in the day. Thanks for coming round with us, Lucy.'

I'll leave Sophie to it – she is doing her best with Nan... The house looks uninhabited, the carers have at least kept it tidy... but there is no real sign of a room being used ... Nan is an empty presence ... She probably doesn't move from her living room, not to eat or sleep ... one chair is her realm, there silently she reflects, grumbles, daydreams, rages against the relentless destruction of her mind, alive only to herself, but still alive, still determined to live, even beyond the vanishing of hope ... Or is this latest tragedy the *coup de grâce* for her?

24 AUGUST

'Well, if you're determined to stay put here, Nan, we can't do any more for you. Sophie will look after you as well as she can, but your great problem is the toilet. You don't always use the bedpan in time ...'

'Disgusting thing, sitting here with that stinking thing next to my chair ...'

'It's better than smelly underpants ...'

'As if I've lost control! I can still rush up to the toilet in time ...'

'No, Nan, you mustn't go up or down the stairs unless a carer assists you. In fact, they tell me you don't want to go up even at night to go to bed.'

'Put to bed like a helpless child and far too early ... I can't just go off to sleep at the press of a button ...'

'I'm going back to Dad's house now to let him know how you are. Sophie will pop into see you once more today. See you again soon, Nan.'

She won't, you know. My family think I'm indestructible ...

My God, what am I doing here at the bottom of the stairs? ... I must have dropped off to sleep before I managed to get upstairs ... I can hardly get myself up, terrible pain in my leg ... must get help ... Mrs Lipton has a taxi up the road, she can take me to hospital ... Just as well I left the front door open ...

'Mrs Robson! What are you doing crawling out of your house at this time of night? Just as well I was on my way in to put you to bed ... I'm Sophie, remember ... You look as though you've broken something badly ... I'll put you in my car and take you straight to casualty.'

25 AUGUST

If only Mother could have used the phone ... And that panic button – she kept taking the cord off her neck and hiding it away in obscure places, didn't know it was there even when it was in place, anyway ... Sophie said Mother was muttering something about trying to get to Mrs Lipton's to be taken to hospital in her taxi ... Mrs Lipton had to give up her taxi service years ago, she can't even drive any more ... Anyway, how did Mother manage even to crawl out of the house with a broken femur? She must have been going up to bed with the house door open ... What mood is she going to be in when she sees me from her hospital bed?

'I was having a row with my sister Maddy, Derek, and she started a fight, causing me to fall down the stairs ...'

'Yes, Mother. I'm afraid you'll have to have an operation ... if you're fit enough for it ... and then you'll be in hospital for a while until the bone sets.'

'I'm as fit as a f ... fiddlestick. I'll be up and out of here in no time. Who's looking after my house and garden while I'm in here?'

'I'll have to, Mother. The carers won't call now that you're not there.'

'Then tell that sweet little thing, Daisy, to call on me one day if she's free.'

26 AUGUST

Mother is stable and they are going to perform the operation. She won't be mobile after the op, but the bone needs setting to prevent constant pain and the threat of gangrene or embolisms. Pneumonia is also apparently quite possible afterwards ... What to make of all this? ... My time will be shared between Mother and Daphne ... and the house will need looking at from time to time. Do I break the news to Daphne?

'Derek, you mustn't spend so much time on your own, brooding. I've been very supportive these last weeks, but I need you to take notice of me, to realise that you still have a wife.'

'Fiona ... I'm sorry, darling, my days and waking nights have been riddled with cares about my mother and sister ...'

'Your career has been ruined by all of this, too. We need to discuss what the future holds for us.'

'Should I return to work and overwhelm my mind with other people's problems? It would at least help to wipe out my own.'

'Derek, you've answered that already by saying that you would be overwhelmed. We have enough money to live comfortably if you retire now. You would probably have stopped working anyway in a few years' time, wouldn't you?'

'But what would I do all day long? Mother and even Daphne are not long for this world, I fear, and then what?'

'There you go again. What about *us*? Won't we get to spend a lot of time together? There are places we'd like to travel to, we still have some interests in common ...'

'You're right, Fiona – thank God I've got you. I think both Mother and Daphne suffered above all from loneliness.'

'Well, I don't want you to sink into some kind of

dementia or mania as well, so you need to shake yourself out of your present mood. Let's start making firm plans for next year.'

'Not until Mother has passed on and Daphne cured ... or ...'

27 AUGUST

Well, the operation has worked to a degree, but her bones are frail. Another fall would be the end. In any case, she has lost her cognitive skills and won't be able to relearn how to walk. She will be insufferable without the ability to get about ...

'Is that you, Derek'

'Yes, Mother. How are you today?'

'Just having a rest. I've been on night duty, a hard shift it was. Are you managing to get yourself ready for school in the mornings?'

'I'm managing fine, Mother.'

'You always were a capable lad, you could always get by. Is there enough food in the house?'

'I go shopping when needed.'

'Ask Gertie or Madge to bring a few things back for you when they go to the shops. Listen to that woman groaning. Nurse! Go and see to her. How long does she have to wait before you stir your stumps? At this rate, Derek, I'll have to work the day shift as well.'

'No, Mother, you look tired. Go back to sleep.'

28 AUGUST

'It is indeed an alarming situation, Mr Robson. Your sister wanders around constantly, keeps falling and banging her head. We need your permission to strap her in her bed. Of course, she would still be able to get out of bed with full supervision.'

'You mustn't ask me to make a prisoner of my sister.'

'Well, we may have to override your wishes in the interests of the safety of your sister.'

'Hello, Daphne – it's me, Derek. How are you feeling today?'

'You're the only nurse who listens to me. My mother has stopped coming to see me. Tell her to come, so that she can see my father.'

'Your father visits you, Daphne?'

'The waves opened their smothering arms and cast him up. The sea knew that I had more use for him. He waded across that field of grass and floated up to my window.'

'Daphne, I've tried to come to terms with your ... your way of thinking about Mother, but I've always failed miserably. You never really came to terms with your father's death ... nor did Mother ... and that affected your relationship with her ...

When her marriage with my father broke down, Mother took on the role of the discarded wife ... Later she assumed the part of the neglected mother, but she still felt love for us, Daphne.'

'If Mother felt love for me, why did she not show it more clearly, why did she not express it?'

'Sometimes pride prevents people from revealing their love, Daphne. Pride demands that the other person take the active role ...'

'True love, above all maternal love should take the

humbler part ... Mother would never stoop to that ... Perhaps I was too proud as well to be the first to show affection.'

Daphne's insanity is deeper than ever, they say, but that was the first time we delved deep enough inside ourselves to search for the root of our affliction ... Even if we fully identified the root, surely we could never eradicate it ... not now, anyway.

29 AUGUST

'Which bed is Mrs Robson in, ducky?'
  'What is your name, please?'
  'Mrs Agatha Partridge – Agatha after that writer.'
  'Excuse me a moment, Mrs Partridge – we're monitoring her visitors.'

'Mr Robson? I'm your mother's charge nurse – I'm calling from the office. A Mrs Partridge is waiting at the desk outside. Wasn't she the lady you wished to have barred from visiting your mother? ... Fine. I'll make sure the note is prominent on our side of the desk. Sorry for the inconvenience.'

'Why would she not want to see me, ducky? I was always doing things for her, the ungrateful cow.'

Oh, a fax – today's bulletin ... Apparently Mother's burst of mental energy after the operation has faded. She's sleeping too much. They have to wake her and move her as best they can to avoid pneumonia taking over.

30 AUGUST

'Why are we all in this ambulance? Why are all you people coming with me? ...'

'We're only here in case you need us, Daphne.'

So, they're taking me to see Mummy. She must have fallen down when she was climbing up the hospital wall to see me. Pity she can't float like Daddy. Why have they put her in another hospital? I remember visiting her in all those different wards when she was a patient before – my brother was sheltered from it ... except that whenever she was in hospital he had to stay with aunts and uncles hundreds of miles away who didn't look after him properly ... Where is he now? He's a young man now ... doesn't need his sister any more ... I can't wait to see Mummy ...

'That old woman is not my mother.'

'But Daphne, there's her name on the clipboard – look, Amy Robson.'

'What made her age like this? Why is she sleeping and wheezing like that, Doctor?'

'She's showing the first signs of pneumonia – quite common after broken bones at her age.'

'You idiots! What's the point of my coming if she can't talk to me? Wake up, Mummy!'

'Don't get hysterical, Daphne, or we'll have to take you back.'

'The patient has been sleeping for some time. We need to move her around, so that might wake her up.'

'Eeh ... I don't mind being a guinea pig while on duty, I know you student nurses need to practise, but that's not the proper way to lift a patient.'

'Oh, Mummy, you're not dying, you can talk.'

'So I look like a mummy wrapped up in all these bed-clothes! Who is this person?'

'It's me, Daphne, Mummy ... your daughter. How did you become so old suddenly?'

'Me old? What about you? You're far too old to be my daughter.'

'I told you it was a mistake. She's not my mother.'

'This visit is having the opposite effect to the one desired. We'd best take Daphne back immediately.'

'Mummy, if it is you, I'm sorry I neglected you, left you to get into this state, it's all my fault, forgive me, please forgive me ...'

'Calm down, Daphne. We're leaving – no, you're not going back to your mother's bed.'

'What is that hysterical woman screaming about?'

'It's your daughter, Mrs Robson, asking for forgiveness.'

'Why? Has she been a naughty girl again? Tell her to stop squawking and look after her little brother, Derek, while I'm having this operation.'

The liars – saying Mummy forgave me. I didn't hear it. She's too cold-hearted for that. Telling me to look after my brother though, yes, that would be true, that's typical of her. Well, he needs to look after me now. It's payback time.

31 AUGUST

All my fault, I should never have pleaded with them to take Daphne to see Mother. Fiona and Lucy advised against it. Lionel thought it was a sign that I'd gone bonkers too ... I thought I could wave a magic wand and bring about the delightful denouement of a Shakespearean comedy ... It somehow comforts me to relate life's absurd events to the world of fiction ... Well, it was more like a Molière play, where the comic slips imperceptibly into the tragic ... Lionel has tried to make me see the funny side of things with Mother, but his laughter has been embarrassingly stifled by ever-worsening events ... Just as well Mother's not here at the cathedral today ... with Tracy's funeral delayed by pathology reports and the police enquiry, this memorial service for her is the only outlet for everybody's grief. It seems as though the whole city wanted to be here ... To think I used to sing in this cathedral, yet I can force no sound out of my ribs today ... Its parts didn't seem to fit well together then, but today with the renovation finally completed it feels like a more harmonious entity, worthy of a celebration of the life of selfless, soft-hearted Tracy, the only one who could really put up with Mother's fiery, cross-grained tetchiness ... And this was the day Tracy was to be wed.

5th September

Dear Freda

This is to inform you that my mother, Amy Robson, succumbed today to pneumonia. I will write again in more detail when I know the funeral arrangements.

Derek Robson

9th October

Dear Stephen

It is with deep sadness that I have to inform you of my sister Daphne's death today. You attended my mother's cremation and will remember what a traumatic day it was for Daphne. She never truly recovered from it. My only consolation is that

Mother did not have to attend her own daughter's funeral. I will write again when I know the arrangements for Daphne. I should also mention that I have made the decision to take early retirement, following Fiona's advice. I need a long period to recover from this year's events.

Derek